Skipping the Scales

Book Two in the
Flipping the Scales
series

Pete Tarsi

This is a work of fiction. Names, characters, businesses, places, events, and incidents are either the products of the author's imagination or used in a fictitious manner. Any resemblance to actual persons, living or dead, or actual events is purely coincidental. Any trademarks, product names, or named features are assumed to be the property of their respective owners, and are used only for reference. There is no implied endorsement if any of these terms are used.

ISBN: 1534925791
ISBN-13: 978-1534925793

Cover by Vila Design
www.viladesign.net
Coral Reef by alexxl | Bigstock.com
Girl on left by kohrhzevska | Bigstock.com
Girl on right by kobayakov | Bigstock.com
Girl on back cover by kohrhzevska | Bigstock.com

This book is dedicated to my mother.
Thanks for always believing in all of my creative endeavors,
and for never skipping any of my stories.

~ Chapter One ~

"Marina, you should *not* be doing this!"

She didn't have to turn around to know her best friend Lorelei was following her. Without responding, Marina flapped her orange tail even more vigorously than before. Water streamed around her as she glided through the ocean, her long blonde hair flowing behind her to halfway down her back. She knew that it would only be a matter of time before Lorelei caught up with her because while Lorelei wore only her typical seashell top, the human covering that Marina wore created too much water resistance.

As Lorelei gained on her friend, she noticed Marina's tail sticking out from under a pink sundress, presumably taken from the sunken yacht they had borrowed human clothes from before. "I know what you are thinking, and this is *not* the proper way to go about it."

"I have made up my mind." Marina caught a glimpse of Lorelei's red hair in her periphery and realized she was now swimming alongside her friend. "Though I appreciate your offer, this is something I must do on my own."

"You have only been on land twice before. I go almost every cycle."

"You forget that I spent half a moon cycle amongst the humans. In that regard, I could say that I have more experience than you."

"You may be correct, but you did not plan it back then." Lorelei took hold of Marina's hand and then slowed the motion of her own green tail, thus decelerating both of them. "You must carefully consider the choice you are about to make. If the consequences are the same as others who have made that choice, then—"

"Sink or swim, Lore." As they drifted into a vertical position, Marina used her free hand to keep the dress from floating upwards while she looked into Lorelei's eyes. "I understand what you are trying to do, and I truly appreciate your concern, but I must not follow anyone other than myself."

Lorelei quickly surveyed the surrounding area to ensure no one had followed them. Since they had returned to the north, Calliope, the purple-tailed daughter of their school's leader, had been keeping careful watch on them. She had grown suspicious when the disappearance of the odd mer Meredith had coincided with Marina's return to the school, especially because they were the only two mers with orange tails. Her father's decision to migrate early was due to Calliope revealing that Meredith had interacted with a human-maid.

Fortunately, the early departure was the only consequence of those events, but Lorelei remained cautious when she and Marina ventured away from the school. Seeing no other mers around, Lorelei said, "I am willing to follow *you*, Marina. Please let me share the experience."

Marina glanced upward and caught glimmers of faint red light dancing on the ripples of the undersides of the waves. She was not only closer to the water's surface, but also closer to the desired time of day. "You will share it, just not the way you think you will." She turned to Lorelei and smirked. "Remember, there are two of us, but only one on the other side."

Dropping her arms limply by her side, Lorelei stared quizzically at Marina. During the awkward pause that followed, Marina seized the opportunity to kick her tail forcefully and thrust herself forward to her destination.

~ ~ ~

Sitting cross-legged on the private beach behind her island

home, Hailey stared out at the eastern horizon and watched for the sun to rise. Awash with fiery colors, the cloudless sky was waiting to change to a beautiful light blue on that Wednesday morning. Waves rustled calmly as they rolled onto the shore, and the seagulls flying by called to each other. For the early time of day, the air was unusually humid, even for late June. Her straight dark hair frizzed a little bit, almost as if there were some static electricity around her. But she hoped that the sensation was a precursor to something much more fantastical.

There was going to be a full moon that night.

She had spent her entire senior year paying close attention to the calendar and circling the date of each and every full moon with orange magic marker. On each of those days, she had written the precise time the sun would rise—information she had easily obtained from an online almanac. She would go to bed as early as possible on the nights before so she was wide awake and outside before the sun came up. As she sat on the footbridge connecting the beach to her yard, Hailey would hope it was *that day*—the day that a mermaid would come back to visit.

Marina had appeared one other time during the previous summer—on the morning of the first full moon after Hailey had helped her return to the ocean—just as promised. And just as promised, Hailey had spent the two weeks researching the painting they had received, but information about it was practically non-existent. Even the strange old shopkeeper at *The Mermaid's Lagoon* who had given them the print wasn't entirely sure how or when it had ended up in her possession.

The painting depicted a baby mermaid with an orange tail being handed to outstretched arms in the ocean. The woman giving the child away, with her blue eyes and long blonde hair, bore a striking resemblance to Marina, and the painting's title, *Coral*, matched Marina's long-lost mother's name. It wasn't a far stretch of the imagination to assume that the baby was Marina, and the arms belonged to Lorelei's father, who had become Marina's adoptive guardian so long ago.

The painting was enough evidence that Marina's mother—and maybe even her father—had once been somewhere on land, but no one knew where.

Though she and Hailey spent from sunrise to sunset together, it was a bittersweet reunion. After almost eighteen years of being orphaned, Marina's first glimmers of finding at least one of her parents had been washed away.

When the waterlogged translucent skirt transformed her legs into a single iridescent orange tail, Marina warned Hailey that she wouldn't be returning again that summer. After rumors surfaced that the mer named Meredith had exposed herself to humans, the leader of the school decided to migrate away earlier than usual. Regardless, Hailey vowed to be sitting on her beach at sunrise on the same day of every moon cycle in case Marina ever wanted to visit.

On the marked days, Hailey awoke to witness the sunrise but sulked away when it was time to head off to school. As the months passed, and summer turned into fall, the sun rose later, and she spent less and less time waiting on those full-moon mornings.

Even through the cold winter, she'd sit outside bundled up. There were some rainy days in the spring, where she sat under an umbrella on the steps of the footbridge connecting her yard to the beach. On one occasion, the morning of the full moon coincided with a birthday slumber party at a friend's house, and she faked being sick to drive home in time to be on her beach at sunrise.

But Marina never came back.

A full year passed. Hailey had graduated high school and received an athletic scholarship to a smaller state university on the mainland to join their swim team. Although she wasn't sure what her major was going to be, she had accepted. Anything that kept her swimming regularly would get her one step closer to her ultimate career goal of becoming a mermaid performer at an aquarium or a water theme park. There were other wonderful developments—and a little bit of information about the painting—that Hailey wanted to share with Marina. Hopefully, that early summer morning would be the day they'd see each other again.

A warm breeze blew as Hailey watched the sun in its entirety hanging low in the sky, and some of her long hair blew into her face. She wove her fingers between the fine dark strands and stared at their colorless tips. For a long time, she had kept the last six inches or so dyed, but due to the additional time spent underwater in chlorinated pools, the color had faded away into bleached streaks.

Sighing dejectedly, Hailey stood and walked toward the wooden footbridge. When she stepped on the first stair, a voice in the distance called, "Hailey! Is that you?"

She turned, and in the distance was a girl with blonde hair wearing a pink sundress that clung to her body. She was skipping toward Hailey, one hand in the air waving and the other hand by her side with a rainbow emanating from it. Only one object could produce such vibrant colors, and Hailey immediately smiled when she realized what it was and who was carrying it.

"Marina?" Hailey took off toward her mermaid friend. "O-M-G, it's really you!"

They met and hugged on the stretch of sand behind Hailey's neighbor's house. Fortunately, Mr. Dobbins wasn't awake yet, and even if he were, Marina had legs, so all he'd do was complain about them being on his part of the private beach.

"I am sorry that I have not visited before now," said Marina. "The school has only recently returned here."

"Don't worry about it." Hailey jumped up and down and clapped her hands. "I'm just so happy to see you again."

"So much has happened, and I—"

Before Marina could say anything further, Hailey took her hand and started leading her to the footbridge. "So much has happened here too. Let's go inside, and we can give each other the four-one-one. I can't wait to show you what I've got! And you're gonna totally freak out when you see what I use it for!" Remembering that Marina didn't always understand human expressions, Hailey abruptly stopped and turned to her. "And I don't mean freak out in a be-angry kinda way. I mean freak out in an O-M-G-that's-really-awesome kinda way, K?"

"Hailey, there is something important I must ask you first."

"Marina!" called a voice from down the beach. "You *cannot* do it this way!"

Approaching them was Lorelei, her wavy red hair blowing behind her as she sprinted across the beach. Unlike Marina, who had removed the tail-skirt, Lorelei was still wearing hers around her waist and was wearing her purple seashell bikini top.

"It is the most sensible solution, Lore," said Marina firmly. "And I have done it before."

"That time was an accident. This is—"

"This is my choice, and it is the only way I may fulfill my dream."

While the two mermaids continued debating in her presence, Hailey's eyes bounced back and forth toward whichever one of them was speaking. In the brief pauses between their statements and responses, Hailey tried to interject but couldn't time herself well enough. All that she uttered were scattered *ums* and *ers* and *buts* until finally she flailed her arms and exclaimed, "I-D-K what you two are even talking about! Can one of you please clue me in?"

Marina took Hailey by the hands and answered, "I have learned more about the disappearance of my parents, so I am going to the mainland to do whatever it takes to find my mother."

Hailey's face beamed. "That's awesome news! I've got a folder with printouts of everything I found out about the painting. It's not a lot, but it's better than nothing."

"I truly appreciate your help."

"I'm sure Jill and Meredith—and maybe even Jeff—will help too. Whatever you need me to do, Marina, I'll do it. You can count on me."

"That is reassuring to hear. My search may take some time, and I do not know how long I will need legs. I do not wish my tail to disappear like it almost did last time." Marina withdrew her hands, leaving the translucent object in Hailey's grasp. "So will you keep it safe until the next full moon?"

~ Chapter Two ~

Meredith stood with the other two interns around the stingray touch-tank at the aquarium, listening to the information of the marine biologist to which they had been assigned. Only three high school students had been selected from a pool of a few hundred applicants nationwide. She felt honored to have been one of them, and it enhanced her applications to several colleges, particularly the prestigious one—the country's best for marine biology—that she had chosen to attend.

They also liked her diverse resume of athletics and other extracurricular activities. After field hockey season in the fall, she tried out for the girls' swim team in the winter and quickly rose through the ranks as one of the team's fastest swimmers. She earned second place in the girls' five-hundred-yard freestyle at a regional meet but would have easily finished first in Marina's tail.

"To protect our human visitors from injury, the barbs of these rays have been humanely removed," lectured Dr. Hatcher. "No harm came to our aquatic friends, as they are significant to the global ecosystem as well."

A tall, broad-shouldered man in his early fifties, he still had a full head of thick but short dark hair, except for the first signs of grey at his temples. Employees wore the standard uniform of khaki shorts or pants and a navy polo shirt, the aquarium's logo embroidered in green and white on the top left, but Dr. Hatcher always wore a stark white lab coat over it, making him look much more distinguished and official.

"I assume that you all have read up on the proper handling and petting procedures for the rays," he continued. "So which one of you would like to dive in first? Figuratively, that is."

Without hesitation, Meredith raised her hand. Appreciating her eagerness, Dr. Hatcher called on her, so she stepped closer to the tank, not seeing the reactions of her fellow interns.

Popping her bubblegum in her mouth as Meredith's hand went up, Brittany went to fold her arms across her chest, but then stopped to check her fingernails. They were painted black, just like her lipstick and her obviously dyed hair, and Meredith wondered what the girl's parents thought of her dark fashion choices.

On the other side of Dr. Hatcher stood Will, who sidled out of sight at the request for a volunteer. For someone so tall—just over six feet—it puzzled Meredith how he could so easily blend into the background. He had short, almost spiky blond hair and pale skin that was a sunburn waiting to happen in some of the outdoor parts of the aquarium complex. Fortunately for him, the ray touch-tank was shaded under a tent.

As Meredith stepped closer to the tank's edge, six-inch thick concrete about waist high, she smiled in anticipation of what was going to happen. Her fingers broke through the surface of the water, and several of the rays immediately started swimming in her direction. Their tails were vibrating subtly, almost like the wagging tails of puppies seeking affection. And that's exactly what the rays were looking for, so Meredith gently stroked them near the backs of their heads. She willingly and gladly petted each and every ray that swam her way, sensing that her touch soothed them.

"That's excellent, Meredith." Dr. Hatcher then turned to the other two—Will watched intently while Brittany thought she had hidden her phone at the last moment before it could be spotted—and added, "Looks like someone knows how to apply the assigned reading."

Since it was easy reading with simple facts and instructions, Meredith had only skimmed through the section about handling the rays. Instead, she spent most of her study time reading ahead on some of the advanced projects and facilities of the aquarium that she hoped to experience. But that morning at the tank, she knew exactly what the rays wanted her to do as soon as she was in contact with their water, as if a telepathic link existed between her and them.

The super-rational part of her mind had struggled even to attempt a scientific explanation for the phenomenon, so she stopped looking for one and merely accepted it as one of a few residual instincts from when she was a mermaid. As she sensed the others watching the rays interact with her, she knew she couldn't keep that skill a secret, but she would downplay it if necessary.

Except with her best friend Jill, who referred to Meredith's new abilities as her "superpowers." She always shushed Jill when the word came up, but it wasn't an inaccurate comparison. From spending those two weeks doing practically nothing other than swimming, she had improved considerably, especially when she swam beneath the surface. She was able to hold her breath underwater for almost two minutes on average, and on one occasion came close to three minutes. Even if she could have taken first place at the regional competition, she probably wouldn't have allowed herself to do so, as it wouldn't have been fair to win using any fantastical gifts.

Dr. Hatcher turned his head from Will to Brittany and then back to Will again. "Would either of you like to try?"

Will hesitantly held his hand over the tank. It quivered when he turned to Meredith and mumbled, "I did the reading, but how'd you know exactly what to do?"

"I just did it," replied Meredith. "And so can you. Watch."

She took hold of his wrist and dunked his hand into the water. Squirming, he shouted, "Cold, cold! Wow, that's cold!"

He tried to pull his hand out of the water, but Meredith leaned toward him and held his arm steady with her dry hand.

"Just stay calm and follow my lead."

When one of the rays glided underneath their hands, Meredith gently guided Will's fingers onto the ray's skin behind its head. She could feel the muscles in his arm tense up, and he seemed to grow taller as he stood on his toes. His eyes, at first closed, opened one by one, and the grimace on his face turned into a grin. "They're kind of soft," he said. "But squishy too. I didn't expect that."

Dr. Hatcher asked Brittany if she wanted a turn, but she quickly answered, "They're not dangerous, so what's the point? Bring on the sharks." Then she popped her gum again.

A couple of aquarium employees entered the tent. One of them started feeding the rays while the other started fiddling around with his headset microphone and the tent's speaker system. Dr. Hatcher glanced at his watch and said, "They'll be opening up to the public in about fifteen minutes. I've got a few things to check on, so why don't you enjoy some of the exhibits for a bit, and we'll meet in my office at about half past nine." He took a few steps away but then came back and whispered to Brittany, "Make sure the gum ends up in the trash. It would be dangerous to our aquatic friends."

As soon as he left, Brittany grumbled and took out her phone, texting as she walked away toward the seal and sea lion tanks.

While Meredith walked to the main gates, Will followed. "I thought I was smart at all this—*Rhinoptera bonasus*, that's the scientific name of those cownose rays—but what you did back there? Wow. I can tell you're going to be Dr. Hatcher's star, and I mean that as a compliment."

"That's nice of you to say." Smiling politely, Meredith then turned her gaze away. "But all three of us must have been the best candidates, so I know you'll do fine."

"Working with Dr. Hatcher, that's wow. He's brilliant and well-respected in the field, and I consider myself lucky to get the chance to work with him."

"Agreed. I hope we spend a lot of time in the rehabilitation complex."

"I hear they're nursing a *Trichechus manatus* back to full health. They found one offshore, and that's rare because—"

"Because West Indian manatees aren't indigenous to these colder northern waters." Though Meredith had interrupted him, she wasn't trying to be rude. The mention of manatees set off a warning bell inside her head. Long-ago sailors supposedly mistook manatees for mermaids, resulting in their folklore, but she wondered if back then the sailors were *actually* seeing what they thought they were seeing.

"You know so much, Meredith. It was amazing what you did with the stingrays, like they *knew* you were friendly."

Her internal alarm blaring, Meredith turned to him and rapidly said, "Sorry Will, but I'm meeting a friend of mine at the main gates, so I'll catch up with you at Dr. Hatcher's office." Then she picked up her pace, quickly taking a glance behind her to make sure he wasn't following.

People had already gathered beyond the gates awaiting entry. Open from nine to five every day in the summer except Sundays, the aquarium was one of the biggest attractions in the area. It was a collection of indoor and outdoor structures sprawling over a few acres of land. Outside were several tanks of water large enough to house seals, sea lions, and a pair of beluga whales, along with the stingray touch-tank. A few buildings were also part of the complex: the main gallery that housed thousands of fish, sharks, eels, and other aquatic animals including an octopus; the sea lion performance theater; and finally, the aquatic observation and rehabilitation complex.

As she scanned the faces in the crowd, Meredith felt a nudge from behind. When she turned, she saw the tall, plush-covered mascot of the aquarium: Sandy the Sea Lion. Also wearing a navy polo over her dark grey fake fur, Sandy was ready to greet the patrons as they entered. Some children outside were already pointing and waving.

"I see you ditched your shadow," said Sandy, the voice muffled by the thick costume. "You know he's totally crushing on you, right?"

"No, he's not," Meredith spoke through tightly closed lips so no one other than Sandy would hear her. "And I thought you weren't supposed to speak when you were in character."

"I'm also not supposed to sweat this much when I'm in character. I've got to get this thing off."

Sandy reached out a hand to take hold of Meredith's hand, but since the costume included fingerless flippers that didn't bend very well, all Sandy could do was jerk her flipper to the side, whacking Meredith's arm as she gestured for her to follow.

When they got to a secluded corner near a restroom pavilion, Sandy reached up to remove the head of the sea lion costume. Tucking the head under a flipper, the performer inside shook her head, letting her mane of uncontrollable dark hair loose in all directions. "That's better," said Jill. "I can breathe again. All those drama classes for *this*?"

"No small parts, Jill. Only small actors." Meredith smirked. "At least it's a job."

"Yeah, yeah, whatever. I think I'm gonna spend most of the day in the main exhibit hall where there's air conditioning."

Meredith giggled at how much of a drama queen her best friend was being, but she was grateful that she had coerced Jill to apply for a job at the aquarium so they could spend time together over the summer. In the fall, they were going to different colleges: Meredith to study marine biology and Jill to study theatre. Even though Jill was commuting home every afternoon while Meredith was staying in the dormitory housing provided to the three interns, it was great seeing her daily. They both had Sundays and Mondays free from the aquarium.

Brittany appeared from the women's bathroom, gave them a snide look, and then popped her chewing gum and strutted away.

"So, Miss Super-Intern, what animals did you meld minds with today?" Wearing a white tank top and denim short-shorts underneath, Jill had wriggled out of her costume enough that she could tie her hair into a ponytail.

"Quiet, Jill!" Meredith reached up to block Jill's mouth while quickly surveying the area to make sure Brittany hadn't overheard. "We don't say that out loud in public!" Satisfied that they were alone, Meredith smiled and answered, "Stingrays. They gathered around my hand, Jill. It was one of the most surreal experiences I've ever had."

"More surreal than when you were a—?" Jill ended her sentence and chuckled, seeing the look of panic in Meredith's eyes. She had no intention of saying the M-word, but she loved watching Meredith's reactions whenever she teasingly almost said it.

While Meredith whispered a rant about hating when Jill did that, Jill reached into her pocket and took out her phone. Since she couldn't use it at work, she kept it in silent mode and often forgot to turn the ringer back on. At least without it ringing or vibrating, she wouldn't have the desire to grab it from her pocket, where she couldn't even reach when she was in costume.

She noticed several missed calls and texts from Hailey starting at about six-thirty that morning. She rolled her eyes, wondering what was so important. Before she could reply, the phone showed her she had an incoming call from her cousin, so she answered.

"Jill! W-T-H took you so long?" shrieked Hailey, loud enough that Meredith could hear her.

"I'm at work; we open soon." Jill shook her head. "The kids won't greet themselves."

"We've got a mermaid nine-one-one here!"

The mention of the word caused Meredith's eyes to bulge. She looked around—the coast was still clear—so she nodded at Jill, who understood to put the phone on speaker.

"You need to pick Marina up from the ferry later. She's gonna look for her mother, so she needs your help."

Meredith knew it was the day of the full moon, but with no contact from the mers in a year, it had never dawned on her that they'd return. "What about Marina's tail?" Meredith spoke into the phone. "She can't just leave it."

"She's letting me borrow it!" Hailey giggled. "I'm gonna be a real mermaid!"

Jill and Meredith locked eyes, their jaws dropping.

"You haven't put it on and gotten it wet yet, have you?" asked Jill.

"G-M-A-B, Jill! I still gotta drive Marina across the island to the ferry, and then—"

While Hailey continued babbling about her plans, Jill muted her phone to talk privately with Meredith. "The sun sets about what time? I can make it all the way there by then, right?"

Meredith replied, "Yes, we can."

Jill put a hand on her friend's shoulder. "Merri, that's sweet of you, but I don't want you to miss a day of your internship. It's too wonderful an opportunity for you. On the other hand, I can afford to take a day off from being a fish."

"Aquatic mammal," said Meredith, as if by reflex.

"Whatever." Jill unmuted the phone. Her cousin was still speaking until Jill interrupted by saying, "Hailey, don't you dare do anything—or transform into anything—until I get there."

~ Chapter Three ~

Though Marina had been inside Hailey's convertible before, this was Lorelei's first time riding in a car so open to the air. Sitting in Hailey's short pink party dress and a pair of flip-flops on her feet, she spread her arms across the backseat and let the breeze blow through her red hair. The two tail-skirts were safely hidden in Hailey's bedroom, its walls and shelves fully loaded with mermaid paraphernalia as she imagined. A day on land was always an enjoyable experience, and she smiled for the entire ride. "This flows so fast!" she exclaimed, much calmer than she was just after sunrise. "No other experience like it."

When they had left their school that morning, Marina hadn't told Lorelei the full extent of her plan, so Lorelei had assumed Marina was deliberately choosing to abandon her tail to remain on land to reunite with her mother. Learning of Marina's offer to Hailey, Lorelei tolerated the idea, and she thought back to her swimming race the previous summer with the human-maid. Knowing that their concealed tails could transform humans to mers, Hailey seemed the most logical choice to preserve Marina's tail in the water. And having done so once before with Meredith, Lorelei was the most logical choice to protect Hailey in the water.

"Are you sure you can convince Jill to help me?" asked Marina. "She and I did not always get along."

Hailey waved her hand toward Marina. "Leave Jill to me. And if she doesn't willingly help you, I'll call her brother. Jeff will *definitely* help you."

Smirking, Lorelei leaned forward into the space between

the front seats and asked Marina, "Is Jeff the human-man who you—?"

"Yes." Marina sighed and smiled as she glanced at the quaint brightly colored houses they passed. "We went on a date. And we kissed. Several times." She sighed again.

Hailey's mouth dropped open. "O-M-G, Marina, look at you, kissing and telling! And about my cousin!"

"You showed me, Hailey, that best friends tell each other everything." Marina switched her gaze from Hailey to Lorelei. "And the two of you are my best friends."

Grimacing after she spoke, Marina turned away to view the scenery and to avoid looking at them. She felt guilty for saying how best friends told each other everything when that wasn't the case. The information she had learned about her parents, she hadn't yet shared with anyone else. Especially not Lorelei.

It took them a half hour to cross the island and find a parking spot near the ferry terminal. Jill had an hour drive from the aquarium to the mainland terminal and then an hour-long boat trip to the island, so it would still be awhile until she arrived. To pass some of the time, Hailey led Marina and Lorelei across the street to *The Mermaid's Lagoon.*

The little bell above the door rang when they entered, and the old woman behind the counter looked up and smiled. "Why if it isn't my favorite customer! What brings you here, dearie?" Clothed in her usual black robe of a dress with its flared sleeves, the grey-haired shopkeeper tottered over to Hailey and hugged her. "I'm afraid I haven't got any new information about that painting since the last time you were here."

"That's okay, Isabel. We're just chilling here till…" Hailey's voice trailed off as she watched the woman hover away from her as if she were on roller skates hidden under her dress.

"It's you, dearie, isn't it? The face from the picture?" She stopped before Marina and reached up to squeeze her cheeks in a grandmotherly way. "The girl with the ocean blue eyes.

Only they're not blue with sadness this time. They're a more turbulent blue, like a tidal wave of mixed emotions inside you."

Unsure of what was happening, Lorelei stepped forward, hoping to remove the strange human's hands from her friend's face.

Sensing the movement, Isabel turned to Lorelei and gazed at her. "But you, dearie, your green eyes are also like the ocean. An ocean that's filled with life but clouded by something you can't fully see. Interesting."

The old woman stood motionless, fixated on Lorelei's eyes. The shop fell silent except for the muted sound of traffic and tourists outside until Hailey bounced up and down with her hand raised like a precocious student, calling, "My turn, my turn!"

Snapping out of her trance, Isabel glanced at Hailey and chuckled. "I don't need to look into your eyes to tell that you'll soon be living out your wildest dreams."

As she waddled back to the counter, Lorelei and Marina felt their bodies tense up as they exchanged worried glances at each other, wondering how the human figured out their secret identities. Not catching the mers' reactions but wanting to protect them, Hailey blurted, "I-D-K what you're talking about."

"You must have another party today, don't you, dearie? Here to buy more stickers for the little girls?"

The two mers simultaneously sighed in relief, and Hailey quickly purchased a few packets of mermaid stickers so they could leave without further predictions being made.

They sat at the beach for the next few hours, watching the people and eventually eating. Now and then, attractive and shirtless boys would pass by and smile at them. Some even stopped to talk. Since tourist season had recently started, Hailey didn't know every guy that approached. For no other reason but to pass the time, they occasionally chatted with them and then laughed at their reactions when Lorelei playfully told them that they weren't from anywhere nearby.

Jill's ferry arrived around half past noon. Before leaving the aquarium, she had limped to her supervisor—one hand clutching her side—and claimed terrible stomach cramps. Her acting performance was award-worthy, and as she keeled over and covered her mouth while heaving, she was immediately granted the day off and any subsequent days she needed to recover. She figured that her supervisor didn't want her to vomit into the costume or onto any visitors.

Weaving around other passengers as she stomped off the gangplank and through the exit gate, Jill went straight to Hailey, only giving Marina and Lorelei a quick but civil hello. Pointing her index finger at her cousin's face, Jill commanded, "You're not going to do this."

"It's already a done deal." Hailey smiled and shrugged. "I touched Marina's tail-skirt-thingy, and I can feel it pulling me to the ocean. B-T-dubs, it feels totally awesome! I wanna go right now."

"But it's for a whole month. Do you remember what happened to Meredith? And she was only there for two weeks!" Jill recollected everything negative Meredith had told her about the experience, particularly that vindictive mermaids chased her and she was later knocked unconscious on the beach by violent waves in a storm. "It's too dangerous."

Lorelei stepped forward and said, "I will guide and protect her. Unlike Meredith, Hailey clearly wants to experience being a mer, so I doubt similar events will occur."

"Jill, I appreciate that you are looking out for your family." As Marina spoke calmly, Lorelei and Hailey moved aside. "Please give me the opportunity to look for my family. I do not wish to sacrifice my tail, and Hailey wants—"

"Wants to be a mermaid more than anything else in the world, yeah, yeah, yeah." Jill closed her eyes and took in a deep breath, thinking back to the complicated ruse they developed the previous summer to pass off Marina as Meredith. When she opened her eyes, she turned to Hailey and asked, "What are we going to tell your mom this time?"

"Oh, thank you, thank you, thank you!" Hailey leaped forward and wrapped her arms around Jill. "That's why I need your help. You kick butt at improv!"

Jill groaned. After Hailey had told the complete truth about the previous summer to a skeptical Aunt Susan, Jill stepped in and quickly fabricated a story: Marina was a runaway they had met on the ferry who eventually decided to go back home, while Meredith stayed home to study until her parents returned from their vacation. Though Aunt Susan sensed that the girls believed they had a strong enough reason to hide something from her, she didn't seem to believe either story. More importantly, she certainly didn't appreciate being lied to, so she had grounded them for the rest of that week.

The four girls got into the convertible, and Hailey drove to her two-o'clock appointment at a big yellow house on the east side of the island. When Hailey arrived and was greeted at the door by a pretty woman in her thirties, she explained that the other three were her nautical helpers for the day. The mother smiled at them all and said, "There's plenty of cake. Welcome aboard."

The woman directed them around the side of the house so they could get to the back without being spotted by her daughter. Surrounded by a concrete patio, their in-ground pool was a large rectangle, twice as long as it was wide. Sixteen by thirty-two, estimated Hailey, who had been in a variety of pools in her lifetime, especially that summer. Stairs led into it at one corner of the shallow end, and a diving board was at the deep end. A small bath house was at the far end of the patio, so the girls went inside.

"Wait till you see this." Grinning at Marina, Hailey unzipped the opaque garment bag she had brought with her—just another precaution to preserve the illusion.

When Marina first saw what was inside, her eyes widened. Though her steps were tentative, she couldn't resist being drawn to it. Hailey held it out for Marina to touch, and Marina ran her fingers over the rubbery bumps of the scale pattern. Definitely not the same texture as a real tail, she thought, but from a distance, the difference wouldn't be noticeable. Expecting the costume tail to have been pink, Marina smiled up at Hailey, joyous tears pooling in her eyes, and said, "An orange tail?"

Nodding, Hailey said, "This way you're not the only one."

Hailey sprang into action. First, she went into the bathroom stall to change into her bathing suit: a pink string bikini bottom and a white plastic clamshell top. She also styled her hair, accessorized with a starfish hair clip, and applied her make-up while she could still stand. While readying herself, she explained how she became a kids' birthday party entertainer.

By her eighteenth birthday the previous fall, she had finally saved up enough money to order a swimmable mermaid costume, custom-made to her measurements with optional design choices—color, fluke shape, and so on. Her parents prohibited her from using it in the ocean, but her mother suggested some other creative reasons to wear it. They had been looking for interesting children's programming at the library, so one evening a month, Hailey would read stories dressed in her mermaid tail. She built up a following, and when the weather got warmer, the mother of an overly enthusiastic little girl offered to pay Hailey to perform at her daughter's birthday pool party. Hailey dove at the opportunity, and before she knew it, she had several similar bookings.

Once out of her flip-flops, she plopped onto the floor and rolled the stretchable material of the tail down to the single two-footed flipper built into the fluke. After putting her feet inside, she unrolled the costume up over her legs, occasionally adjusting it and smoothing it out. She had to lie down, arch her back, and suck in her stomach to pull the waistline of the costume over her hips as if she was trying to fit into a pair of extra tight jeans.

Releasing the material which snapped against her skin, Hailey audibly exhaled and sprawled flat with her arms stretched to her sides. Her flipper-fluke loudly smacked on the floor. "Will someone bring me to the pool, please?" she asked, propping her "human" half up with her arms.

Without hesitation, Marina and Lorelei each stood on a side of her and lifted her off the floor. They each had an arm placed under Hailey's knees and one across the back of her waist, and Hailey had her arms around their necks.

"Does this seem to flow upstream to anyone?" asked Lorelei.

"I get it!" giggled Hailey, swinging her fluke back and forth. "L-O-L! I'm a girl dressed like a mermaid being carried by mermaids dressed like girls!"

They sat Hailey down near the steps so she could dip her tail into the pool. The vertical blinds on the inside of the house's sliding doors were drawn closed to keep the birthday guests contained until the big reveal. One little girl was peeking through the blinds, and when Hailey noticed, she grinned and waved, eliciting a wide smile from the girl.

The doors opened shortly after that, followed by a stampede of eight-year-old girls, wearing a rainbow of brightly colored one-piece bathing suits. Stay-at-home moms for many of the children followed closely behind, carefully watching their children near the swimming pool while enjoying how they interacted with the mermaid performer.

First, Hailey let the girls come close to her, either sitting beside her or standing in the shallow end. They were all fascinated by her tail, which she swished around in the water, and some of them eagerly asked if they could touch it. Then she took the birthday girl for a swim on her back before giving the others rides.

She had to be lifted out of the water by her helpers and deposited onto the bench of a long picnic table for individual photographs, a story, art—pages from a mermaid-themed coloring book—and then presents and birthday cake. "This really flows," mumbled Lorelei, globs of chewed chocolate cake in her mouth.

After the cake, the young party guests wanted to watch Mermaid Hailey swim. Happily, she dove under the water and swam all the way across the pool without coming up for air, her hands by her side as her undulating tail propelled her forward. When she finally popped her head back up to tread water with her tail dangling below her in the deep end, all the girls clapped and cheered.

"Your cousin is a natural at this," said Lorelei to Jill.

"It seems she is." Jill stood straight, hoping her height advantage would intimidate Lorelei, but when she looked into the mer's green eyes, Jill relaxed her shoulders. "Promise me you won't let anything happen to her down there."

"You have my word."

The remaining time was unstructured, so all of the party guests were in the water with Hailey. Marina and Lorelei sat on the pool's edge at the shallow side to dip their feet into the water, but it didn't smell or feel right to them. The youngest girl there, wearing inflatable floaties around her arms, made her way over to them and asked, "Are you mermaids too?"

Marina and Lorelei glanced at each other, wondering how to respond, until Marina replied, "Not today."

The child pulled herself out of the pool and then skipped away and into her mother's outstretched arms. The mother kissed the girl's cheek while the girl pointed at the other children gathered around the mermaid. Hailey sat on the other edge of the pool, smacking her fluke onto the water's surface and splashing all the girls around her. They were all laughing and egging her on to do it again.

"So you are going on this adventure, Marina?" asked Lorelei. "Sink or swim?"

Marina's gaze remained on the little girl and her mother, their arms happily embracing each other. "I have never wanted anything more."

~ Chapter Four ~

"You're gonna need clothes for the month," said Hailey, removing her suitcase from the closet and laying it open on her bed. Then she started packing for Marina, first a pair of denim shorts before remembering that the previous summer, Marina had only worn skirts and dresses.

Leaning against the door and barricading it shut, Jill watched Hailey fill the suitcase. "She doesn't need much more than a few days' worth, tops. She can borrow Meredith's clothes once we're off-island."

"But what if Jeff wants to take her out on a date? She'll have to look pretty." Hailey dashed to the closet and fingered through the party dresses still hanging there. "What's his favorite color? She should wear that!"

Jill rolled her eyes and replied, "Blue, but I don't think—"

Hailey squealed and hopped around when she found the perfect one. It was royal blue with a single shoulder strap, a tight-fitting bodice, and a flared skirt. "This will look super hot on you!" She bounced across the room to hold the dress in front of Marina. "S-W-I-M?"

Picking up the shorts and feeling the texture of the denim, Lorelei asked, "What does S-W-I-M mean?"

"It's just the way Hailey talks," answered Jill. "You learn the acronyms after a while."

"It stands for See. What. I. Mean." Hailey enumerated the words on her fingers. "See what I mean? Marina's gonna look pretty in the dress. That's what I mean."

"S-W-I-M." Lorelei pondered the explanation before smiling. "Something I now know."

Hailey giggled. "Hey, that's S-I-N-K. That spells *sink*, and mine spells *swim*!"

"Sink or swim," said Lorelei.

"That. Is. Too. Cool!" Hailey leaped to Lorelei and hugged her. "You and I are gonna get along so well under the sea! We'll be B-F-Fs!"

"Best friends with fins, I remember that one from last northern season." Still holding the shorts, Lorelei walked over to Marina. "In many ways, I envy you. I know you have already walked among the humans for longer than I have, but you are going to travel to places I can only dream of experiencing."

"There's a way you both could stay here." Hailey skipped over to Jill and elbowed her in the side. "What do you say, Jill? Sink or swim?"

Jill watched Hailey clasp her hands together and bat her eyelashes. Then she turned toward Marina and Lorelei, who were standing there in anticipation. Feeling the pressure of all of their stares, Jill shook her head. "No way. My feet stay on land, and my feet also stay on me. You need a mermaid guide down there, and I haven't figured out what to tell your mom yet."

"Chill out, Jill. J-K, okay?"

Hailey finished packing, needing to sit on top of the suitcase to close it. Marina reached to take it, but Hailey wouldn't let her do it on her own. As far as Hailey was concerned, Marina was her guest on land and deserved special treatment. Lorelei retrieved her tail-skirt from Hailey's drawer and slipped it on underneath the dress she was wearing. Then she took Marina's, and the girls went downstairs and outside.

They assumed that at some time after Jill gave her improvised explanation, Hailey's mother would drive Marina and Jill to the ferry terminal. Hailey loaded the suitcase into the convertible's trunk, but before closing it, she realized there was one more thing she needed to give to Marina. She jogged to the back deck of the house and retrieved her costume, which had been laid out to dry on a beach chair.

"I know it's not the same, but if you're out there and you want to feel like a mer, well then you can wear this." Hailey handed her costume tail to Marina. "I'm borrowing yours, so it's only fair that you borrow mine."

"That flows," said Lorelei.

"I don't know what to say." Marina held the tail close to her, and she could smell a mixture of scents: the bitterness of the flexible material with the sharpness of the strange odor from the swimming pool—chlorine, she believed Jill called it—but there was a faint sweetness of Hailey's perfume. "I will take good care of it."

"And I'm gonna take great care of yours," said Hailey, taking Marina's shimmery tail-skirt from Lorelei. She turned to Jill and asked, "What time is it?"

"Almost five-thirty," answered Jill as she glanced at her phone. Then she scrolled through a few messages from Meredith, who was wondering what was happening.

"O-M-G! We've gotta go," squealed Hailey, tossing off her cover-up to reveal the plastic clamshell top and pink bikini bottom she had been wearing at the party before sprinting toward the water.

Glancing at the late afternoon sun still high in the sky, Lorelei sighed. "I was hoping to stay on land until sunset."

"You can't go yet! Your mom's not—" Jill looked up from her half-texted status report and was suddenly whacked in the face by a floppy orange silicone tail fluke.

"I did not mean to do that, Jill," said Marina, leaving the costume in Jill's arms. "Could you kindly hold this for me so I may assist Hailey."

"Whatever." Grumbling, Jill dumped the tail costume in the back seat of the open convertible and took off after her cousin. "Hailey, you can't just swim away and leave me to explain everything to your mom!"

Though Hailey heard Jill's call, she kept her eyes focused on the shoreline. When her feet touched the foamy water, she quickly jumped back onto the sand, fearful about getting the skirt wet before she was wearing it. Sensing that Marina and

Lorelei had joined her, she clutched the smooth material in her quivering hands and asked, "What do I do now?"

"Put it on," answered Marina. "The ocean will do the rest."

The wave receded, so Hailey gingerly bent down and stepped one foot inside the tail-skirt, followed by the other. Lifting it all the way up her legs and over her bikini bottom, she released it, and it conformed snugly around her waist and hips. Slowly, she stepped forward into the oncoming wave. As the cool water tickled her feet, she bounced up and down, leaving imprints of her toes in the damp sand.

"What are you waiting for?" asked Jill, a tone of contempt in her voice. "Isn't this what you always wanted?"

"Well, *yeah!*" Her hands on her hips, Hailey glared at her cousin but couldn't keep the angry look on her face long enough. "But Meredith said it was really painful." She turned toward Marina. "This isn't gonna hurt, is it?"

"If it will ease your concerns, you may watch me first." Lorelei lowered herself into the next wave as it rolled onto the beach, and the water seeped through her dress and onto the tail-skirt. As she felt her transformation beginning, she sighed. "The sensation is quite pleasant."

Hailey's eyes widened as she watched a green light emanating from underneath the dress Lorelei wore. Within moments, green scales were starting to crawl their way down Lorelei's legs.

"This is really gonna happen to me! I'm gonna be a mermaid!" She turned to Lorelei and Marina. "Oh, sorry, my bad. A *mer*." Then Hailey squealed.

Lorelei patted the film of sea foam and said, "Sit beside me so you may watch your legs change."

"Oh, T-R-F! That. Really. Flows!" Hailey giddily jumped up and down until she lost her footing and landed on the damp sand.

When water from the incoming wave touched the skirt, it started glowing, and Hailey watched in awe as its translucence was replaced by an opaque shade of orange. Her legs started to tingle until the skirt suddenly constricted around her waist and hips. The pinching sensation startled her so much that her backside sprang up off the ground and splashed when it landed back on the water of the next wave.

Clapping her hands, she giggled. "It's happening. Like, really happening. It feels like it's attaching itself to me."

"That is what you should be feeling," said Lorelei, her legs completely replaced by a green tail. Her fluke was starting to appear.

Hailey felt the strings of her bikini bottom unravel, and the next wave carried it away. "I'm naked!" she shrieked as she brought her legs close together.

But when she looked down at her bare thighs, she only saw one scaly mass in front of her. She caressed the iridescent disks the wrong way, so they felt sharp and jagged instead of smooth. Her fingers recoiled as if receiving an electric shock, and she burst into giggles again. Reflexively, she separated her knees, but they were drawn back together like two powerful magnets.

The feeling of pins and needles ran down her legs as they were connected and coated with more scales. "I'm being zipped up! Can't feel my legs, but I can still wiggle my toes. See?" She demonstrated for them.

Marina put a hand on Hailey's shoulder. "I know I asked you to protect it, but it is odd watching my tail appear on another."

From the house behind them, a voice called, "Jillybean? Is that you?"

Jill turned and saw her aunt at the wooden footbridge. "Aunt Susan?" she muttered as Hailey simultaneously said, "Mom?"

Her tail fully formed, Lorelei lunged forward into the rising tide. Marina crouched down and said, "Hailey, you must leave now. If your mother sees—"

"Yeah, it's nine-one-one, I get it." Hailey looked out to the ocean past her uncooperative feet—the only human anatomy below her waist that remained. She released audible *oomphs* as she scooted forward before groaning in frustration. "I'm all numb down there. I'm not done yet."

"I'll see what I can do." Jill took a deep breath before jogging toward her aunt.

Marina reached under Hailey's tail to lift her but almost instantly dropped her back onto the ground. "I did not realize mers were so difficult to move out of the water."

"Tell me about it. Carrying Meredith around last summer was like moving a beached whale." Hailey sheepishly looked up at Marina. "Oh, J-K. I didn't mean—"

"Let it float. We have more important matters to attend to."

Instead of trying to carry Hailey, Marina reached under her arms and rotated her halfway around. The surf crashed against Marina's legs, but she kept her balance and dragged Hailey backward into the water.

"Hey, there go my feet!" Hailey cocked her head forward at the flattened and flimsy appendage growing outward at the end of her orange scales. She tried to control it, but it flopped and drooped.

She looked toward her house and saw that her mother had met Jill at the bottom of the stairs. Even across the beach, with the sounds of the waves and seagulls, she could clearly make out parts of their conversation.

Susan embraced her niece. "What are you doing here, Jillybean?"

"Had the day off, so I thought I'd come by and see Hailey. She's inside. Why don't we go in there?" Jill quickly turned Aunt Susan around so she wouldn't be looking at the ocean and tried to guide her up the stairs.

"Hailey's down the beach. I saw her with you and some other girl." Susan adjusted her librarian glasses, which had been jostled during the hug, and then stared directly at Hailey.

Recognizing the glare on her mother's face, Hailey gulped. "I gotta get out of here A-S-A-P!"

"Hailey Elizabeth!" called Susan, stomping through the sand. "I thought I told you that costume was only for swimming in pools!"

"Oh no, she middle-named me." Hailey's fluke had almost fully formed, but when she tried to flip it, it just hung limply. "Can I swim in this thing yet?"

"Perhaps, but your mother would see you leave." Marina was suddenly almost knee-deep in the water as the next wave came in. "I do not see Jill. Why is she not doing her improv for you?"

"You know the rules, Hailey. No mermaiding in the ocean." Susan leaned over and waved her finger angrily. "And you're not going to encourage my daughter to do dangerous stunts like this." When Susan looked up and saw Marina's face, her mouth dropped in instant recognition. "You! You're that fake-Meredith girl from last summer. I'm not surprised someone like you is responsible for this."

Like an apprehended criminal, Marina held her arms up, so Hailey's arms fell until they splashed the receding wave.

"Mom, Marina's one of my B-F-Fs," said Hailey. "She's really sweet, remember?"

"Sweet? She got you and Jillybean to lie to me." Susan grabbed her daughter by the ankles and struggled to drag her away from the water. "When I get you onto dry sand, you're taking this costume off, young lady."

"But Mom, I *can't* take it off!"

"You'd better take it off, or you'll be grounded all summer."

Hailey chuckled at the thought of being grounded, imagining herself being kept in the bathtub every day. Her laughter stopped when her mother gave her tail a yank, causing her mermaid parts to jerk forward but her human parts to fall back until she was lying horizontally with her head submerged in the next wave coming in.

When she was dragged out of the surf, she spit some of the salty water out of her mouth, secretly thrilled that it hadn't made her gag. "It's not coming off. It's part of me, Mom."

"I know your mermaid fascination has been a part of you

since you were younger, but I'm serious. If you don't take this tail off this minute, then I'll take it off myself."

Finally away from the waves, Susan let go of Hailey's ankles. The tail smacked the ground and scattered some sand. Susan knelt beside her daughter and tried to pry the costume away from Hailey's waist, but she couldn't find a gap between the orange material and Hailey's skin.

"They really make these things form-fitting," she muttered in frustration while Hailey giggled.

"Mom, that tickles!"

"Hailey Elizabeth, I swear I'll cut you out of this thing if you don't get out on your own."

Propping herself up with her elbows, Hailey grinned sheepishly with her eyes wide open. "If you'd just listen to me, Mom. I'm going to be a mermaid for the next month. A *real* mermaid."

"Mermaids don't exist."

"Yes they do, Aunt Susan." Jill arrived with Hailey's costume tail in her arms. "You're looking at one."

Marina bowed her head. "I am a mer, and I am trusting Hailey to protect my tail until the next full moon."

Susan's head jerked around while she looked from Marina to Hailey to Jill. With one hand, she squeezed the thick, rubbery fabric of the costume in Jill's hands—the costume that clearly looked like Hailey's. With her other hand, she stroked the hips of the costume she thought Hailey was wearing—first toward the fluke and then back toward Hailey's waist. Smooth and then scaly, like a fish.

"This can't be real."

"But it is. I don't have to pretend to be a mermaid anymore." Hailey squealed in delight. "I really am one."

Then Susan's eyes rolled back into her head, and she collapsed onto the sand.

~ Chapter Five ~

"Mom, I'm doing fine." Meredith shook her head, almost causing the phone balanced on her shoulder to fall off.

"I'm always going to ask you those questions," said Meredith's mother. "It's my prerogative to worry about you when you're away for a long time. I've never gone this long without seeing you."

"I've only been here a week. You and Dad went on a safari for two weeks last year, remember?"

Thinking back to her adventure the previous summer, Meredith glanced at the figurine on the corner of the desk in her dormitory room. It was an orange-tailed mermaid that had made its way into her suitcase. Hailey had purchased it as a gift for Marina, who had forgotten about it in all the commotion. Instead, Meredith opted to keep it for herself as a memento of the two weeks she was a mermaid with an orange tail.

She reached for the statuette and traced her fingers along the jagged scales sculpted into its tail. When she reached the fluke, which flared outward around the rock the mermaid was perched upon, she stopped at the tip which had been chipped away. The figurine had broken in the suitcase. Had Meredith known it was inside, she would have wrapped it better to preserve it. The piece that had chipped off had crumbled into a few pieces too difficult to glue back together, so the mermaid would forever be incomplete.

"Meredith, are you still there?" asked her mother through the phone.

"Sorry, Mom."

"You seem distracted. Are you positive you're doing fine?"

"I told you I am, Mom." Meredith looked around and found the perfect scapegoat—an open reference book—on the desk in front of her. "I'm studying."

"Now that sounds more like my girl. What are you studying?"

Meredith looked down at the color photographs. "Manatees. The aquarium is nursing one back to health. I'm hoping I can impress Dr. Hatcher with my knowledge of them, so he lets us see it before they release it."

"Still setting impressive goals. I'm proud of you, Meredith. I'll let you get back to your work. I'll call tomorrow night."

"Mom, I'm fine, and I'm busy here. I promise we can talk in a few days."

"All right. A few days. I love you."

"Love you too."

Meredith hung up the phone before her mother could ask if she had been eating well, sleeping well, and making friends with the other interns. She groaned at her mother's recent clinginess. No matter how many times Meredith reminded her mother about the length of time they were apart the previous summer, her mother didn't relent. And her mother would have had more reason to worry about her back then if she had known the truth about how far away she had swum as a mermaid. Her mother would have grounded her if she knew how unsupervised she had been out in the open ocean.

At the aquarium, Meredith and the other interns never had unstructured time lasting longer than a half hour. In the nearby university, they had a little more free time and could even explore the surrounding area as long as they signed in and out with the dormitory's house master.

Meredith was bright enough to understand what had changed during the year. While her parents were on their vacation, Meredith had still been living with them. After the internship, Meredith would be leaving for college and only returning for holiday breaks. Her mother was obviously dreading the day she'd move out for good.

"Sorry that your little bird is leaving the nest, Mom," muttered Meredith to her phone as she placed it face down on the desk. Her eyes turned to the mermaid figurine. "Or that your little mer-baby is leaving the school."

She sent a quick text to Jill asking for a status report before turning back to the open reference book. On the next page was a diagram of the internal anatomy of a manatee, so she started memorizing the names of the structures. Her peripheral vision caught the figurine again, almost like its tail was glimmering in the early evening sunlight coming through the window. Experiencing things firsthand had just as much value as studying, but in this case, the only way she could hope to gain any first-hand experience with the ailing manatee was to study.

As she leaned over the book, the images went out of focus, so she pushed her eyeglasses back up to the bridge of her nose. The truth was that she didn't need them to read anymore, her vision having been enhanced since her time as a mer. Another one of her newfound superpowers, but she chose to wear them during her senior year at home to keep her teachers, friends, and especially her parents from getting suspicious.

However, her fellow interns and the marine biologists at the aquarium—people she barely knew—wouldn't know the difference.

As she removed her glasses, she dislodged some locks of hair from behind her ear, and they fell in front her face. Groaning, she brushed them away from her eyes and undid the bun to release her long hair. Another side effect of being a former mermaid was that her hair grew at a much faster rate than before. She had gotten it cut short just before graduation, but only a few weeks later, it already hung past her shoulders.

Frustrated, she tied her hair into a ponytail, but before she could return to her work, she heard the slightly ajar door to the room creak open.

"Again you're studying?" Brittany popped her bubble

gum. "How did I end up in a program with the two biggest dorks in the world?"

"You must be intelligent also, or you wouldn't be here." Though Meredith spoke the words, she doubted they were true based on Brittany's attitude and poor work ethic.

"You're here without parents breathing down your neck, and all you want to do is study? We might have to do marine biology stuff at the aquarium, but this is after hours, and I'm away from all that surveillance. But I'm stuck with dorks who don't want to enjoy the independence like we'd have in college."

"Maybe you should embrace your inner dork."

"Maybe you should keep your comments to yourself." Brittany turned to go but stopped upon seeing the figurine. She snickered as she picked it up. "A mermaid? What are you, like, eight years old?"

"And what's wrong with liking mermaids?" Meredith tried to snatch the figurine from Brittany, who quickly raised her hand into the air.

"Nothing's wrong with it, if you're still a little girl."

As Meredith stretched to retrieve her statuette, there was a knock on the door. "I thought I heard you both in here," said Will. "We should study together. I brought chips and soda."

"What a lame party," snarled Brittany. She slammed the figurine onto the desk, popped her gum, and strutted to the door. "Let me know if you two dorks change your mind and want some real action."

"Wow. What's wrong with her?"

Meredith didn't hear Will's question because she was examining the figurine for any further cracks. Fortunately, there wasn't anything new. Just the chipped tail.

"Did she break it?" asked Will.

Break the mermaid? No, thought Meredith. *Break my spirits a little bit? Maybe.* "She's just a crabby blowfish, I guess."

"You've got your book open to manatees, you've got this little mermaid on your desk, and you're making fish puns. You're really into this stuff, aren't you?"

"Aren't you? You're doing this internship too. What got you into marine biology?"

Will sat and recalled a story from when he was twelve years old. His family lived in the Pacific Northwest, not too far from the ocean. One summer day after a big storm, they went to a beach where half a dozen humpback whales, *Megaptera novaeangliae*, had washed ashore. There were people—mostly unsupervised teenagers and college kids—touching, teasing, and taunting the poor creatures instead of helping them. His parents covered his younger sister's eyes, but Will couldn't stop watching. He remembered being angry on the drive back and at home that night when they watched the news, only to learn that though a few of the whales had been saved, most of them had died. Some of them had been severely injured by the people.

"After that, all I wanted to do was help the animals in the ocean." Will leaned forward. "What about you?"

Meredith had spent most of the story focused on Will's face, which had brightened as he told his story. Finally snapping out of her trance when he asked his question a second time, she replied, "I went swimming with dolphins last summer."

"*Tursiops truncates*, I assume. So you're a dolphin girl?"

"What's that supposed to mean?"

Will shook his head and held his arm forward, waving it like he was erasing a chalkboard. "I didn't mean anything by that. I've heard that swimming with dolphins can be a life-altering experience." He quickly stood up. "I just thought that…well, you're really good with the rays, and I'm sure you'd be good with dolphins too…and, well—" Nervously pacing the room, he raked his fingers through his short hair all the way back until his palm grabbed the back of his neck. "I don't really know what I mean."

Stifling a giggle, Meredith said, "It's all right. The dolphins were part of the reason I decided to study marine biology."

"What's the other part?"

After a glance at the mermaid figurine, Meredith quickly

turned around and focused on the open book before Will could connect the dots. "Manatees," she said abruptly.

"Manatees? You've swum with them too? Wow."

"I haven't swum with manatees. Not yet, anyway." She smirked. "But I do have to learn about them."

"Oh, yeah, sorry." Will got up and headed for the door.

Assuming he had left the room, Meredith instinctively reached for the figurine and let her fingers stroke the mermaid's tail. Swimming and communicating side-by-side with dolphins had been more than a life-altering experience; it had been as significant a career-path transformation as the physical transformation that had made her a temporary mer.

"Maybe someday you'll be the one to find them."

Will's voice startled her, and her body tensed as she withdrew her hand. "I thought you had left." She glowered over her shoulder at him until her pulse rate returned to normal. "Find what?"

"Mermaids." He winked at her and wandered down the hall.

As Meredith sighed, she wondered if she was already the first person to find them.

~ Chapter Six ~

The tide was still coming in, so Jill and Marina carefully sat Susan up and dragged her a little further away from the water. The abrupt movement jostled her back into consciousness. "What happened?" she asked groggily.

"I think you passed out," said Jill. She sat beside her aunt and put an arm around her to keep her supported. "Can't say I blame you. I'm still not sure how I kept my wits about me when it happened to Meredith last summer."

"So it's all real?"

Susan's eyes scanned the immediate area. Rumpled on the dry sand on one side of her was the costume tail. The silicone material was a dull shade of orange compared to the bright sparkling scales covering Hailey's lower half.

Shaking her throbbing head, Susan looked up at Marina. "And you're a mermaid?"

"We prefer to be called *mers*." Marina knelt beside Susan. "You should be proud of your daughter and niece. They have faithfully kept our existence a secret. I am honored to call them my friends."

Unable to keep her eyes off of her daughter's new form, Susan remembered how ecstatic Hailey had been when her swimmable tail arrived in the mail. She wanted to try it on immediately in the living room, and the first picture of her lying on the sofa in costume was instantly uploaded to her social media profile pages and then printed and hung on the fridge. But Susan was still trying to wrap her brain around watching her daughter flap an actual fish tail up and down on the sand.

"Myths, legends, folklore. I can tell you what aisle in the library they're in." She drew a hand to her mouth as she gasped. "I'm going to have to reclassify some of those books."

Hailey shook her head. "No one can know. That's why we made you think Marina was Meredith. We were kinda covering for both of them. You see, Marina hid her tail on the beach, and Meredith found it and put it on, and then got stuck that way until…"

As the girls put the events of the previous summer into the correct context for Susan, she blinked rapidly and raked her fingers through her hair, trying to process all the information. The truth made complete sense to her, even though the situation was utterly unbelievable.

"…and Marina needs the time to find her mom, so I'm gonna watch her tail. You gotta promise not to tell anyone else any of this. C-Y-H." Hailey traced an X in front of her heart.

Susan stared into Hailey's eager and pleading brown eyes. "There's no way to reverse this and still preserve Meredith's—I mean Marina's—tail until the next full moon?"

Hailey shook her head enthusiastically, and the other two girls followed suit.

"What am I going to tell your father?"

Jill clapped her hands once to get everyone's attention. "You can tell Uncle Greg that Hailey got a job as a mermaid at the aquarium I work at so she'll be staying with me for the summer."

"Now that's the kind of Jillybean improv I was hoping for!" Hailey flipped her tail and gave Jill two thumbs up.

Susan shook her head. "I'm not going to lie to him."

"Look at it a different way." Jill wrangled up her hair that was blowing in the sea breeze and tied it up behind her. "Hailey's playing a *role*, just like I do in my plays. She's a temporary mer."

"I admire your integrity, Aunt Susan," said Marina. "And I know you are trustworthy. If you feel you must tell Uncle

Greg the truth, then you may."

Turning to Jill and Hailey, Susan cocked an eyebrow. "Why is it that the only one of you talking rationally is the one who's mythological?" She took Marina's hand. "Thank you, but if you're going to be out here, who's going to take care of Hailey out there?"

Marina stood, turned toward the ocean, and called, "Lore, you may show yourself."

"I'm gonna have the best mer-guide ever," said Hailey. "Lorelei watched Meredith last summer, and I can't wait to go swimming with her."

The rising tide reached Susan's feet, so she removed her sandals and handed them to Jill. Standing over her daughter, Susan smiled as Hailey laughed and splashed the foamy water with her fluke. "I understand that you've got to do this, both for Marina and yourself, but when you get back, it's only a month or so until you go off-island for college. I was hoping to have you here before you went off to school."

"I will be taking her to school." Lorelei was gliding to shore upon an incoming wave.

Upon seeing the green-tailed, red-haired mermaid appear out of nowhere from the water, Susan felt herself getting woozy. She started to sway, and Jill rushed to her side to steady her.

They introduced her to Lorelei, who once again made a promise to keep Hailey from danger. Then everyone crowded around Susan, awaiting the final permission to leave, but she cleared them away to talk privately with Hailey.

"Please, Mom?" Hailey clasped her hands together and bounced in the water. "P-P-S-O-T! I want to do this more than anything I've ever asked you for."

"I know you have, ever since you were a little girl." Susan sat beside Hailey, not caring that the water was soaking her skirt. "And you're good at it. I watched you on your first story time at the library with all those little kids. All I could see were little versions of you, completely enraptured by the beautiful, magical creature before them."

Hailey blushed as she shyly looked away. "You thought I was beautiful?"

"Oh, Sweetie, I've always known you were beautiful." Susan gently brushed some of Hailey's dark hair away from her eyes. "But those days at the library, you were positively glowing. I had never seen you happier. I wish I could have seen you swimming at some of the birthday parties, live instead of on video. The little girls must love it."

"They do. There was this one time—"

"And my little girl must love it too." Susan stroked Hailey's cheek and then wiped some tears away from her own. "You must be in your element right now."

The wave receded, keeping Susan in ankle-deep water and Hailey's tail covered. "I can feel the water pulling me like I'm supposed to go there. Like I'm supposed to be a mermaid for real. Marina and Lorelei watched me swim in my tail at the party today. B-T-dubs, they think I'm an awesome swimmer. For a human-maid, they said. L-O-L!"

"Just promise me you'll be careful and do everything you're told."

Hailey nodded and then crossed her heart. "Of course. And I'll be back here next full moon, I promise."

"The house is going to be quiet without you, and your father's not back on-island until later next week."

"You and Dad can go away together! Take a trip! It's your anniversary soon, isn't it?"

Susan chuckled. "In November, but I'm sure I can get some time off from the library."

"You totally deserve it! Don't worry about me. I'm gonna be fine 'cause I'll be in my element." Hailey squealed in excitement as the water rose to her waist and covered her tail with sea foam.

"Susan?" asked a voice from the back deck of the house next door. "Is everything all right out there?"

Upon hearing the sound of the stranger's voice, Lorelei submerged herself.

"Nosy neighbor alert," said Jill, running toward the water.

"I think it's time for you to sink and swim."

"It is sink *or* swim," said Marina.

Hailey quickly threw her arms around her mother and squeezed tightly. "Thanks for always supporting me, Mom, even when my dreams were a little…well, you know…"

"Crazy?" Susan reluctantly broke the embrace and stood. She turned toward the houses and called, "Everything's fine, Mr. Dobbins. You can go back to doing whatever you were doing."

He nodded and lurched away from the railing of his deck.

Susan turned back to Hailey, but she wasn't there. The water rose to Susan's knees while she frantically looked around, but Hailey was no longer on the beach. "Where…?" she huffed, stopping her question when she noticed Jill and Marina pointing toward the southern horizon.

Even with her glasses on, Susan could only barely make out the two heads that bobbed up and down in the distant water. The glare of the sun off the waves made it impossible to tell which waving arm belonged to Hailey, but Susan waved goodbye all the same. Before the two heads disappeared into the deep water, the wind carried Hailey's voice to a misty-eyed Susan.

"T-T-Y-L and I-L-Y, Mom!"

A split second later, their two flukes broke through the surface. Before they could vanish, Susan squinted as tightly as she could. Sunlight caught the brighter color of the tail on the right, so it glowed with a golden hue, and Susan wistfully smiled knowing it was Hailey.

She felt a warm hand on her shoulder. "Are you gonna be okay?" asked Jill from behind.

"I'm going to have to be." Susan wiped her eyes and then took a deep breath. "I suppose I have to drive you two to the ferry now."

"I have never been on a boat before," said Marina. "This is going to be an exciting adventure."

Jill quickly checked the time on her phone and noticed another inquiring text from Meredith. "Next one leaves in about forty-five minutes. Think you can make it on time?"

"Just give me a moment first." Susan stared out at the water and breathed in the salty air. Memories of Hailey's childhood filled her mind, and she wondered how eighteen years could have passed so quickly. Whether Susan agreed with the decision or not, Hailey was old enough to plan her own future.

Spotting the orange fluke one last time far in the distance, Susan wiped away a melancholy tear and whispered to herself, "She's not a little girl anymore."

~ Chapter Seven ~

"So Hailey's officially a mermaid," said Jill into her phone as the ferry pulled away from the dock. "Or a mer—whatever they call themselves. Naturally, she's overjoyed."

Meredith said, "Of course she is. I'll bet she's as happy as a clam."

"Yeah, yeah, yeah, no fish jokes, okay?"

"Sorry." Meredith paused, and there was the sound of a door closing. "Hailey's going to have a blast. I know I had a great time, but she's been wanting this since she was little."

"Whoa, back up a few steps, Merri! How can you say you had a great time? You hated it at first, and at the end, you were almost run out of the ocean."

"But the dolphins and the—"

"Or would it be *swum* out of the ocean? You're the grammar expert."

"What did you end up telling your aunt?"

"Let's just say that last summer makes a lot more sense to her now."

"You told her the *truth?* What does Marina think of that?"

"She's fine with it." Jill glanced over at Marina, who stood at the ferry's back railing beside Hailey's suitcase with the garment bag draped over it. She was waving at whatever people were at the terminal and the nearby beach. Rolling her eyes, Jill said into the phone, "Right now she's smiling like she's the queen of the world or something."

"What are we going to do with her? Where's she going to stay? We had the perfect combination of situations to pull it off last summer, but how do we explain her this summer? For a full moon cycle?"

"Tonight she'll have to stay at my place. We'll figure the rest out later."

"Your place? Does she know about—?"

Jill didn't hear the rest of the question, so she covered her other ear and spoke louder into the phone. "You're breaking up, Merri! I don't get good reception once the boat leaves the island."

The connection went dead, and Jill verified that she had no signal bars showing. With no other choice but to call Meredith back later, she put the phone in her purse and walked over to Marina.

Her long blonde hair blowing wildly in the wind, Marina was still leaning forward and waving at the island. Then she looked down at the white-capped lines of waves leaving the back of the ferry.

"This is magnificent! I have never seen waves being made from above before." She pointed at the island. "The humans over there—they look so small I can barely see them. Even the island appears to be getting smaller."

"It's getting further away," said Jill. "That's what happens."

"Yes, I understand, but I thought Hailey's island was a large land. We typically stay further out in the ocean, so I have never seen otherwise."

"Then you'd better be ready to have your mind blown when you see the mainland."

Jill led Marina away from the back of the boat and to the lower level to get a bag of popcorn from the snack bar. Once they emerged from the stairway at the front of the boat, Marina ran to the front railing and stared into the distance. The pale blue sky met the edge of the water, but she couldn't tell where one ended and the other began.

"The island's not what's large," said Jill when she leaned against the railing beside Marina. "It's the ocean that's large. The whole earth is three-fourths water. Or is it two-thirds? I don't remember exactly, but I bet Meredith could tell you the exact percentage. If you want, you can ask her when we see her tomorrow."

"Will she be helping us search for my mother?" asked Marina. "Is it possible to see Meredith sooner?"

"We're going straight to my house. I'm already late coming home as it is. I'm supposed to be there now. Oh no!" Spilling some popcorn on the deck, Jill dug out her phone and held it high in the hopes she could get at least a faint signal. "My mom's probably calling right now wondering where I am. She's gonna freak out."

Jill handed the popcorn to Marina and told her to watch the horizon for the mainland, and then she excused herself to look for someplace on the ferry where her phone worked.

Marina reached into the bag and took out one of the puffed kernels. She rolled it between her fingers and it left a slippery residue on her. When she brought it closer to her face, its aroma tickled her nose. She had watched Jill eat it by the handful, so she placed it on her tongue. The slight taste of salt reminded her of home—a home that she was floating over on the boat. A home from where she would be journeying farther than any mer she knew. A journey to find the one mer she had never known.

As she ate more of the popcorn, her thoughts wandered to Jill's mother wondering where Jill was. Was her mother out there wondering where she was? Had her mother been worrying about her all those moon cycles—over two hundred of them? Would her mother recognize her? Would her mother even remember her?

The questions popped into her head rapidly, one after the other like the kernels in the machine that had mesmerized her at the snack bar. She didn't have the answers. They were ahead of her on land, and when she looked forward, the scenery had changed. An endless dark line stretching across the horizon separated the ocean from the sky, and it grew as the boat approached it.

The mainland? Jill had used that phrase, but Marina hadn't been able to imagine the size of land equaling the size of the ocean. She kept her gaze focused ahead and lost track of how much time was passing and how much popcorn she was eating.

Her trance was broken when Jill cleared her throat and said, "Mind blown yet?"

"There is much land out there." Marina crunched on a handful of popcorn. "I would never have known."

"You looked like you were watching a movie."

Marina only vaguely remembered what a movie was from her lessons pretending to be Meredith the previous summer, but she didn't care. She kept looking forward as she reached into the emptying bag. "How will I ever find her if there is that much land?"

"We've got that folder with Hailey's research." Jill handed Marina a napkin to wipe off the popcorn butter from her fingers and around her mouth. "That's how we start."

As the ferry approached the mainland, Marina watched the distant trees swaying in the wind. Just beyond the terminal was a large parking lot filled with cars—many more than she had seen gathered together on Hailey's island, and in a variety of colors closely matching the various tails of the mers in her school. None were orange.

Jill led her to a dark blue car called a minivan, though Marina had no idea why Jill was apologizing for it. While Jill drove, Marina kept her attention on the scenery passing by.

First, there were shops like the ones near the main beach of Hailey's island, followed by a series of quaint houses with green grass lawns in front of them. Eventually, the car turned sharply, causing Marina's body to lurch to the opposite side. When the roadway straightened, the vehicle's speed increased and the bushes and trees lining the sides of the road smeared together into a blur of green.

"Why are we traveling so quickly?" she asked.

"I'm already late as it is," answered Jill. "Besides, that's just what you're supposed to do on a highway."

"A highway?" Marina leaned against the window and looked at the flat dark surface below the car. "But we are not high. We are on the ground."

"Yeah, I know we're on the ground. It's called that because you can travel at high speeds here. Get it?"

After a brief pause, Marina replied, "I do not. Why *must* you travel so fast? Lorelei often encourages me to let it float and enjoy the experience. How can I when everything rushes by?"

"But there's not much to see here. Only trees."

"There are no trees where I am from." She turned back toward the window and sighed, unable to make out the details of her view.

Groaning, Jill moved into the right lane and slowed down. A loud horn honked behind them a few times until Jill drowned out the sound with music from the radio.

"Thank you." Marina smiled as she noticed how the trunks of the trees were arranged in rows and how the larger branches split off from the trunks. Other details were still obscured by the speed of the car, but Marina was happy to see what she could. "How much more distance will we travel to your home?"

"If we go this slowly, it's gonna be a while." Jill released a long breath and muttered to herself, "Let it float, Jill. Just let it float."

Jill drove without starting up a conversation, and Marina kept watching the scenery. She looked ahead, behind, and even out the window on the other side of Jill. There were trees, occasionally interrupted by roads turning away to the side or roads under or over them—and she wondered if they would be called *lowerways* and *higherways*, not that it made much sense to her. Sometimes she could see buildings along the roads leading away but never any water, though they had been driving for some time. When on Hailey's island, they had never journeyed for so long without seeing the ocean. If the mainland was so large that there was no sight of her home, Marina hoped finding her mother wouldn't be impossible.

By the time they pulled into Jill's driveway, the color of the sky had darkened to the purples of dusk. The gray house was two stories tall with a wraparound front porch which included a two-seat swing. As Jill led Marina up the front walkway, she whispered, "Let me do all the improv."

As soon as Jill opened the front door, her mother called from the kitchen. Wearing a navy blue business blazer and skirt with a string of pearls hanging over her shimmery cream blouse, she briskly entered the hallway, her matching heels clicking loudly on the hardwood. She tapped her watch and asked, "Do you have any idea what time it is, young lady?"

Jill sprang forward. "You see, Mom, I was at the aquarium, and then Hailey called…"

"Aunt Susan?" asked Marina, looking straight ahead at Jill's mother. Minus the glasses and with shorter, pulled-back hair, the face was the same.

Putting a finger in front of Marina's lips to silence her, Jill spoke curtly through clenched teeth. "They're twin sisters."

"Speaking of your Aunt Susan, she called precisely an hour ago." Jill's mother nodded as Jill's shoulders slumped. "I know all about your unscheduled excursion to visit your cousin. A word with you in the kitchen, please?"

"Stay here," said Jill before she gulped and followed her mother.

Marina studied the large room. There was a stairway leading up and four doorways: one on either side of her to other rooms, one straight ahead where Jill and her mother had gone, and a closed door underneath the top few stairs. Hanging on the wall were three images in wooden frames. She recognized one of Jill from the amount of hair. The center picture had four figures including Jill and her mother, and then a human-man—Jill's father, she assumed—with no hair on the top of his head but hair around his mouth, and finally a younger human-man with somewhat unkempt brown hair that made her smile: Jill's brother Jeff.

The third photo was of him alone. Seeing his face made her heart beat faster and her feet feel lighter, like they could float off of the floor. She sighed and touched her lips, remembering the sensation and taste of his lips on them. Maybe he'd kiss her again, she hoped.

Suddenly startled, she jumped when she felt something rough like barnacles come in contact with one of her ankles. Looking down, she saw a four-legged creature like none she knew from the ocean. Its tail curled upward as it circled her feet and tickled her legs with its brown-and-black striped fur.

"Who are you?" said Marina. "And why are you doing that?"

The animal looked up, revealing a face with two pointed ears and crescent moon shaped eyes. The only answer it gave was a single *meow*, and then it resumed licking her ankle until she giggled.

"Look, Sparky's found a new friend. He usually avoids new people," said Jill's mother as she reentered the hallway. "Welcome to our home. I'm Stephanie, Jill's mom."

Marina bowed her head. "It is nice to meet you, Aunt Stephanie."

"Just Stephanie will be fine. My sister Susan—you can call *her* Aunt—told me you'd be coming back with Jill. I hope you find what you're looking for."

"As do I."

Stephanie introduced Marina to Jill's father, who was sitting on the sofa in the living room and thoroughly engrossed in a baseball game. With only a quick glance to Marina, he greeted her and then returned his attention to the television.

"George, that wasn't very polite of you. We have a guest for a few days." Stephanie marched into the room to block his view of the game. "This is the girl that Jeff wouldn't stop talking about last summer."

At the mention of her brother, Jill quickly said, "That's okay, Mom. I'm sure we don't want to embarrass Marina with that kind of talk, so let's keep that quiet. Besides, she's traveled far today, and I'm sure she'd like to unpack and get some rest." She put her arm around Marina to extract her from the living room. In the hallway, she snatched up the suitcase and garment bag and then rushed Marina to the stairway.

"Is it true?" Marina asked, looking over her shoulder at Jill. "Did your brother talk that much of me?"

"Yeah, yeah, yeah." Jill kept nudging Marina up the stairs.

"Can I see him?"

"He's not home. He's at his evening job. And because I didn't have the car back in time, my mom had to give him a ride. That's one of a bunch of reasons she's not so pleased with me right now."

"Will he be home soon?"

Jill pushed Marina into her bedroom and quickly closed the door. "No. You're coming to where Meredith and I work tomorrow, so we have to get to bed early tonight—before he even gets home."

The bedroom was a similar size to Hailey's but was much neater and had fewer wall decorations. A small fabric-covered board hung on one side of the room, and crisscrossed ribbons held small booklets in place. Jill explained they were the programs for different plays in which she had appeared.

The bed with a white metal frame was against the wall by a window overlooking the front of the house. Jill knelt by the bed and pulled a mattress out from underneath it.

"I'll sleep on this one." Jill indicated the bottom one. "You'll sleep on the other. That way I'll know if you get up in the middle of the night to try and sleep in the bathtub. I don't think Aunt Susan noticed you doing that last summer, but believe me, my mom would find out and ask too many questions."

Marina frowned. "The bed at Hailey's house was uncomfortable, and I missed being in the water."

"There's a pool out back if you need to swim. You can even wear Hailey's costume if you want." Jill moved some of the pillows from the main bed to the trundle while she muttered, "I hope I can explain why we have it."

When bedtime ultimately came, Jill fell asleep almost instantly out of sheer exhaustion. Marina, however, lay on her back under the thin bed sheet. Like the previous summer, the lack of water around her kept her wide awake. Longing for the support of the water and the steadiness of the current, she closed her eyes to force herself to sleep, but nothing worked.

She tossed and turned until she heard a familiar voice from the darkness outside. "Thanks for the ride home," he said.

Jeff!

She turned toward the open window and let the light breeze cool her face while the sound of his voice calmed her nerves. The roof over the front porch blocked her view of him, and she tuned out the other voice as she imagined Jeff talking to her. She didn't fully understand what he meant when he talked about work, but it didn't matter. His warm voice lulled her to sleep.

On the porch, Jeff kissed the girl who drove him home before saying goodbye and entering the house.

~ Chapter Eight ~

Effortlessly flipping her fluke, Hailey curled her tail and swam in a corkscrew pattern that left a swirl of bubbles in the water behind her. "This is awesome!" she gleefully shouted. "Wheeeeee!"

From behind, Lorelei maintained a slower pace so she could watch and enjoy Hailey relishing in her recent transformation. Smiling, she said, "It is clear that you do not need swimming lessons."

"I figured out how to swim with a fake tail." Hailey arched her back, curving her path upwards and ultimately back. At the top of her loop, she said, "It's so much easier when the tail's a part of you."

"You shall blend in easier than Meredith did last northern season. You may be mistaken for a true mer."

"O-M-G, you really mean it?" Completing the circle, Hailey dove back down until she was beside Lorelei.

"In appearance and skill, yes. However, your speech will be viewed as foreign to our school."

"O-I-C. Oops, my bad. I mean *Oh, I see.*"

"Nothing was wrong with what you just said. You said the same words twice."

Hailey crinkled her forehead until she realized what she had said, and then she laughed. "Maybe I talk differently because I'm from another school. Can't you tell them I'm on vacation or something?"

"I doubt others will believe that. We never encounter other schools and only rarely find stray mer families."

"Then is your school the only school? Or are you the only

school in the Atlantic? Could there be other schools in other oceans?"

"I do not have the answers to those questions, and once we are in the school, it may be wiser for you not to ask them."

As much as Hailey wanted to know everything there was to know about the mermaid world, she knew she was a guest—an unexpected one and perhaps an unwanted one by some—so she decided not to ask why she couldn't ask those questions. Still, it disappointed her that Lorelei didn't seem willing to discuss it in a private location. Rather than dwell on it, she shrugged it off as a new idea flowed into her head.

"Lore, watch this!" Hailey clasped her hands together and stretched her arms in front of her. She flapped her tail more vigorously than before and torpedoed forward.

"When in the school, it is considered impolite to swim with your arms extended. Maids keep them by their sides."

"R-U-K-M?" Hailey made a sharp U-turn and floated in place while Lorelei approached. "Oh, sorry. *Are you kidding me?* That's the way to go super-fast. Meredith told me so herself."

Hailey thought about the conversations she had with Meredith after her return the previous summer. Like a sponge, she absorbed all the factual details of being a mermaid in case she had ever gotten her chance. She had gotten the impression that her constant phone calls and texts had ultimately frustrated Meredith. In the end, it really didn't matter because Hailey was finally getting to live out her dream.

Lorelei calmly said, "There is no need to swim so quickly. Take your time and enjoy the experience."

"I'm already enjoying it!" Hailey curled her tail and dove underneath Lorelei, only to circle back above her and continue forward. "I can't wait to go to all the cool places you're gonna take me to, and I can't wait to see all the other—"

Her swimming stopped as abruptly as her speech, and she

stared open-mouthed into the distance until she finally mustered up the breath to whisper, "O. M. G."

Lorelei caught up and grinned upon realizing why Hailey had become so silent. "Welcome to the school. We arrived in these waters several daylights ago."

Hailey watched the hundreds of mermaids before and below her. From her vantage point, they appeared as small as fish in a household aquarium tank. Though they were far away, Hailey's heightened eyesight could clearly distinguish the colors of their tails—almost every color she could imagine except for two. Her favorite shades of pink weren't exactly naturally occurring colors, so their absence didn't particularly surprise her, and orange was missing because she had the only tail.

The mermaids of the school weren't traveling as one in any particular formation, but instead, there were small groups in various locations doing various activities or simply going about their own business. Several groups were swimming, some casually and others more purposefully. One group seemed to be playing some game that involved throwing and swimming after something too small for Hailey to see. There was one with a silver tail who flitted from one stationary group to another before settling down with other similarly tailed mers.

Hailey noticed the green-tails and blue-tails mixed nicely, and the red-tails seemed to be scattered throughout, but the mers with purple tails seemed to interact exclusively among themselves. Seeing that every other color had a somewhat large population, Hailey couldn't help feeling sad for Marina, who would have spent her entire life as one of a kind. *How lonely that must have been*, she thought.

But Hailey was determined not to spend the month lonely. "When do I get to meet them? I want to meet that merboy that Meredith became friends with. What was his name?" While she scratched her head, her fluke wiggled back and forth. "Barney! Yeah, that's it."

"In due time," said Lorelei. "I think we should consult

with my father first."

"I know I'll be here awhile, but look at them all!" Hailey thrust both of her arms forward. "They're right there! Can't we go there now? Please?" She brought her hands together with a flourish of bubbles. "Please, please, please."

Lorelei cringed at the noise Hailey was making. "You sound like an ill seal. You should quiet down before you draw attention to yourself."

"But they're so far away. How could they hear us?"

"Sounds travel quickly in the water." Lorelei lowered her head and flicked her tail to enter into a dive directed toward the outskirts of where the school had congregated. "Let us see what my father says."

Disappointed for only a moment, Hailey followed, unaware she had been heard.

A purple-tailed mermaid saw them. Instantly recognizing them by the color of their tails, she swam away in disgust, her two friends following close behind.

Shortly after that, Lorelei and Hailey arrived at a submerged cavern with rocky green bioluminescent walls.

"This place is incredible," said Hailey, exploring the inside perimeter before floating up to the top and soaring back down to the cavern's opening. "You really live here?"

"Yes. My father, Marina, and I inhabit this cave when we spend the northern season near your island."

Hailey flitted over to Lorelei. "Will your father let me call him Finn? All I want to do is meet every mer I can. I know I can't tell the others who I really am, but in here, with you and your dad—well, we can talk openly about it all, right? I want to know everything there is to know about being a mer so I can be even better at parties and whenever else I wear my tail. So where's your father?"

There was silence, and Hailey felt the pressure of the water increase as if something was behind her. She was too anxious to look, fearing that a mer had overheard her secret. Lorelei's head was down, almost sinking into her slumped shoulders, and she pointed toward the entrance. "He is here."

Hailey's face filled with a buoyant smile as she pirouetted in place, swooshing a vortex of water bubbles around her that obscured her view of the cavern. When her twirling ended, she turned to Lorelei's father, ready to introduce herself, but the muscular outline of his body and the stern look on his face caused her stop her tail flapping.

"I can only presume that Marina has misplaced her tail once again," said his deep voice.

He hovered vertically forward by curling the bottom half of his green tail back and twisting his flapping fluke sideways. Gazing at the handsome merman with the square jaw and spiky dark hair, Hailey could only squeak out a quick introduction.

"I expected the two of you to be more careful this time." He swam past Hailey and addressed his daughter directly. "How could you let her make the same mistake a second time?"

"It was not a mistake, father," said Lorelei, her voice a mixture of guilt and defensiveness. "This time, Marina willingly lent her tail to Hailey."

Hailey raised her hand as she spoke up. "Yeah, and I willingly borrowed it. I've dreamed about being a mermaid—I mean a *mer*—since well, forever."

"She should not have given it to you."

The grave tone of his words frightened Hailey, as Finn wasn't acting like the kind and understanding mer that Meredith had made him out to be. Glancing nervously at the entrance behind her, she considered escaping. Would she be chased? Sure, she knew how to swim somewhat fast—Lorelei had said she could pass as a mer—but Finn's tail was strong, and he'd easily overtake her. But if she stayed, what kind of punishment would she receive for impersonating a mer?

She refused to believe that Meredith's recollections of him had been a lie, so she hoped Finn—the only father figure Marina had ever known—would be lenient with her, especially with Marina's tail at stake. Before facing him, Hailey prepared herself with the tactics that always seemed to dissuade her father from reprimanding her: quivering her bottom lip and batting her eyelashes like she was about to cry. But would Finn even notice any tears underwater? She'd have to find out.

When she finally turned to face Finn, he didn't seem as angry as she expected. Instead, one of his shoulders was shrugged, and one side of his mouth was curled up into a kind of smirk.

"I am truly sorry, Hailey," he said calmly while he took her smaller hand in his. "Marina told me all about your desire to be a mer and about the heroic way you restored her tail."

"Heroic?" Hailey felt her herself slowly rising upward. "You think I'm a hero?"

"Undeniably so. I would want nothing more than for you to experience the adventure of a lifetime, but this is a difficult time within the school. We almost did not return here."

Sensing bad news coming, Hailey let herself sink like a slowly deflating balloon. "Well, I'm really glad you did," she said before quickly flailing her arms in front of her. "Not because I'm being all selfish and wanted to be a mer, or anything like that. I'm glad that Marina has the opportunity to look for her Mom."

"Coral was a dear friend of mine. I had come close to giving up hope that she was out there somewhere." Finn sighed. "When Marina told us of the image she saw—"

Hailey nodded eagerly. "The painting?"

"Yes. Once Marina told me, I spent several moon cycles persuading Ray to return to these waters—that they were safe for the school once again. If he knew that my intentions were to assist Marina in her search, then…"

Finn's voice trailed off as he swam to the cave's entrance to make sure there weren't any other mers in the vicinity. Shivering as she suddenly felt chilled by the change in the conversation, Hailey turned to Lorelei and asked, "Who's Ray? Meredith didn't mention meeting any mer named Ray."

Lorelei looked toward her father and waited until he nodded to answer, "He is the leader of the school."

"A mer that we should not anger." Finn returned and whispered. "He became suspicious when his daughter Calliope told him about the other orange-tailed mer who had communicated with the human-maid."

Hailey remembered the night of the previous summer's storm. While she and Marina were at Isabel's shop receiving the painting, Jill had sneaked out to talk to Meredith. Unknown to them, Calliope had been eavesdropping and chased Meredith to bring her to Ray.

Finn continued, "He did not want to return because he feared humans had discovered our existence."

"Well, they kinda did." Hailey pointed at herself. "Me and Jill and Meredith. Oh, and I guess Aunt Susan knows now too."

"It is worse than I thought." Finn brought his hand up to his face and groaned. "Ray must not see that there is yet a new orange-tail in the school. With Marina absent, he will conclude—quite correctly—that you are not truly a mer."

Hailey frowned. Only hours earlier, Lorelei had praised her swimming abilities by telling her that she could pass as a mer, but the compliment drifted away with the obvious fact that she wasn't really one.

"If Ray's suspicions are confirmed, he will believe a human infiltrated our school. He will relocate the school and banish you at no moon, so Marina's tail disappears. Then there will no longer be an orange-tail, and *we must not allow that to happen.*"

"I don't really want to leave, but if I had to, I would. Anything for Marina. But I can't exactly take this tail off now. It's kinda stuck on me." Hailey sniffled and wiped tears away from her eyes until they disappeared into the ocean depths. "So what am I supposed to do for a month?"

Finn floated over to Hailey and stroked her cheek in the comforting way only a father could. "I am sorry, but until the moon cycle has ended, you must remain here in the cave."

~ Chapter Nine ~

Meredith found Jill just inside the closed aquarium gates and asked, "Is Marina here?"

"She's out there." Jill leaned to one side while pointing with her other plush flipper. "It's not like I could get her in before the place opened."

"So what is she doing? Where is she?"

"At the picnic tables. I told her to wait there until you came to get her."

Meredith glanced at her watch. "I think I can get her inside before I have to get back to Dr. Hatcher. We're watching videos all morning, but he usually doesn't start till nine-thirty." She fumbled around in the pocket of her khaki shorts and removed a laminated aquarium visitor's pass. "This should do the trick."

The two of them stood and watched a security guard unlock the front gates. As people filtered into the ticket lines, Jill nudged Meredith aside with her flippers. "Now shoo. This is my part of the day." Then Jill waddled forward and waved, much to the delight of the younger children entering with their families.

Meredith walked against the traffic of patrons until she was outside the gates and looking at the parking lot. To the right were picnic tables—visitors were encouraged either to bring a lunch to eat outside or to eat at the slightly overpriced snack bar.

She found Marina sitting alone, an orange folder stuffed with papers clutched against her chest, while she stared at her feet. "Still getting used to them?" asked Meredith. "It took me a few days to readjust to walking when mine came back last summer."

Marina looked up and smiled. "It is good to see you, Meredith." They hugged, giving Marina a closer view of the ponytail hanging behind Meredith's head. "Your hair has gotten longer."

Grunting, Meredith backed away and bunched up her dark brown locks once more into the elastic. "It's frustrating. I don't like it this long, but it won't stay short."

"I think your hair looks good."

"You and the rest of your school can pull it off—maybe you even have a genetic predisposition for it—but it's a nuisance out here when it gets too humid." Meredith looked up at the blue, cloudless sky. "Fortunately, the weather's going to cooperate. Best day of the summer so far. I think you're going to enjoy it here today."

Meredith escorted Marina into a ticket line, flashing her identification badge and indicating the visitor pass was for her friend. As the woman in the admission booth issued her a ticket, Marina asked where Jill was.

After taking Marina's ticket from her and passing it to the white-haired gentleman collecting them, Meredith said, "She's over there. We can get our picture taken with her if you'd like."

Jill stood before a tall wooden board painted a bright shade of green, the color to be digitally replaced later with an image of swimming sea lions. A harried woman was trying to organize her three children into a pose. Her oldest, a boy about seven years old, ran circles around Jill. The middle child, a girl about four, sidled away and pouted, almost on the verge of tears. The youngest child, a toddler in his mother's arms, kept trying to reach for the mascot's nose.

"I do not see her," said Marina.

During the one split-second when all four of them were in place, a middle-aged man at the camera snapped the photo. Then the chaos resumed, and the mother had an equally challenging time placing her two youngest children in the double stroller while containing her oldest's orbit around her instead of Jill.

"Really?" asked Jill when Meredith placed Marina beside her.

Marina's eyes widened and looked up at the smiling face stitched into the costume. "Is that Jill in there? Have you been eaten by this creature? No sea lion I have ever met would devour a human. Or walk on its back flippers."

Jill turned toward Meredith and tried to shrug another *really?* at her, but due to the bulky costume, her flippers only extended straight outward.

"Marina, it's a costume," said Meredith. "Jill's wearing it; she's only pretending."

"Your culture is quite bizarre. Hailey has dressed as a mer several times, and Jill is dressing as something like a sea lion. Do all humans wish to live under the sea?"

While Meredith quickly shushed Marina, Jill attempted another shrug.

"We shouldn't talk about that until lunch." Meredith looked at her watch as she moved to the other side of Jill. "Can we meet at noon?"

Jill agreed, but Marina asked, "Noon? When is noon?"

"It's noon. Twelve o'clock p.m." Jill turned to Meredith. "Noon's p.m., right?"

"Right," answered Meredith, who then glanced across Jill's stuffed belly at Marina. "Noon is when the sun is at its highest in the sky. Does that help?"

Marina nodded in understanding as the photographer took their picture. Behind him, Brittany passed by and glared at Meredith before raising her nose in the air and walking off away from them.

The gathering crowd had grown impatient with the amount of time to get the picture taken, so Meredith ushered Marina away from Sandy and toward the main aquarium building. Marina opened the orange folder and asked questions about when they were going to start helping her look for her mother.

"I'm sorry, Marina, but we can't yet. At least not today." Closing the folder, Meredith then explained that both she and Jill had their respective jobs so Marina would be on her own for most of the day. "But it's all right. We're at an aquarium, and I think it may even remind you of home."

They entered the main gallery, and their eyes immediately adjusted to the dim lights inside. While being led to the center of the large room, Marina's head rotated back and forth quickly, and her mouth slowly dropped open.

Sharks, rays, and fish of all shapes and sizes swam all around her, and water surrounded her as if she was submerged in it, yet she remained dry. Curiously, she approached the closest school of fish until she noticed a clear barrier between their water and her lack thereof. Like she was separated from her home, the sea creatures were separated from her.

Marina's voice wavered. "What is this place? Why can they not swim freely?"

"They're swimming freely." Meredith pointed at an angelfish that was reversing its direction. "The tanks are designed to give them a large enough living habitat."

Marina looked at the other tanks in the room. "They cannot interact. How can you say they swim freely?"

Nervously fiddling with her watch, Meredith said, "I wish I could stay and assure you that they're all safe while we study them, but I don't want to be late for my internship." She squeezed Marina's shoulder. "I'll see you at lunch. My treat."

Meredith disappeared into the crowded darkness of the room, leaving Marina standing there. As much as she cared about the ocean life around her, she had left the ocean to find her mother—the mother that had left her for some unknown reason. Jill and Meredith were also leaving her adrift, but only temporarily. She had arrived unannounced and couldn't expect them to let their commitments float. They would assist her when they were able, and until then, she had the orange folder from Hailey to study.

She found a place to sit—a rectangular bench that

extended up from the floor and was covered in the same carpeting. The first item in the folder was the image of her mother handing her to outstretched hands in the sea. Underneath was a stack of papers, which had bulked up when she opened the folder. Some papers contained small color images not much larger than her thumb, others had dark printed words on white paper bent at the corners, and others had one side comprised of jagged, fraying pieces but had lines crossed by illegible pink scribbles. After a long time of flipping through the pages, not much of it made sense to her, and she closed the folder and looked at the tank before her.

It was large and cylindrical, filling the center of the room. Inside was what looked like a coral reef. She curiously approached, drawn in by the myriad of beautiful colors.

She hoped the swaying of the coral in the current would lull her into a more relaxed state, but there wasn't any such motion. The tank obviously didn't have the same strength of waves as the ocean, but with a majority of the fish inside swimming in the same direction around the tank, there had to be a current. Squinting, she noticed places where the bright oranges and pinks of the coral had flaked away to reveal a dirty white underneath. Nothing but a lifeless model, another false way the human world tried to represent hers like all the little statues in the shop on Hailey's island.

Returning to her seat and opening the folder, Marina chose to look at words she couldn't translate instead of an undersea world she didn't recognize.

Her internal daily rhythms, still in sync with the sun and moon cycles, told her when it was time to meet the others. The sun was almost directly overhead when she went to the designated meeting place, and she didn't wait long before Meredith arrived and asked, "Have you been enjoying the aquarium?"

"I am confused by this place," answered Marina. "The fish appear to be content, but I cannot be certain through the glass. I would have to go into the water—"

"So what would you like for lunch?" Meredith spoke

loudly to drown out Marina's comments. Looking around to make sure no one was listening, she continued, "You can't go in the tank, but don't worry. We have professional marine biologists that take good care of all the animals."

"But they should be free."

"I'm so glad to be free of that costume." Jill was fanning herself by pulling at the front of her sweat-soaked tank top. With her other hand, she gathered up some of her wild, matted-down hair. "Even if it's only for a half hour."

They proceeded through the line at the snack bar. Meredith emerged with a Caesar salad, and Jill and Marina opted for burgers and a shared large order of fries. Their salty taste was familiar yet deliciously different, and Marina devoured more than her share.

"I have been sitting inside looking through what Hailey gave me about my mother." Marina opened the folder and removed the print she believed showed her mother. "But I need help deciphering its meaning."

Seated between them at the square table, Jill took the folder from Marina and laid it open on the corner close to Meredith. They scanned the first few pages of images taken from an internet search of the phrase *Coral, acrylic on canvas*. It was the one-hundred and twelfth page of Hailey's search when she had finally found the print, although she had printed a few pages before it. Then there was a full-size printout of the same image and the home page of an art gallery where the painting had been featured.

Jill took the page. "I've heard of that town. Maybe an hour or so from here?" She pulled out her phone and started typing the address into a driving directions app.

"Never mind." Meredith pulled out the next sheet of notebook paper—a series of dated and detailed log entries in Hailey's handwriting. "According to this, there's no answer at that phone number. Hailey tried calling there almost every week. She also called information and gave the address, but there was no longer a listing for the gallery."

"I wish I could show Hailey how grateful I am for all her

help," said Marina.

Jill put her hand on Marina's shoulder. "You already have. You're letting her be a…" She purposely trailed off her voice and turned to see Meredith squirming in her seat. "Your scaly-sense is tingling again, isn't it? Afraid I was gonna say the M-word, weren't you?"

"Will you please stop doing that?" Meredith was thumbing through the papers and skimming them. "Hailey's already printed a map of the area with directions from the highway. There's even a picture of the gallery's exterior."

"Then we go there. It's a start." Jill pushed a small handful of fries into her mouth.

"May we go after you have finished with work?" asked Marina, her blue eyes wide open and wistful.

Meredith and Jill looked at each other, and their silence stood out among the background chatter of the visitors at other tables. Breaking the awkwardness first, Meredith said, "If the gallery still exists, it would probably be closed by the time we get there."

Jill added, "My mom won't like me going out that late on short notice. Our next day off is Sunday when the aquarium's closed. When we get home, I'll schedule the car. Three days is usually enough advanced warning for her."

Three days? Marina gazed at the picture. She only had one moon cycle, but with all the information in Hailey's folder, it would be more than enough time. Three more days without her mother was nothing compared to her lifetime, and she thanked her friends for their willingness to help.

"Is this seat taken?" asked Will, a tray of food in his hand.

Meredith quickly slammed the folder shut on top of Jill's hand. "Sure you can sit here." She gestured toward Marina. "Will, this is…"

"My cousin Marina," said Jill without missing a beat. "She's visiting for the month, so I thought I'd bring her here for the day."

"Nice to meet you, Marina. The aquarium's a great place." Will ripped open a ketchup packet and drizzled it onto his fries while he turned to Meredith. "What did you think of that video Dr. Hatcher showed us? The way they trained the dolphins to find lost divers—that was just, wow."

"You sound surprised," said Marina. "Dolphins are quite intelligent. They are also helpful and kind and playful."

"Wow, you're a dolphin girl like Meredith." He wiped ketchup off his mouth and noticed the picture in Marina's hand. "What have you got there?"

Before he could take a look, Brittany walked over and hovered behind Marina. Able to see the picture, she groaned. "More mermaids? Guess there's no room for me at the *kiddie* table." She released an audible humph and strutted away.

Will glanced at the baby mermaid in the photo and then grinned at Meredith. "Hey, are you sure Marina's not *your* cousin? You two seem to have a lot in common. Dolphins and mermaids, wow."

Jill clapped her hands together once, getting their attention and effectively ending the conversation before Meredith convulsed. "I've got to go and get back into character. Will, Meredith, why don't you tell Marina about all the aquarium's attractions? She's gonna be spending a lot of time here the next few days."

After Jill left, Will itemized almost every single species by scientific name, enthusiastically inserting a *wow* at the aquarium's most popular exhibits. Marina listened intently, occasionally stealing ketchup-drenched fries from Will's plate. Meredith's nervous breathing had returned to normal, and she nodded and smiled at Will's descriptions, especially when he mentioned that the beluga whales were his favorite.

Eventually, Meredith and Will had to return to Dr. Hatcher. Left alone at the table, Marina wondered if she was like all the other fish in the aquarium: confined inside with nothing to do but wander aimlessly.

~ Chapter Ten ~

"Nowhere to go, nothing to do," muttered Hailey to the walls of the cave, to the water around her, to no one in particular, and mostly to herself. "Nowhere to go, nothing to do…"

Staying still for too long was boring, so Hailey flitted around the cave. Once she reached a wall, she'd push off with her hands while doing a backflip U-turn to head toward the opposite side. The constant motion gave her something to do during the times she was alone. After three days, her speed had increased, but her trajectory was more erratic, like a pinball bouncing off of the bumpers and flippers.

"It's driving me nuts being in here. I'm getting…oh, W-T-H is it called?" She grunted in frustration at not finding the right words and in contempt at herself for speaking in text when she promised she'd try to do so less often. "I mean what the—? Cabin fever! Yeah, that's what it's called, from being stuck in this…" She looked around. "Well, I guess it's not a cabin. Mers don't have cabins; they—well, the ones I'm with, anyway—live in a cavern. Cavern fever! Yeah, that's what I'm getting. A bad case of cavern fever." She nodded proudly, but before long, her fluke started twitching. "I gotta get outta here!"

Almost out of her control, she shot forward, but when she got to the mouth of the cave, she calmed the spasms in her tail. "Let it float," she said to herself, taking quick inhalations until she stopped moving. Turning around and heading back for the farthest point from the entrance, she said the words again. "Let it float, Hailey. Let it float. You're staying put for Marina. That's what matters most."

Thinking somewhat rationally again, she remembered and understood why she was alone. Finn was the school's most trusted scout, and Lorelei had a reputation for being adventurous, so if they didn't make regular appearances, the school would get suspicious. Apparently, Marina being missing for the same amount of time—or even longer, like the two weeks on land the summer before—wasn't an issue. It upset Hailey that the school didn't seem to acknowledge Marina, one of the sweetest and dearest friends she had.

At least she hadn't been left by herself for the three days. Most of the time, either Finn or Lorelei stayed with her. Sometimes even both of them. Hailey enjoyed hearing the stories they told, especially about Lorelei and Marina's childhood. Finn never mentioned the disappearance of Marina's parents or the death of Lorelei's mother, just like none of the mers recognized Marina as one of them.

And why was that, she wondered while glancing behind her to watch her fluke flutter back and forth. *Was it all because Marina had an orange tail?*

"That's not fair!" she cried out, hoping the others would hear her condemnation of them.

She jetted toward the cave's entrance, and maybe she would have made it outside if Lorelei hadn't appeared and asked, "What is not fair?"

Bubbles appeared and popped as Hailey swerved and screeched to a halt. "Nothing," she said, backtracking to the center of the cavern.

"I do not disagree with you," said Lorelei. "It is not fair that you must remain here. You have wanted this experience for such a long time."

Unsure if she had heard correctly, Hailey rubbed her ears to unclog them. The water still stayed inside, so she asked, "What did you say?"

"I would like to stay longer than a daylight time on land, but I must return to the ocean before the sun sets. It is not fair that I stay while Marina has a second adventure out there. I imagine you are feeling the same way."

"Yeah. What good is having a tail and being a mer when I can't, you know, go out there and use it to be a mer?" Hailey was pointing at the exit before bringing her arm back to her side. "In here, I kinda feel like a fish in a tank. Who wants that?"

"You are here to experience, and so you shall." Lorelei took Hailey's hand and guided her toward the entrance.

Before they could cross the threshold to the open water, Hailey pulled back. "I shouldn't do it. What if your father finds out?"

"You were willing to leave your mother without much of an explanation. My father will not be back until after moonrise. He will never know."

"Parents eventually find out. Besides, I can't do this to Marina. What if someone sees me?"

"I have brought a mer we can trust who will watch the waters and keep us away from other mers." Lorelei swam forward until she was outside the cavern, and then she looked off to the side. "Barney, is it clear?"

Hailey remembered Meredith talking about Barney and how he was the first friend she had made on her own in the school. From Meredith's description of him, Hailey envisioned Barney to be kind and helpful, but clumsy, nervous, and scrawny. But his appearance didn't matter to her. She was thrilled to meet someone else after being stuck in the cavern for three days, so she excitedly swam forward.

At the same time Hailey emerged from the cave, Barney glided into view from behind the right side of the cave's opening. To avoid a head-on collision with him, Hailey veered to the left, only to whack him in the face with her fluke.

"O-M-G, I'm so sorry!" She quickly reversed her direction until she found herself face to face with his stomach.

His stomach wasn't rippled or muscular, but he wasn't as thin as Hailey had imagined. She floated upward, and her view rose up to his boyish face, where he was rubbing his jawline.

"I didn't mean to hurt you." Reaching out to console him, Hailey grasped his upper arm and was surprised by how strong his biceps felt.

As electric tingles coursed from the fingers of the hand touching him all the way to the tips of her tail, Hailey withdrew. Embarrassed, she turned away.

"I should be sorry. I got in your way," he said, his quick sentences coming out in rapid-fire succession. "You did not know I was there. How could you know? You cannot see through cave walls. Or can you? Is that something humans can do?"

His voice and personality matched *exactly* how Meredith described him, and Hailey giggled. "You are far too cute." Instantly, she covered her mouth. "Did I just say that out loud?"

"I think you did. I heard you say it. Did you think you did not say it? Or is it difficult for you to hear down here?"

"She can hear perfectly well," said Lorelei. "If we do not leave immediately, we risk being seen floating here."

"Lorelei is correct," said Barney. "But where are we going? What would you like to see?"

Hailey gazed into his eyes and couldn't turn away. Since they were out of the cave without anything blocking the sunlight from reaching the depth they were at, Hailey noticed Barney's gray irises sparkling with what looked like flecks of silver. "What would you like to show me?"

"You are the visitor. What would you like to see?"

Shaking her head in frustration, Lorelei spouted, "I will decide where we go! Follow me." She started swimming in a direction away from where most of the school congregated but had to turn back to get them to follow her.

Hailey and Barney swam side by side, and he asked her several questions about herself, the human world, and why she wanted to be a mer. As much as she enjoyed talking about finally having her dream come true, she wanted to ask him questions too. Every time there was a pause in the conversation—which wasn't often—she tried to formulate a good question, but he seized the opportunity to ask her something else. Eventually, she stopped worrying about it because a boy was displaying genuine interest in her. And not just any boy, but a *mer* boy. An adorable mer boy with a shimmery silver tail.

While they kept following Lorelei, Hailey sneaked a quick glance behind her to take a look at Barney's strong tail, but it looked more like a dull gray. As she looked around, everything was darker. As far as she could tell, they had left sometime in the morning. Had they been swimming for so long that the sun had already set?

"Have we been getting deeper?" asked Barney. "The water is getting darker. Lorelei, do you know where we are going? I have not been paying attention."

"Neither of you has paid any attention to anything but each other," said Lorelei with a teasing lilt in her voice.

Barney swam forward and in a defensive tone, said, "What do you mean? I have been watching the waters as you asked. No other mers are near us."

"No other mers are near us because I am taking you to a place they do not know. Your head has been in a whirlpool since you met Hailey."

The mention of her name knocked Hailey out of her trance, mesmerized by watching the undulating flukes of the mers in front of her. Particularly the silver one. She shook her head and asked, "Did I miss something? What about me?"

Barney swam back to Hailey and said, "You should ignore what Lore is saying. She should learn to let it float."

"Yeah, she should!" Even in the dimness around her, Hailey was sure she saw Barney blushing.

Lorelei slowed down until she hovered in place, and Hailey and Barney diverged until they stopped on either side of her. "Why did you stop?" asked Barney. "You heard me say let it float? I did not mean to stop swimming and start floating."

Hailey's laugh was a shrill squeak, and she covered her mouth in embarrassment.

"We are here," said Lorelei, gesturing into the distance. "My father discovered this when he scouted ahead. As far as we know, the rest of the school does not know it is here."

A collection of dark red, orange, and yellow pillars and blobs grew on the rocks ahead of them. Their tentacles swayed rhythmically with the steady underwater current. The area wasn't much larger than Hailey's beach, but their arrangement was a maze-like pattern upon the rocks where they grew.

"Is this a coral reef?" asked Hailey. "I thought they were only in the tropics."

"It is rare, but they can exist this far north." Lorelei swam forward, closer to the coral. "But they are only found this far down and do not grow into large colonies."

Hailey followed. "But isn't the water, like, too cold for it?"

"Cold?" Barney zipped forward to join them. "What do you mean by cold?"

"You know, cold. Like, not hot." Hailey noticed the confusion on Barney's face. "When you're not warm, so you shiver. Brrr." She wrapped her arms around her chest and shook to demonstrate, but both Barney and Lorelei looked at her strangely. "Oh yeah, silly me, we don't feel the cold."

"Now that we are here, what would you like to do?" asked Lorelei.

Hailey grinned. "Ever play hide-and-seek?"

Lorelei and Barney had never heard of the game, but when Hailey explained the rules, they said that it was similar to a game that younger mers played. Hailey insisted that the labyrinth of rocks and the various colors of coral would provide plenty of possible hiding places. Hailey appointed Barney as the first to be *It*, and then she and Lorelei swam to the reef.

He turned to face away from the reef and started counting. Water streamed by as Hailey swam into a crevice between two of the larger rocks in the center of the reef. Some coral, almost the same color as her tail, extended up from the top of the rock and expanded outward into a mushroom shape. She dove deeper to grasp onto the base of the rock, flipping her tail up so it was right behind the coral. Keeping herself as steady as she could, the current caused the thin, translucent webbing of her fluke to drift. Some little fish swam by, so Hailey whispered hello to them and was shocked when it sounded like a few of them returned her greeting.

When Barney reached twenty, without calling "Ready or not, here I come" because Hailey had forgotten to tell him to, he turned around. Hailey sensed him approaching her hiding spot. The water was too dim for his shadow to pass over her as he turned away without seeing her.

Lorelei was lying on the ocean floor, nestled in a crag below a rock on the far end of the reef. Barney found her first when he circled the perimeter, and then the two separated to search for Hailey.

Barney swam upward to get an overhead view of the reef while Lorelei swam low to the ocean floor through all the passages between the rocks. She soon found herself face to face with Hailey, who moved a finger to her lips to keep Lorelei from revealing her hiding spot.

"I sense that you like Barney," whispered Lorelei.

"Well, he's sweet and nice and funny. Cute too. All that's cool. I mean, that flows. Now get outta here before he finds me." Hailey tried to shoo Lorelei away, but with only one arm clutching the rock, buoyancy took hold of her, and her tail started to float upward.

"I have known him for many moon cycles and can tell that he likes you. I believe that you like him too. Why else would you be playing deep to get?"

Hailey dug her fingers into the rock and pulled herself downward to conceal her tail once again. "Four-one-one, Lore. Meredith told me she kissed him last summer. I can't like him *that way*. That wouldn't be fair to her."

"I do not think she will return." Lorelei cocked an eyebrow and smirked. "He is in open water for you."

"Yeah, but I'm leaving at the next full moon. I can't—" Suddenly, Hailey imagined herself back home, more willing to flirt with tourist guys visiting for the summer than the boys from her school. In the mer world, *she* was the tourist, so why couldn't she get to know him better? "I guess I can, but I-D-K, Lore. He's—"

"I found you, Hailey!" Calling from above, Barney darted to them. "That was excellent hiding. I would not have thought to look there. I saw that Lorelei stopped swimming. Why would she have stopped? Only if she was talking to you! That is how I fished you out."

"Gee, thanks, Lore." Hailey burst into laughter, unable to keep a look of mock contempt on her face. She floated back into an upright position. "You found Lorelei first, so now she's *It!*"

They played a few more rounds of the game until the already dim water got dimmer. Lorelei insisted they leave because they needed to be in the cavern before Finn returned. On the way back, she swam ahead to keep an eye out for other mers and to let Hailey and Barney talk to one another.

When they got to the cave, Barney promised he'd visit Hailey again soon. She thanked him as he swam away, and then she thanked Lorelei for allowing her the opportunity to swim freely like a real mermaid, even if was only for a few hours.

They were chatting and laughing as they entered the cave, so they didn't see Finn floating there with his arms folded across his chest.

His voice boomed and echoed off the cavern walls. "Where have you been, young maid?"

Lorelei froze. "Father! We were only out playing."

"It's my fault." Hailey swam forward and started batting her eyelashes. "I was, like, going crazy being cooped up in here."

"No, it is my fault." Lorelei swam ahead to nudge Hailey away from Finn. "I decided to take Hailey on an adventure to the reef we found. No other mers in the school know about it, so we would not have been seen."

"But you *were* seen." Finn leaned forward, and he

tightened his stare on them so his eyebrows slanted inward to form a V. "And we have been summoned to see Ray."

~ Chapter Eleven ~

When the sun rose on Sunday, Marina sat up in bed and bounced upon the mattress, eager for the adventure that was about to begin. The squeaking of the springs so close to Jill's ears knocked her out of her slumber, and her eyes forced themselves open. "What time is it?" she groggily asked.

"Time to start the search for my mother." Marina's face was beaming as she reached for the orange folder on the nearby nightstand. "We can go now, correct?"

Jill groaned. "Not yet. It's too early." She rolled over, face first into the pillow until only a twisted mass of hair was visible where her head was.

"But how much longer must I wait? The earlier we leave this morning, the more time we shall have."

"Snooze button. Ten more minutes, please."

Crisscrossing her legs, Marina turned her attention to the digital clock. Though she didn't fully understand the human measurement of time, she could count on her fingers whenever the symbol on the display changed. Ten changes were ten minutes, she figured, and when she reached her second thumb, she bounced again.

"Are you ready now?"

After another grunt, Jill's arms appeared from under the bed sheet. She lifted her head and parted her mane of hair to see the clock. Then she dropped her head back into the pillow. "Day off," she mumbled. "But I've got the early mer wanting to catch the worm."

Then she remembered that if she stayed in bed too long, there'd be a chance that Marina would see Jeff. He had been dating his girlfriend for about a month now, and though Jill didn't have an opinion one way or another about her—she was friendly enough—she didn't want him to get all starry-eyed if he saw Marina once again. He had talked endlessly about her for months after meeting her the previous summer, and it took him a few more to get over the fact that she had never called him back. He used to sulk about her disappearing into thin air.

Or deep water.

As far as Jill knew, her mother and father had yet to mention to Jeff that Marina was staying with them. Between his two summer jobs and the time he spent with his girlfriend, Jeff wasn't home much. On weekdays, Jill's father left early to take a commuter train to his accounting firm in the city, and her mother left at precisely the same time every morning, whether or not she had new buyers looking for a home or an open house to run.

Fortunately, Jill had been able to keep them apart because he had worked late each night and she had to get to aquarium early enough in the morning while he was still asleep. But Sunday was both her *and* his day off. The only way to avoid Marina seeing him was to leave as soon as possible, even if it was an earlier departure than she had scheduled with her mother.

She had no idea how Marina would react upon seeing him. For all Jill knew, Marina would be heartbroken knowing he had moved on. The last thing she wanted was a sulking mermaid on her hands all summer, so she stood and stretched her limp arms and legs. Through a long yawn, she said, "Shower first. Stay. Right. Here."

Marina obeyed, and before anyone else in the house seemed to be moving, they left to pick up Meredith at her dormitory. When Jill called her, Meredith had already been awake and researching rescue dolphins.

Seated at a table in a doughnut shop, Meredith tore off a piece of her cranberry muffin and popped it in her mouth. "We should go to the address of the art gallery first," she said before taking a sip of orange juice.

Marina stared at the delicious powdered round pastry on her plate. Dark reddish-purple goop was oozing out of the place where she had taken a bite. "I thought Hailey wrote that it had closed down. Does that not mean it is gone?"

"Maybe, but chances are someone in the neighborhood remembers it. If there are other businesses, we ask the manager or whoever's working. Or we knock on the doors of people's houses. I'm sure Jill can improvise a reason we'd be knocking. Right, Jill?"

Face down on the table with her hair splayed out, Jill tightly clutched an almost-empty foam cup. "Whatever," she mumbled. "Need more coffee."

"Are you awake enough to drive?" asked Meredith. "It's at least an hour away."

Jill lifted her head and nodded, grumbling something that sounded like "I'm up," before inverting the cup at her lips and pouring the final drops of coffee down her throat.

For most of the trip, they drove northwest, so the bright glaring sun was in the opposite direction. Jill wore her sunglasses to hide the puffiness of her sleep-deprived eyes. In the passenger seat, Marina watched the scenery pass by, frequently asking when they'd pass any water.

The address was only a few miles from the highway—first down the state route from the off-ramp. They drove into the center crossroads of a small town with sidewalks lined with various storefronts, some of which had closed. They approached an intersection, and at the four corners were a gas station, a restaurant, a beauty salon, and a hardware store. They turned right, passing more shops, which became less connected to one another and further apart until replaced by trees and houses of a residential area.

Watching the numbers on the mailboxes, Meredith noticed that they had passed the address. After turning the car around, Jill pulled into the empty lot and parked the car in front of a dance studio.

"Not an art gallery." Jill pulled the lever at the base of her seat and leaned back until she was in a reclined position. "Wake me when you figure out what to do next."

Marina removed a paper from the folder and held it up in front of the windshield. Her eyes alternated between looking at the printed image on the paper and the building in front of her. "Do you think this is the same place?"

From the middle seat of the minivan, Meredith leaned forward to compare the two. The picture and building had the same shape—the gabled entryway extended forward from the main building, and the two side wings were symmetric. But the dark wooden shingles in the photo had been replaced by off-white vinyl siding.

Meredith and Marina got out of the car and walked to the door of the studio. Just as Meredith expected, it was locked. The sign beside the door displayed the studio's hours; they were closed on Sundays. Leaning her forehead against the glass door, Marina looked into the entryway and saw some framed pictures hanging on the walls. "There are images inside," she said. "Could this be the place?"

"Unfortunately not." Meredith checked the time and studied the neighborhood. She thought it was too early to knock on people's houses, but some shops seemed to be open. "Come on."

One of the pictures captivated Marina's attention. A woman appeared frozen in the air, held by a man's arms—one under her shoulders, and the other at her knees. He wore dark pants with a red open-buttoned shirt and that matched the color of her loosely flowing dress. One of her legs was kicked straight upward. Marina could easily tell they were enjoying the closeness from their smiles and the way their gazes met.

"Come on, Marina." Meredith took hold of her arm.

Marina pointed at the photograph. "What are they doing?"

Meredith peered inside. Even without her glasses, she could see the picture. "They're swing dancing. Some kind of lifting and dipping move, I would guess. Now let's go ask some of the neighborhood shopkeepers."

As Meredith pulled her away, Marina imagined herself in the lady's position, floating outside of the water yet supported in someone's strong arms. She grinned, knowing exactly which young man she wanted to hold her.

They methodically went from store to store down the street to the intersection, where they turned the corner and continued. When there weren't any more places to ask, they crossed the street and started on the other side. Responses varied from vague recollections of the gallery to no knowledge to rude questions about whether they were going to buy something or not.

The beauty salon on the third corner had just opened, and they asked the young stylist, whose lavender-streaked dark straight hair curved inward at her collarbone, but was short enough in the back to expose her neck.

"I don't live here in town," she said in a pleasant voice. In the mirror, she made eye contact with her customer, an older woman who was getting her gray hair dyed. "Esther, do you know when the art gallery down the street closed down?"

"Frances MacPherson's place?" Closing her eyes, the woman folded her hands together and tried to bow her head, but the stylist held it in place to continue working. "It was sad the day her children sold the property."

"You mean that she passed away?" asked Meredith.

The woman's eyes popped open. "Oh, goodness gracious, no. I play cards with her every other Wednesday!"

Meredith sighed in relief.

"She couldn't keep up with the gallery anymore—the bills, lack of clients and customers, and her failing memory. It was sad that her children had to put her in the nursing home."

With an address in hand, Marina and Meredith happily stepped out of the salon. Stopped at the red light, Jill honked her horn a few times and leaned her head out the window. "How's the search going?"

Marina was about to run into the street, but Meredith pulled her back as a car passed. Then they jogged to Jill's minivan, Marina a few strides ahead, and she bobbed up and down when she got to the window. "We have discovered someone who should know about my mother's picture!"

Visiting hours for the nursing home started at three in the afternoon, so the girls stopped for lunch. It gave Jill enough time to create a new character: a granddaughter who hadn't seen Frances all year because she was away at college. They figured the story would at least get Jill past the check-in station. After that, if her memory was what the old couple implied it to be, then maybe Jill could convince her they were related. Then Jill would casually reminisce about her favorite picture in the gallery, the one of the sad woman giving away the mermaid baby.

They arrived precisely at three o'clock. Security was somewhat lax, and the nurses revealed her "grandmother's" room without hesitation. They even believed Jill's not-entirely-untrue story that she brought two friends along because she didn't want to be alone for the long car ride.

Outside the room, Jill turned to Marina and Meredith. "You two wait out here, and leave the acting to me."

After knocking on the door, they heard a scratchy voice say, "Come in."

A frail woman with thinning white hair sat in a wheelchair and played solitaire at a table. She finished laying out her cards before looking up and crinkling her already wrinkled forehead. "Who in the blazes are you?" she barked.

Cautiously, Jill approached. "Don't you recognize me?"

The scowl on the woman's face didn't budge.

Jill knew that even an award-winning acting performance wasn't going to convince her skeptical audience of one, but always committed to a show-must-go-on philosophy, she said, "I'm…your…granddaughter?"

The woman carefully studied Jill from her feet all the way up to her head. "No, you're not. My good-for-nothing kids gave me seven grandsons and only one measly granddaughter. She's still in diapers, nowhere near as tall as you, Beanpole, and has nothing like the mangled mop you call hair!"

Her mouth dropping open, Jill turned to the others

standing just outside the open doorway. The look on her face told them to run away, but Meredith stepped inside with the orange folder.

"We have a question about a painting that used to hang in your gallery." Meredith sat at the foot of the nearby bed, hoping that a face-to-face conversation would calm the woman. "We don't mean to bother you, Frances. May I call you Frances?"

"No, you may not," snapped the woman, waving a thin, bony finger at Meredith, who scurried away. "I don't know you, I don't know your beanpole friend, and I don't know why you're bothering…" Her voice trailed off upon noticing the picture on Meredith's lap. She fiddled with the pointed-rim eyeglasses hanging on a chain around her neck until they rested on the bridge of her nose. "I haven't seen this picture in…goodness, I don't know how many years."

Her frail hands quivered as she took the matted print from Meredith. The crow's feet around her eyes were more prominent as she scrutinized the image. Then she grinned, and some wistful tears flowed through the crevices of her face.

"So you know who painted it?" asked Jill.

Furrowing her brow, Frances glared up at Jill. "Of course, I do! My Danny Boy painted it. Daniel's my youngest son. All that boy ever wanted to do was draw and paint. Drove his father—rest his soul—crazy. Said he needed to learn a trade, not a hobby. Didn't take my gallery too seriously either, but it helped pay the bills, and I outlived him anyway." She snickered.

"Lucky him," muttered Jill, without being overheard.

"The original hung in my gallery for years. I wouldn't let anyone buy it, no matter how much they offered." Frances's face beamed with pride as she held the print close to her face. "It was his best piece—his favorite too—because it was painted with so much love."

"Love?" exclaimed Marina from the doorway.

Frances lowered the print to her table, displacing some of

her playing cards. "How many hooligans did you bring with you, Beanpole?" She turned to Marina, and then her eyes glanced at the image in front of her. "Come here, lassie, so I can get a better look at you."

Giving up her seat on the bed, Meredith nodded subtly to let Marina know it would be safe to approach. Probably.

"Now you, I remember." Frances took hold of Marina's hand, squeezing three fingers in her tiny fist. "You still look as young and angelic as you always did. It's like you haven't changed at all."

Marina's voice wavered as she said, "I am afraid you are mistaken. We have never met."

"Of course, we've met." Frances laughed until she coughed. "You're Carol."

~ Chapter Twelve ~

They swam in a triangular formation, with Finn silently leading the way and maintaining a brisk pace.

"Are we in trouble?" asked Hailey, swimming ahead of Lorelei and trying to keep up with Finn. "What's gonna happen to Marina's tail? What's gonna happen to *me*?"

Finn didn't answer.

Lorelei flipped her tail a little harder until she had gotten close enough to Hailey to take her hand. "Do not worry. We will not let anything happen to you, sink or swim."

Though Lorelei's words were reassuring and her touch was comforting, Hailey was still quivering. "But what if something does happen? How often do mers get summoned to see Ray?"

"My father regularly consults with him—"

"Yeah, because he works for Ray. I bet it's bad when regular mers get called in. Have you ever been summoned?"

After a pause, Lorelei answered, "Never."

"S-W-I-M? This is *really* bad."

"You should not speak like a human," said Finn without looking back at them. "Neither of you should speak at all unless Ray asks you a question. Keep your answers short and as truthful as possible."

Hailey asked, "You want me to tell him the truth? What if he asks where I'm from? Or why I'm here?"

"If he summoned us, he may already think he knows those answers."

Before long, they arrived at an overhang built from remnants of sunken boats, and Hailey's eyes bulged when she saw it. The hull of what looked like a pirate ship from a movie was inverted and tilted forward at a steep angle. Several masts—wooden and metal—from a variety of different types of boats kept it from tipping over. Anchors, ship steering wheels, and other nautical artifacts were placed in decorative patterns around the area, and two mermaid figureheads flanked the apparent entrance. Unlike the coral reef which was teeming with life, there weren't any other fish around.

A merman with a dark blue tail blocked their way. He blew into a conch shell, creating a low tone that echoed within the overhang.

"Come!" called a deep voice from inside.

The mer floated aside, and Finn swam forward, followed by Lorelei and Hailey. Inside, along with other scattered human belongings, there were collections of seashells, arranged by color and shape.

Sitting on ornate chairs at the far end of the overhang were three mers with purple tails. In the center and highest chair, with a mermaid on both sides of him, the single man held up his shoulders and chin so he appeared taller and more imposing. He had short, pitch black hair on his head, but none on his bare, chiseled chest. His fluke pivoted from side to side as Finn swam ahead. Even in the distance, he appeared much larger than Finn.

"He's obviously Ray," Hailey whispered to Lorelei. "Who are the other two?"

Without it altering her course, Lorelei cocked her head to the side indicating the mermaid seated at Ray's right. "That is Calliope. I am sure Meredith told you about her."

Calliope sat back in her seat, with her tail floating forward. There was a smug grin on her face, and her long dark hair hung behind her. She folded her arms across her chest, just under her shells, which were held in place by thick, black netting tied around her neck.

"Ooh, she's got good fashion sense," said Hailey. "I might have to try that fishnet-halter-top-thing for my next party. Is the other her mom?"

Lorelei nodded. "Her name is Shelly."

Unlike her daughter, Shelly wore her dark raven hair up and twisted around a nautilus shell atop her head. A necklace made of shark teeth strung through a strand of seaweed extended down to the two starfish that served as her bikini top. She clutched the arms of her chair, and her tail curled tightly around one of its legs.

"Swim closer, orange-tail." In Ray's deep voice, the command sounded grim and foreboding.

Hailey gulped as she glanced at Finn, who gestured for her to approach. She knew she didn't have a choice and that she had to follow his orders or risk being banished, but she trembled with fear.

"This is the maid you have told me about?" Ray spoke slowly and then turned to Calliope. "And she is not the same orange-tail you encountered when we were last in these waters?"

"No, Father," said Calliope.

Ray left his chair and floated forward until he loomed right in front of Hailey, his chin slightly higher in the water than hers so he could stare down his nose at her. "You are not part of this school, and I cannot fathom why an orange-tail would leave her school."

"Well, I..." Hailey's heart pounded inside her. She didn't know the correct thing to say. Lorelei and Finn hadn't prepared her for direct questioning. All she knew was that she was petrified.

"You are aware that orange tails are exceedingly rare?"

Hailey nodded briskly. The only reason she knew was that Marina had told her so the summer before.

"Our school has only one. Do you know who that is?"

Afraid to answer but equally terrified not to answer, Hailey said, "Marina."

"So you have heard of her?"

"Finn and Lorelei told me about her," Hailey spoke quickly and cracked a nervous smile, wondering if Jill would be proud of her quick-thinking improv skills.

"Yet she is not with Finn and Lorelei, just as she was not when the other orange-tail was here. That is curious."

"Curiosity killed the catfish," said Finn. "I strongly recommend you let it float and allow me to handle the situation."

With a violent flip of his tail, Ray swooshed through the water until he was face to face with Finn. "You dare question my authority in this school? You are a mere scout."

"Your most trusted scout, or so I have been led to believe." Finn maintained eye contact with Ray, who eventually backed away. "I have trained my daughter and Marina well, and Marina is scouting ahead for us now."

Hailey turned to Lorelei, who brushed her long, flowing red hair behind one ear. As her hand crossed in front of her face, she held a finger in front of her lips. With the signal, Hailey understood that Finn was making up the story to protect Marina, and she hoped that Ray would be convinced.

"How convenient." Ray swam back to Hailey and circled her, slowly sinking to examine her fluke. "The color of your tail makes you drift out among the school. Tails have unique scale patterns, thus making mers easy to identify."

"And dear, you of all mers would recognize Marina's tail," said Shelly.

Ray shot upward and glowered at Shelly, who sank into her seat. "Of course," he said. "And this tail—"

"Hailey will remain under my supervision." Finn swam in front of Hailey and blocked Ray's view of her. "I have advised her to stay in the cave while she is here."

"I find it odd that for two consecutive northern seasons, an unknown orange-tail visits our school." Ray narrowed his gaze at Finn. "And in both cases, you have harbored her."

"We have extra space in our cavern, and we enjoy the company of visitors. They have interesting tales of adventure."

"Your family has always enjoyed adventures, perhaps too much. Unfortunately, adventure sometimes leads to tragedy."

He swam back toward his chair and nodded at Shelly before looking back over his shoulder at Finn. "You should understand that more than anyone else here."

"You leave Pearl out of this discussion," said Finn angrily.

Hailey was afraid to ask who Pearl was—she was afraid to ask anything given the situation in which she found herself—but Lorelei's pose, with her mouth dropped open and her head hung low, gave a clue. She figured that Pearl must have been Lorelei's mother.

"Those events were many cycles ago, but it is still a cautionary tale." Ray returned to his seat. "Shelly had tried to stop them. Is that not correct, my dear?"

In a meek voice, Shelly replied, "Yes, but they would not listen."

"I would not want any further loss in the name of adventure. Have I made my point?"

Through clenched teeth, Finn answered, "Like a swordfish."

"I will now tell you what I hope is not the truth. When we were in these waters last, an accident occurred, and Marina was temporarily stranded among the humans. Her tail was discovered by a human, who spent the time in our school. However, this was *not* brought to my attention." Ray swam to Finn and Lorelei, his eyes drifting back and forth between them and waiting for at least one of them to flinch in an admission of guilt, but no such motion came. Grinning, Ray continued, "If that were the case, withholding the information was a wise idea. Mostly."

Lorelei turned to her father and shrugged in confusion.

Ray asked, "Do you think my words flow against the current? Imagine the panic that would ensue had the school learned a human-maid swam with them."

"There are some who might consider it a fair exchange," said Finn. "We have the ability to walk among the humans, some of whom are kind."

"Others seek to trap fish in their nets, so there are also humans who are unkind."

"As there are also mers who are not kind."

Finn and Ray maintained their stares with their nostrils flaring and their fists clenched. Their flukes waved back and forth, keeping them afloat and ready to swim if the other pounced first. Grinning broadly, Calliope swam up from her seat like a cheerleader jumping up to applaud her father. Disgusted, Hailey looked at Lorelei, who watched Finn with a shocked look on her face as if she had never seen him so furious.

"Please end this float-off," said Shelly, timidly but loudly enough to be heard.

Ray glared at her then turned back to Finn, who hadn't moved.

"There is nothing more you need to concern yourself with." Finn flicked his tail to swim slightly upward. "Hailey will be safe in my care, and the rest of the school need not know she is here."

"It is decided, then. You may stay." Ray swiftly swam to Hailey. "I expect you will be on your best behavior and keep your tail wet until the moon cycle is over."

"Really?" Hailey's mouth and eyes popped open in surprise.

"If you are indeed a mer, then allow me to express my humblest apologies." He placed his hands on his hips and extended his elbows outward such that his shadow appeared to loom larger over Hailey, never breaking eye contact with her. "But if you are a human in disguise—and for your sake, I hope you are not—then I recommend you keep your interactions with the mers in *my* school to a minimum. Have I made my point?"

Trembling, Hailey replied, "Like a swordfish?"

"You learn quickly." He swam back to his seat. "Finn, you may escort the maids back to your cave."

Finn bowed and thanked Ray, and then Lorelei and Hailey did the same. When they had swum away from the overhang, Hailey let out a long sigh before saying, "Now that went better than I expected. I'm sure it could've been *a lot* worse."

Letting Hailey drift behind her, Lorelei swam to catch up to Finn. They cast each other silent glances, signaling to each other that they didn't trust Ray's behavior but weren't going to discuss it around Hailey out of fear of upsetting her.

"We shall let it float," said Finn.

Meanwhile, under the overhang, Shelly hesitantly put her hand on top of Ray's. "You were quite generous, as a true leader should be. Age and wisdom seem to have tempered you."

"Perhaps they have, my maid." Ray leaned over and planted a quick kiss on her forehead. "Now swim away so I may drift in my thoughts for a wave."

Shelly bowed her head and swam away, followed by Calliope.

Before they left the overhang, Ray said, "A word with you please, daughter?"

Calliope looked at her mother, who shook her head disapprovingly before leaving, and returned to her seat. "Yes, Father?"

"What do you think of this maid?"

"Her tail is orange," said Calliope, a contemptuous tone in her voice. "She is not to be trusted."

"I have raised you well." Ray smirked and stroked his daughter's cheek. "It is clear to me that the tail belongs to Marina, so I need you to alert me of anything questionable done by our *visitor*." He twitched upon uttering the final word.

"How long would you like me to tail her?"

"The time of no moon is approaching." He released a burst of laughter. "If you can catch her before, then we may finally rid the ocean of the last orange-tail."

~ Chapter Thirteen ~

"Coral," said Marina, sitting at the foot of the bed.

"What?" blurted Frances. "No, your name is Carol."

"*My* name is Marina. You must have known my mother. *Her* name was Coral."

"You're mistaken, lassie. I remember it clear as the break of day, and the name was Carol."

Jill clapped her hands once to silence the discussion. "Carol, Coral. They pretty much sound the same. Can we just get on with it and find out how you knew her?"

Her face aghast, Frances stared up at Jill. "You might want to stop your yapping, Beanpole. This is between me and Carol here."

Marina leaned closer to Frances and clutched her hand. "Please tell me what you remember."

"We were visiting family on that island…" Frances spun her wrist around and tried to snap her bony fingers. "I haven't the foggiest what the name of the place was. My memory for names isn't what it used to be."

Jill nudged Meredith in the side and muttered. "No kidding. Carol, Coral."

"Watch it, Beanpole!" Scowling, Frances waved her finger at Jill.

"But her hearing's perfect," whispered Meredith.

"What was that?" asked Frances. Shaking it off, she turned her attention back to Marina. "It was the summer Daniel graduated art school. That's when we met Carol. He loved that girl with all his heart. Carol never came right out and said it, but you could tell by the look in her sad eyes that she must've loved my Danny but couldn't find the words to tell him before she left."

Marina stood and felt herself getting dizzy in a whirlpool of confusion. As the color drained from her face, Meredith rushed to her side to catch her before she fell over.

"Do you know where she went?" asked Meredith.

Jill added, "Does your son know where she is?"

"You won't bother my Danny Boy! You understand that, Beanpole?" Frances backed her wheelchair away from the card table. "He was crushed when she left. Took him years to get over Carol. I don't want to put him through that pain again!"

"Please," whimpered Marina. "I need to find my mother."

Frances wheeled to the nightstand and picked up the phone receiver. "If you don't leave here now, I'm calling security."

Before Jill could protest or Marina could bawl her eyes out, Meredith ushered them out of the room and back to the minivan.

Meredith hoped a trip to a nearby ice cream parlor would placate Marina, but the bowl was untouched until it was filled with chocolate goop. Jill stalled them there, discreetly texting home to confirm whether or not her brother had gone out.

On the drive back, the mood in the minivan was subdued until Meredith exclaimed, "Why don't we just call him?"

Rolling her eyes while driving, Jill said, "Merri, that's kinda difficult without his phone number."

"But we know his name is Daniel McPherson. We look him up in the phone book." Meredith watched Jill's face contort in confused ignorance. "Thick book with small print and thin pages, some of which are yellow?"

"What are you even talking about?"

"Before people had cell phones and used their land lines…oh, never mind. Your mom will know what I'm talking about."

When they arrived at Jill's house, her mother graciously supplied them with a short stack of phone books from a drawer in the hallway. There were three Daniel MacPhersons in the vicinity, and Jill came up with a plan to enact the next morning.

They returned to the nursing home and sat in the park across the street. In a nasal voice, Jill played the role of a staff member trying to get Daniel to visit Frances. The first call was to the wrong Daniel, but the second call was right.

Speaking in a nasal voice, Jill said, "Please hold for your mother." She waited a few moments while she loosened her mouth muscles in typical vocal warm-up fashion. When she spoke next, her voice was extra gravelly. "Danny Boy, why haven't you come and visited your mother?"

Marina started giggling at how similar Jill sounded to Frances, so Meredith covered her mouth.

"I want you to come and tell me all about that painting again." Jill paused while Daniel spoke. "The one with that girl we met on the island." Another pause. "Whatever happened to her? How is the lassie doing? Do you know where she is?" Pause. "You know the girl. Her name was Carol." Jill winked at Marina. "Don't talk back to your mother! I'm pretty sure it was Coral!" She glanced at Meredith, who was trying to stifle her own laughter. "Uh-huh." Jill's smirk faded away. "Well, no." She was quiet for an extended period of time, and then her impersonation of Frances ended, and she spoke normally. "Oh, okay." She ended the call as the color drained from her face.

"Is something wrong?" asked Marina.

Jill stood there with her mouth agape until Meredith said, "Don't tell me we blew it."

"His mother called him last night and told him all about us." Jill turned to Marina and grinned warily. "He gave me his address. He wants to meet you."

~ ~ ~

Jill parked in front of a light blue, one-story ranch-style house with rows of hedges separating it from the neighboring properties. There wasn't a car in the driveway, but a figure sat at an easel under an oak tree in the front yard. The man was middle-aged and showed the signs of it: a slight paunch in his belly and a receding hairline. But his facial expression was still boyish.

A light breeze blew when Marina stepped out of the minivan. Her long, fine strands of hair covered her face while the wind rustled the papers on the man's easel. He stood to clip the papers together and saw the girls on his lawn. When Marina gathered the hair from her face and brushed it behind her ears, the man stumbled forward as if he had been blown over by the wind.

He approached slowly, a glint in his hazel eyes. "You're really her—Coral's daughter—aren't you?"

Marina's face beamed, not only because the man knew who she was but also because he had correctly pronounced her mother's name. *Coral.* She nodded.

Meredith stood close to Marina. "Are you Daniel?"

"Yeah," he answered, never redirecting his star-struck gaze from Marina. "You look just like her, you know?"

"I have been told that, but sadly, I have never seen her."

"You sound like her too." The man smiled. "I remember years ago like it was yesterday. You talk in the same speech pattern."

"You mean all stilted without contractions?" muttered Jill, eliciting an elbow to the side from Meredith.

Daniel glared at Jill. "You must be the one who pretended to be my mother. Your performance was a little stilted."

Jill crossed her arms and pouted, but Daniel ignored her and returned his gaze to Marina.

"I meant to say your voice is lyrical, with a rhythm like calm ocean surf. I met your mother on a beach, you know." An awkward silence followed, except for the chirping birds and occasional passing car. Then he snapped his fingers. "Come see what I was working on."

He jogged back to his easel while the girls followed, Jill putting on her sunglasses and lingering behind. He turned the easel around and revealed a charcoal drawing of a woman's face, and Marina gasped when she recognized the face as her own, though she knew it had to be her mother.

"It is like I am staring at my reflection in the water's surface." Marina reached out to stroke her mother's cheek, but she smudged the image and her fingers. "I am sorry. I did not mean to ruin it."

"You didn't ruin it." He paused, once again captivated by the resemblance between Marina and her mother. "Even if you had, I can always make another from memory. I'll never forget Coral."

He recalled the summer after graduating art school when they visited his uncle on the same island as Hailey. After dining one night in the middle of their vacation, they returned to his uncle's beach house to find Coral sitting alone on the beach and sadly staring out to sea. Daniel claimed his mother was a people-person who'd talk to anyone, so she struck up a conversation. Coral gave cryptic answers to the questions, but Frances inferred that she was homeless—perhaps even abandoned—and needed a place to stay at least for the night.

One night led to another and then another, and when the vacation ended, Coral went to stay with them on the mainland. Despite the objections of Daniel's father, Frances insisted there was plenty of room in the house since Daniel's older brother and sister were both married and living elsewhere. During the two years that Coral stayed with them, she worked for Frances at the art gallery, and she and Daniel grew closer until he fell in love with her.

"What about my father?" demanded Marina. "Did she tell you about him?"

"She was always private about her life before us, and I don't think she ever mentioned anything to my mother, but she told me about him. How he was lost at sea, and I saw in her eyes how much she still loved him."

"Love triangles," said Jill, rolling her eyes. "Hate stories with them."

"All I wanted was for Coral to be happy. That's when I

painted her portrait."

Meredith removed the print from the folder and held it up. "This one?"

He grinned as he took hold of the print, and then he breathed out the words, "It worked."

Confused, Marina and Meredith stared at each other.

"The picture is a clue for him to find your mother." Daniel explained how the stormy water in the background symbolized being lost at sea. He never knew Coral had a daughter, but that a baby mermaid—painted to her specification with an orange tail—being given back to the ocean would be a message that he'd recognize. "I taught her how to draw, and she drew a lot of mermaids. She was pretty good, too."

"Do you know where she is?" asked Marina.

"When she had saved up enough money, she moved closer to the ocean. She believed he'd have a better chance of finding her there." He held up the print. "That's why I had these made. I gave them to souvenir shops in as many seaside touristy towns as I could. And *you* found me."

"Yeah, but where is *she*?" asked Jill impatiently.

Handing a folded slip of paper to Marina, Daniel said he and Coral had regularly exchanged letters for a few years. She had never gotten a computer to send email. But then Daniel got married and had two sons, and correspondence with Coral ultimately ended.

"I love my wife." He said she worked as a paralegal and dropped their sons off at their summer day camp that morning before going to work, while he worked from home as a freelance graphic designer and illustrator. "My dad went fishing a lot when I was a kid, and he always told stories about the big ones that got away. Your mother was like one of those for me."

"A big fish?" asked Marina, innocently. "Did she tell you that she was a fish?"

Jill couldn't control the laughter that burst from her mouth, so Meredith quickly dragged her closer to the car.

Daniel wiped his eyes. "No, she was the one that got away. You never forget your first love." He walked to the easel and tore the sketch along its perforations. "Give this to her, from me. And tell her I say hello."

Thanking him, Marina took the drawing and returned to Jill's car. The address was in a coastal town, once again too far to attempt driving there immediately. Because Meredith and Jill had to go to work the next morning, the search wouldn't be continued until the following weekend.

Disappointed, Marina leaned her head against the passenger window and asked, "Do you think my mother…loved him?" There was a catch in her voice on the word *loved.*

From behind, Meredith placed a hand on Marina's shoulder. "She may have, in her own way, but it doesn't mean she was *in love* with him."

"I do not understand. Is there a difference?"

"She may have loved him like a brother, or even as a really close friend that you care deeply about. I'm sure you have similar feelings for Lorelei."

Watching the world go by outside, Marina thought about Lorelei, who was about as close to being her sister as possible. They had shared almost everything over the years—many adventures together—and they had much in common, both being raised by Finn because they had both lost a mother when they were young. The prospect of finding her mother suddenly made Marina feel conflicted, as Lorelei would never get hers back.

After dropping Meredith off, Jill drove home and parked the car at the end of the driveway so they could enter through the side door to the kitchen. Before she stepped inside, Marina heard Jeff's voice around the corner of the wraparound porch. She took off for him before Jill could stop her.

Turning the corner, Marina froze when she saw Jeff and another girl sitting on the front porch swing and kissing.

"Marina, wait," called Jill.

Jeff was standing with his back to her, but upon hearing his sister's voice, he pulled out of the embrace and glanced over his shoulder. "Marina?" he asked.

Her arms still around Jeff's neck, the girl tried to turn his face back toward hers. Marina stepped back and stormed past Jill, into the house, and up to the bedroom, where she collapsed on Jill's bed.

As Marina thought about Jeff kissing that girl, the feelings she had upon imagining her mother loving someone else came flooding back to her, and she couldn't stop her tears from flowing.

~ Chapter Fourteen ~

After returning from Ray, Finn wouldn't let Hailey be unsupervised for any prolonged stretch of time. Like an overprotective father, he made sure that either he or Lorelei accompanied her outside the cavern. *More like babysitting*, thought Hailey. They treated her like an ignorant child and abruptly ended certain conversations if she was hovering too close to them. All their tight-lipped discussions did was convince her that she was in trouble—that Ray knew she was a human girl with the rarest of mermaid tails. If not for Barney's daily visits, Hailey would probably have cracked from all the added pressure surrounding her.

"I can't take much more of the way they're avoiding the subject around me," she told Barney while they were the only two in the cave. "It's like they're walking on eggshells."

Barney stared at her quizzically. "I do not understand. What do your words mean? I have never—"

"That's right. You wouldn't get it. My bad." Hailey's eyelids fluttered while she wondered if fish eggs had hard shells. Then she grinned upon figuring out a more appropriate expression. "How 'bout walking on *barnacles*?"

"That would hurt." Imagining the pain, Barney winced. "But I have never walked on them. I have never walked at all. I have only swum."

Hailey groaned as she flitted around the cave. "Never mind. I know they're protecting Marina's tail—and me too—so I probably shouldn't go anywhere without them, but come on. I'm here on vacation, or mer-cation, or something."

"Have you told me everything Ray told you?" Barney

watched Hailey nod. "He did not say you have to stay in the cave. He said not to interact with other mers. We can go where they will not be." He swam to the cave opening.

Hailey slowly followed. "Uh, F-Y-I, that's what we did the other day with Lore. We got back and got summoned. No thanks. Not gonna do that again. Ray's kinda scary."

"It will not happen again. You have swum out with Lorelei and Finn." Flicking his fluke and rolling his shoulders, Barney swirled through the water until he was bobbing up and down outside the cavern. "This time, let me take you out."

Upon hearing his words, Hailey froze and watched him beckoning to her. He wore a crooked smile on his face that looked somewhat mischievous, and as her gaze caught his, she saw a silver sparkle in his eye. His final words echoed in her head: *let me take you out.* She gasped when her mind translated it as him asking her out—on a date. It had been a long time since she had gone on a date. She wasn't interested in any of the boys back home because she had known them all since elementary school, but Barney was sweet and funny, and she couldn't deny how cute he was.

"Of course, you can take me out." She giggled as she swam out of the cave. "But we shouldn't go too far away."

"Then we will not. Follow me," said Barney as he dove downward.

Hailey followed into the bubbles floating up from behind his flapping fluke. They tickled her nose, but she continued in their wake since they provided a path as the water darkened. Their course ran parallel to the slanted rock face below the cavern until they reached the ocean floor. When Barney slowed down, the stream of bubbles ceased. Unable to see him before her, Hailey came within inches of colliding with his flipper before swerving to the side.

"Now lie down," said Barney. "And look up. Tell me what you see."

She curved her fluke, which twisted her entire body until she was facing upward, and then she relaxed her muscles and allowed gravity to float her down until she settled into the cushion of the loose, sandy surface. The opening of Lorelei's cavern was high up the rocky hill—which appeared more like a mountain from her vantage point—and at some distance in the water above that, there were many faint points of light.

"Fireflies?" she asked, stretching out the word with a mixture of uncertainty and curiosity. But when she noticed the sun, appearing as a small dot hovering in the sky beyond the peak of the rocks, she realized it wasn't the right time of day. "No, can't be."

Barney shook his head, sweeping some of the sand underneath into the murky water. "I do not know what fireflies are. Look closer. What *would* be up there?"

Squinting didn't help Hailey. She was too deep and far away from the points of light. Like viewing diamonds, there were individual bursts of every color. Reds and greens and blues and purples. She gasped and pointed when she figured out what they were. "They're mers. Sparkly scales. It's the school!"

"That is right. But from down here, you cannot tell. We are all small. The waters are large and vast and deep."

Soothed by his profound words, particularly in the slower than lightning-speed pace he was saying them, Hailey released a sigh.

"I would like to explore," said Barney, "To scout like Finn, and to visit land like Lorelei."

"Then why don't you?"

"My parents say I should not shed my tail. They say humans cannot be trusted." Barney rolled onto his side. "I have only met two—you and Meredith—and I trust you both. You are my friends."

Friends. The word disappointed Hailey a little. She knew she'd be leaving in a few weeks, so anything deeper would just wash away with the tide unless she could convince him to visit her regularly. She bolted up, and in her excitement, drifted above the ocean floor. "At the next full moon, when I go back, come on land with me. Let *me* take *you* out for a day!"

"I would like that, but my parents might not let me. I am to stay in the water. When I am of age, I will gather like they do."

"Gather? W-D-Y-M?" Hailey floated back down to the sand. "Er, sorry. What do you mean?"

"I have a silver tail. It will be my responsibility to help gather building materials for shelters."

"So does that mean you find parts of sunken ships, and then you build places to live like Ray's upside-down boat fortress thingy?"

"We gather the materials. The red-tails build."

"Your job's decided by what color your tail is?"

Barney started explaining the hierarchy of the other tail colors. Yellow-tails harvested plankton to make sure the school's waters were nutrient-rich. The blue-tailed mers were in charge of monitoring dangerous animals, such as sharks, and keeping them away from the school. Hailey correctly stated that mers with green tails, like Finn and Lorelei, were in charge of scouting safe locations for the school to stay. Parents were expected to train their children not only in proper swimming and behavior but also in their predetermined lifetime career.

"You didn't mention the purple-tails. Let me guess. They're in charge." Hailey watched Barney nod his head. "Who made them the boss—or, um, the bosses?"

"I do not know." Barney shrugged. "Whenever I ask my parents, they only say that is how it is."

Grunting in frustration, Hailey leaned back and smacked her tail on the ocean floor. Along with the sand rising, another question arose. "What about orange? If Marina's the only one with an orange tail, what's she supposed to do? What's gonna be her job in the school?"

Again, Barney didn't know because his parents had always evaded that question too. Just like Finn and Lorelei had been avoiding discussion about Pearl. Though Hailey wanted to experience everything about being a mermaid, there were far too many secrets in the school. She doubted she would discover any answers while she had Marina's tail. In any other color, she wouldn't have stood out—and probably not have gotten summoned by Ray—so she could have investigated. Not just for her own curiosity, but also for Marina's benefit. Did Marina even know what the color of her tail meant? Or was she kept in the dark as well?

Suddenly, a long shadow was cast over them. "What's happening?" she asked, propping herself up with her arms.

Barney looked up and pointed. Following his arm, Hailey saw that the sun had crossed the sky to the point where the mountain eclipsed it.

"Do you think anyone will ever know why there's only one orange tail?" Hailey flipped her fluke. "Will Marina ever be able to just kinda blend in with the rest of the school?"

"I think you are blending in."

"No, I'm not. I'm a human, an outsider. And I'm pretty sure Ray knows it."

"I mean the color of our scales. They seem to have blended together." He gestured at their side-by-side tails.

Hailey looked at her lap and all the way to where her ankles would be. The usual iridescence of her orange scales had disappeared, leaving only a dull gray color. In the shadows of the bottom of the ocean, nothing sparkled. Barney's tail also appeared pale and gray, exactly the same shade as hers.

"It would flow if the color of a mer's tail did not matter," said Barney.

"It sure would." Hailey took a relaxing breath. "Thanks for taking me out."

Hailey turned to him, and his gaze met hers, but just as their tails weren't glistening, neither did the usual glint of his eyes, so Hailey had to imagine them twinkling. Her heart and fluke fluttered as she closed her eyes and leaned closer to him, hoping that he was doing the same. She puckered her lips, waiting for them to come into contact with his.

"Hailey, is that you down there?" called Lorelei from above.

When her eyes popped open, Hailey saw Barney's face directly in front her. Startled, he backed away, jerked his chin back, and yelled up to the cavern. "She is down here, Lorelei! She is with me! I have been with her all this time." Once again, Barney's short sentences quickly flowed from one to another, and his attention ricocheted between Lorelei above him, the ocean floor below him, and Hailey in front of him. "You should go back. Lorelei is waiting. Maybe Finn is there also. I am afraid we went too far."

He swam upward, and as his gray fluke passed by her face, Hailey groaned and then followed. "But not far enough," she muttered.

~ Chapter Fifteen ~

The interns were expected at the Investigation Station in the aquarium's main exhibit hall a half hour before visitors entered, so Meredith probably wouldn't be able to meet Marina when the front gate opened. As Dr. Hatcher approached her and Will with obvious urgency, Meredith knew she'd probably be occupied at least until lunchtime.

"Change of plans, everyone," he said, frowning when Brittany finally arrived through the nearby door for authorized personnel only. "We had someone call in sick today, so you're getting a quick lesson on our aquatic friends here, and then we're going to man the station for the morning. We'll see how well you do with our human visitors." He snickered playfully when he referred to the kids as human.

The Investigation Station was an octagonal tank only about two feet deep but on a raised platform about waist high. It was the perfect height for pre-teens, and there were step stools for younger children. Over the inner rim on most of the eight edges were smaller, shallower tanks housing sea stars and a variety of small crabs. Two blue lobsters crawled around the center out of reach of curious fingers.

"What are those?" asked Brittany, her face all scrunched up. "Aren't lobsters supposed to be bright red?"

"They're only red when you cook them." Dr. Hatcher derisively shook his head. "And even those lobsters are typically dark green or deep red, almost murky brown. We won't be cooking our friends in this tank, as they were gracious gifts to the aquarium. Do any of you know what causes the rare color?"

Meredith's hand immediately shot straight up, and Dr. Hatcher smiled and called on her to answer.

"A genetic mutation," she said. "DNA contains the instructions for creating proteins. When a mutation changes the code, sometimes a different protein is made, and in this case, the pigmentation—which is caused by some of those proteins—is changed."

"Correct. This shade of blue occurs approximately once in every two million lobsters. Not counting lobsters without pigmentation, does anyone know what colors are rarer than blue?"

During the question, Meredith's thoughts drifted to Marina's orange tail, the only one in her school. Was the color rare like the blue lobster? She hadn't counted the number of mermaids in the school, and the first time she saw them swimming from a distance, she estimated there were several hundred of them, no more than a thousand or two. But what if there were other schools?

As she had learned in her Advanced Placement Biology class, even eye color wasn't as simple as usually taught in introductory lessons; two blue-eyed parents could still produce a brown-eyed child. She knew nothing of mermaid genetics, and without knowing the color of Marina's parents' tails, there wasn't any way of knowing if an orange tail was an inherited trait or a mutation.

"The rarest coloration of *Homarus americanus* is…oh, wow, I know I read it somewhere." Will furiously scratched his head until he remembered. "Is it yellow?"

"Excellent answer, Will," said Dr. Hatcher. "About one in every thirty million. Equally rare is a mottled black and orange lobster."

The mention of the color orange broke Meredith's concentration. "What was that?"

"Something little miss aqua-dork doesn't know," muttered Brittany.

Meredith ignored Brittany's insult and focused on Dr.

Hatcher teaching how to handle the small, delicate animals. His explanations were quick, but he assured them he'd be supervising while the guests were there. It would be more of a trial-by-fire morning for the interns, and Meredith was thrilled by the hands-on nature of their impromptu assignment.

The kids flooded in, followed by their parents, grandparents, nannies, camp counselors, or whoever brought them on the warm summer day. Meredith dove right in, encouraging the children—and showing them how—to interact with the animals. She helped some of the younger, reluctant, and squeamish kids gently scoop the starfish from underneath without taking them out of the water.

Brittany flinched and squealed every time a crab pinched her. Dr. Hatcher spent a majority of his time reiterating the proper procedures to her, and he intervened once when she picked up a starfish by one of its five arms. Whenever he wasn't looking, she flipped the crabs over and laughed while they struggled to turn themselves upright.

Whenever she had a chance, Meredith looked over at Will. He shuddered the first time he dipped his arm in the cold water, but as the morning went on, it seemed to bother him less. Because of his height, he adopted some odd or uncomfortable poses to interact with the kids. Sometimes he knelt, sometimes he leaned over the tank, and sometimes he stood with his feet spread far apart on the floor. She laughed at how the children stared at him quizzically while he enthusiastically identified the animals by their scientific names. When it came to teaching the children how to touch them, his instructions included pointing at Meredith and saying, "Listen to her," or "Do what she's doing."

"Come on, Will," said Dr. Hatcher. "Trust yourself. You know what to do."

Will was letting a little girl put a starfish back in his hand because she thought it was too icky, and his other hand was helping to keep his balance. He cocked his head toward Meredith and said, "But she knows a lot more."

"If you want to know more, ask her if she can help you study." Dr. Hatcher glanced at Meredith. "And while she tutors you, listen to her and do what she's doing."

Turning away, Meredith tried to conceal her laughter. She would have covered her face, but her submerged hands had a few crabs crawling over them, much to the enjoyment of the young spectators.

"You've got quite an audience," said Dr. Hatcher from behind her.

Meredith looked at the dozen or so kids crowded around her. "All here to see the crazy crab lady, I guess."

"I don't just mean the children. The lobsters have taken an interest in you as well."

Meredith leaned forward to look in the main tank, and the lobsters weren't in the center. They had crawled to the side where she was, and one of them was tapping a claw on the tank wall as if it was knocking on a door.

"Would you look at that?" Meredith laughed nervously. Not wanting to call any further attention to her superpower, she gently shook the crabs off her hands and changed the subject. "How's the manatee doing?"

"His physical condition has improved, but we're going to keep him under observation until he's fully healed." Dr. Hatcher flashed a smile, showing off his white teeth. "I'll tell him you asked."

Their replacements arrived, and Brittany proclaimed, "It's about time. My fingers are prunes." She snatched a paper towel from a dispenser at the nearby clean-up sink and stormed through the aquarium employee door.

Dr. Hatcher joined Meredith and Will at the sink. "The two of you did quite well this morning. Our aquatic friends appreciate that."

While drying her hands, Meredith asked, "Is there any chance we'll be able to see the manatee before you return him to the ocean? It would be a great opportunity."

"That it would. Probably not until he's in better health, but something can probably be arranged." He smiled at

Meredith and patted Will on the back before leaving through the door.

Will's usually pale face turned pink with glee. "Wow! Did you just…?" He threw his arms around Meredith, but once he realized he was hugging her, he stepped back. His face had blushed to deep red, and he anxiously shuffled his feet. "I don't know what came over me. I'm sorry, Meredith, I didn't mean to."

"It's okay." Meredith tried to give him a friendly squeeze on his shoulder, but he jumped back. "I'm thrilled about it too."

Brittany appeared among the crowd, in the opposite direction from where she had exited. "How did you—?" asked Will, his head jerking back and forth as he looked from her to the authorized-personnel-only door. "Get there so fast?"

Brittany ignored him and upturned her nose at Meredith. "Your stuffed-sea-lion friend's cousin is causing a scene by the main tank. Just sayin'." She popped her gum.

Excusing herself, Meredith wove her way through the crowd, taking quick and sharp turns to avoid crashing into children until she came to the enormous cylindrical tank in the hall's center. She had an unblocked view of the coral reef replica inside because no one was standing on that side of the tank, but more disconcerting to her was the lack of fish.

A crowd had gathered on the opposite side, so Meredith walked around the tank. Marina was leaning forward with one palm against the glass, and all the fish inside floated almost frozen in place in circles around her hand. They were all pointed toward the center of her palm like they were awaiting further instructions on which way to swim.

The spectators were mesmerized and arranged in semi-circles around Marina just like the fish. They talked in hushed tones, collectively understanding that loud noises would disturb the scene, but some had their phones in their hands and were taking pictures. Meredith knew it was too late to stop some of the people from uploading photos or videos to the internet, but she pushed her way through the crowd to retrieve Marina.

She tripped over someone's foot and stumbled forward but used the wall of the tank to brace her fall. As soon as her hand touched the glass, the formation of fish inside changed. The circle seemed to split into two—almost like the division of a cell, thought Meredith—until it surrounded both of their hands. The fish watched both girls, their eyes flicking back and forth until Meredith took hold of Marina's wrist and slowly withdrew their palms from the glass.

The fish instantly scattered, returning to their usual swimming patterns in the tank. Some of the gathered spectators applauded while others groaned, but Meredith ignored them all. She pulled Marina through the crowd, weaving through their arbitrary walking patterns. They passed the jellyfish tank and entered a family restroom, where Meredith locked the door.

"I would like to go home," said Marina, tears trickling down her cheeks.

"Hailey's still got your tail. The new moon is about a week away, but we don't have any of your scales to recharge it—or whatever happened last summer." Meredith watched Marina give a little shrug. "Besides, we're getting closer to finding your mother. You wouldn't want to give up now."

"I want to find her more than anything else, but I cannot stay at Jill's house." Marina's face quivered, and more tears started flowing. She plopped onto the covered toilet seat. "Jeff is with a new maid now."

"You can stay with me in my dorm room if you want." Meredith sat and put her arm around Marina.

"You would do that for me?"

"Of course, I would. I wouldn't have this internship if it wasn't for your tail coming into my life. I can't thank you enough. I'm here because of you."

"I am still not sure what I think of this place."

"If there's a day you don't want to come here, you can stay in my room. No worries, Marina."

For the rest of the day, Marina waited at the picnic tables outside the aquarium, regaining her composure. When the aquarium closed, Jill apologized for never mentioning Jeff's girlfriend, insisting she was trying to shield Marina from getting hurt. Once Marina thought about the painful secret she was keeping from Lorelei, she accepted the apology and was grateful when Jill lent her a sleeping bag from the back of the minivan.

On the shuttle bus ride to the dormitory, Brittany glowered at Marina and asked, "Why's she coming too? She's not your cousin."

While Meredith fumbled for a response and wished her improvisational skills were as quick as Jill's, Marina started answering, "I can no longer stay in that house. The—"

"The cat!" blurted Meredith. "Marina's allergic, and even though she was taking her medication, the dander was getting to her."

"I do not like the cat," said Marina, though Meredith wasn't sure if she was playing along or speaking in her usual innocent manner. "It liked to lick my feet."

"Mine too! And my ankles. What's bizarre is that it never came near me before, not until last summer after I—" Meredith immediately broke into laughter upon realizing the cat's affinity for her started after returning from her time as a mermaid, and Marina giggled along with her.

"Are you sure *you two* aren't related?" asked Brittany before popping her gum. "Because you sure act the same. It's really fishy."

"Fishy," chuckled Will. "Wow, Brittany. I didn't expect puns from you."

"You know you're all dorks, right?" Brittany popped earphones into her ears and turned up the volume of her heavy metal music.

In the dormitory room later that evening, Meredith offered to sleep on the floor in the sleeping bag, but Marina refused the uncomfortable bed. As Meredith zipped her inside, Marina felt the dark blue fabric envelop her, almost like the supportive waters of home, but she would have felt more buoyant if the distinct smell of the sleeping bag didn't instantly conjure up memories.

The scent reminded her of Jeff.

~ Chapter Sixteen ~

The bursts of colored light in the sky high above the water were slightly distorted by the ripples of the gentle waves. The slight downward slope of the submerged sand not too far out from the beach provided the perfect spot to recline and watch the island's Fourth of July fireworks display. Hailey lay between Lorelei and Barney, and she spent less time watching the fireworks and more time watching their—particularly Barney's—reactions to them.

"Should we be this far from the cave?" he asked. "We are very far. We are almost on land. What if we are seen? What if we are caught? What if the humans—?" He gasped upon seeing an impressive explosion of red and yellow, followed by its loud boom. "That flows!"

While the crowd on the beach applauded, Lorelei asked, "Are you sure we will not be noticed? It sounds as though there are many humans out there."

"No problem." Hailey flicked her wrist above Lorelei. "They usually close the beach for swimmers, and it's already really dark. No one will be looking in the water. They'll be looking at those." She pointed straight up at a spiral of white light whinnying through the air.

"It is smarter to be watching from down here where we cannot be seen," said Lorelei. "We were farther away last time, but Meredith insisted that we sit on some rocks."

"You sat on rocks?" asked Barney, incredulously. "Mers are not supposed to sit on rocks. That is against the rules. What if you were seen? Why did she make you do that?"

"Chill out, Barney." Hailey reached and took hold of his

wrist. "L-I-F…er, let it float."

"But they may have been seen. It is good that they were not. Are you sure—?" He flinched after hearing the loud boom that followed the blue and white flashes. His wrist slipped out of Hailey's grip, but he quickly grabbed her hand. "That was unexpected." His speech slowed down while he sighed. "And amazing too."

As Barney's fingers interlocked with hers, Hailey felt her fluke flutter. "Totally unexpected and amazing," she said with a giggle.

While the display continued, they lay there watching. Whenever a sound startled Barney, he squeezed Hailey's hand—not enough to hurt her, but enough to surprise her and cause her to kick her tailfin.

The lights dimmed, and when the lingering blasts stopped sounding, their vision beyond the surface of the water disappeared into blackness.

"Is that all?" asked Barney. "That flowed. We should probably leave. It is dark now. No one will see us. But I wish there were more."

Hailey had been counting in her head. When she reached ten, she pointed up at the night sky and said, "Wait for it."

A succession of explosions filled the sky with enough light that the three of them could clearly see the color of their tails fading in and out as the colors above them changed. Between the ripples of the ocean surface and the smoke hovering in the sky, the lights sparkled like their scales. Too loud to be muffled by the water, the continuous bursts sounded like waves thrashing onto the shore during a storm.

The final sequence started with only red fireworks, bright enough to make Barney's silver tail reflect the light such that he appeared with a red tail.

"I look like a builder mer," he said.

The lights in the sky turned white, so their three tails shone vibrantly in their original colors.

"Good thing no one's right above us," said Hailey. "We're, like, super neon mers right now!"

In accordance with the holiday, the white fireworks transitioned to blue. Lorelei's tail seemed to disappear, and Hailey's turned to a dull gray, but Barney's again reflected the color above.

Snickering, Lorelei said, "Now you look like you should fend off some nearby sharks or jellyfish."

Barney shuddered. "You let that float, Lore. Sharks are scary. Jellies sting. I am no blue-tail."

The fireworks finale faded away, leaving them in dimness once again, so there was no way to distinguish between their scales.

"I wish I could become a scout," whimpered Barney as the sound of the last explosion was heard. "But I shall never be."

Hailey felt his hand slipping out of hers, so she snatched it back and turned him toward her. "Don't you dare let go of that dream! All my life, I wished I could be a mermaid—a real, live mer instead of just a little girl in a costume. Now look at me." She swam a quarter loop and took him with her until they were upright in the dark water. "My dream finally came true, so maybe someday yours will."

"Is this the closest you have ever come to land?" asked Lorelei, appearing beside them.

After Barney nodded, Hailey said, "Well that's one small step—er, swim—for merkind, and one…uh…" Hailey flailed her hands in front of her trying to complete her thought.

Then Lorelei said, "One giant flip of the fins forward for Barney."

Laughing, the three of them started swimming away from the island and back toward the cavern. Having caught glances of Hailey and Barney holding hands, Lorelei took the lead in their triangular formation, keeping herself far enough ahead to give the two little love-mers some time alone to talk.

About a third of the way home, a snide voice called out to them. "Why did you swim out so close to those filthy humans? You know you might have been seen."

Leaving the others, Lorelei swam toward the familiar voice. "We stayed in dark water, Calliope, watching one of their most beautiful customs. There is far more adventure beyond the sea than in your deepest imagination."

"If you think it flows so much, then maybe you should leave the school and live out there." Calliope folded her arms across her seashells and flicked her tail to rise slightly above Lorelei. "Permanently."

"Hey, hey, no fighting." Hailey swam between them, causing Calliope to recoil in disgust. "This is supposed to be a happy night. They're all celebrating out there." She pointed in the general direction of the shore.

"How would *you* know that?" Calliope swam around Hailey.

Hailey felt her extended arm go limp, but due to the buoyancy of the water, it slowly floated down to her side. "Well, you see, they…" She bent her elbow to point again, uncertain about where she was trying to gesture. "It's their…um…well, it was really easy to tell that…er…"

"We could hear their cheers," said Barney, swimming beside Hailey and taking her hand.

Calliope's head turned sharply toward Barney. "If you were close enough to hear them, then they were close enough to hear you."

Hailey shook her head. "We weren't making any noise, and even if we were, the fireworks were so loud, no one would've been able to hear us."

"Fire-works?" As Calliope slowly repeated the foreign word, a scowl formed on her face. "You know what they are called, and you say other strange words. Either you have been on land many times, or you are from there."

"Let it float," said Lorelei forcefully, hovering above Calliope and looking down on her. Before there was a response, Lorelei quickly dove behind Calliope, who ducked to avoid getting whacked in the side of the head with the incoming green tailfin. Smirking, Lorelei turned to Barney and Hailey. "We should leave this blowfish alone before someone says something they may regret."

Hailey flipped her fluke extra hard as she swam past

Calliope on one side, and the ensuing current of water spun Calliope around. When Barney did the same as he passed Calliope's other side, she was turned the other way. By the time she slowed herself down and overcame her dizziness, the three other mers were far in the distance.

She swam as fast as she could but knew she wasn't going to reach them, so she called to them. "You should be careful where you swim! Even the smartest fish runs the risk of getting caught!"

~ Chapter Seventeen ~

The first thing Meredith noticed when she woke up that Monday morning was Marina sitting at the desk. "You're up early," she said, wiping the sleep out of her eyes.

"Are we not leaving soon?" asked Marina.

Yawning, Meredith glanced out the window at the pale sunlight and then at her alarm clock. It was just before seven. "Jill probably won't be awake for at least another two hours."

"If I were still in the ocean, I would not have to depend on others." Marina carefully picked up the mermaid figurine—the one Hailey had given her the previous summer. Its tail was colored like hers, the only orange-tail in the school. "If I could search on my own, I might have found her by now."

"I know you're frustrated, and I don't blame you. If Jill didn't need the job or I didn't need the internship at the aquarium, we'd be taking you wherever you needed to go, whenever you needed to go there."

Meredith felt guilty that Marina had spent the previous few days waiting patiently but alone in the dorm room with little to do. When Meredith had returned each evening, she found Marina sitting on the bed and sulking. Hoping to cheer her up over the weekend, Meredith arranged for them to join Jill at a local Fourth of July fireworks display, but Marina remained sullen. The night only reminded her of the summer before and her first kiss with Jeff.

Marina looked at the open textbook on the desk. "I still do not understand what you do there or why you would want to be in such a place."

"I'm there because of you, because I was somehow drawn to put on your tail last summer. Being underwater changed my life, and I figured out what I was meant to do. I want to be a marine biologist to care for and protect all the creatures in the ocean, but I can only do that up here by studying them, both in books and at the aquarium."

"I have learned much about those creatures, as you call them, by swimming and communicating with them, without needing to keep them closed in."

The escalating tone of Marina's comments alarmed Meredith, and she didn't want to start an argument. She considered redirecting the conversation but wasn't sure where to take it until she saw the book on the desk. "Then you can help me. Teach me everything you know about manatees."

Marina took a deep breath and recalled the few times her school encountered small groups of manatees. Most of the time, the manatees left them alone. They weren't threatening or unfriendly, but they weren't particularly social either, preferring to remain with their family units.

Eventually, Jill called to tell them she was on her way. Her voice sounded groggy, so Meredith decided to surprise her with some breakfast. The sky was overcast when Meredith and Marina stepped outside of the dormitory, but it wasn't raining yet. They walked half a mile to a coffee shop and had Jill meet them there. Jill grumbled a sleepy thank-you as Meredith handed her a cup.

Meredith navigated from the front passenger seat while Marina sat in the middle row and gazed outside. Everything looked dreary, and before long, droplets were streaking the windows. The rain seemed to annoy Jill and Meredith, but Marina let out a relaxed sigh. Though she remained dry inside the car, it comforted her to be surrounded by the water.

The address Daniel had given them was in a small seaport town, and Jill drove along a road right on the edge of the water. Against the backdrop of the gray sky, several fishing boats were docked on one side of the small harbor and many sailboats on the other.

Staring out to sea, Marina said, "This is a better place for my mother to live than further inland."

"Maybe that's why she came here." Meredith switched her gaze from the small shops—many of them closed down—on the other side of the road to the water. "And if she's here, we'll find her."

"There it is." Jill turned left onto a side road and immediately parked the car when they saw the address on the other side of the street.

The entryway was wedged between a sandwich shop on the right and a corner convenience store on the left with its entrance on the main road. Above the shops were three floors that looked like they were made up of apartments.

Standing in the alcove at the doorway, Meredith scanned the names alongside the doorbell buttons for the twelve apartments. When she announced that none of them indicated that Coral lived there, Marina asked what to do next.

Jill sauntered over to them through the drizzle and said, "We do this." She ran her hands down the two columns of buttons, pressing them all. "And we hope someone lets us in."

Before Meredith could complain, the entry buzzer sounded, and Jill opened the front door. Inside was a narrow staircase leading up to a dingy hallway containing doors to four apartments and stairs up to the floors above. They decided to start at the top, where they were immediately greeted by a pair of college-age guys who had let them in thinking they were delivering their pizza. Jill chatted with them until their lunch finally arrived, and they gave her their phone numbers.

Meanwhile, Meredith and Marina knocked on the other doors on the floor. Two out of three opened, but both sets of tenants were relatively new to the building and didn't recognize Coral from the painting. The third door matched the apartment number from the mailing address Daniel gave them, but the college guys referred to the person who lived there as the "weird, cranky dude."

The floor below provided better information. A woman holding an infant in one arm answered the door. Her husband was in the background, playfully chasing his toddler son. A third child, probably about six years old, clung to her mother's leg while peeking from behind. The girl smiled at Marina and said, "It's her, Mommy. She's back." Then she called for her father.

As the husband and son appeared in the doorway, Marina introduced herself. The wife stated that Coral occasionally babysat for the two older children but had moved out before she had gotten pregnant with the third. That placed Coral's departure at least a year and a half earlier.

"She talked a lot about a Marina," said the woman, eliciting raised eyebrows and a smile from Marina. "Especially before she moved out."

An older woman in the apartment across the hall described Coral as the sweet young lady from upstairs who would feed her cats when she was away. Meredith and Marina exchanged grins when the lady told them how the cats had grown especially fond of Coral. And though the lady couldn't remember exactly when Coral left, she remembered discussion about Marina.

They learned a more precise timeline from a man who smelled like he had dumped an entire bottle of cologne on himself. The top three buttons of his shirt were undone, revealing a hairy chest. He had moved in just under two years earlier and recalled being disappointed that Coral had moved out a week later before he could properly introduce himself and ask her out.

And finally, a middle-aged woman not only recognized Coral from the print but also recognized the print itself. She explained, "Your mother gave me several copies and told me it was a message for your father. I don't have them anymore, but she said that if he ever came looking to tell him she was moving on, but she didn't say where exactly." She scratched her head and then snapped her fingers. "Working on finding a Marina, that's what she said, or something to that effect."

When they walked back outside into the drizzle, Marina wiped her misty eyes. "We have come this far looking for her, but she is somewhere looking for me. She should have known where to find me in the waters." She turned her attention toward the harbor. "But she could not look for me there without her tail."

Meredith put her arm around Marina. "We've gotten one step closer. I promise you we're going to find her."

"I have swum greater distances than I have walked today, yet my feet ache more than my tail ever did."

They returned to the parked minivan, and Meredith encouraged Marina to lie across the back seat. Meredith removed Marina's flip-flops and started rubbing her feet.

At the first sensation of pressure, Marina recoiled with bent knees and curled toes. Meredith straightened Marina's legs and resumed the massage until Marina could feel the tension in her muscles melting away.

"This truly flows, Meredith." She sighed. "Thank you. I have never been soothed like this in the water."

From the driver's seat, Jill said, "Well, you've never really had feet like those in the water."

They laughed, and as the foot massage continued, Marina eventually dozed off.

"How much hope can we keep giving her?" asked Jill.

"As much as we have to." Meredith was stretching out her overworked fingers. "We made progress today. The clues brought us to people who knew Coral."

"I hate to say it, but how far will the next leg of this wild goose chase be? And the way this car guzzles gas—" Jill stopped herself when she saw Meredith raise her finger. "I know you're splitting the cost, and I appreciate that, but we both should be saving for college. I don't exactly get paid a lot playing a mascot."

"I don't get paid at all for my internship."

"You've got scholarships, and you're going to do wonderful things."

"So are you."

"I'm going to study acting. That's not making a difference in the world. Who knows where you'll intern next summer? Or the summer after that? I wanted to spend the summer after senior year with my best friend—"

"We are spending the summer together."

"What about Hailey? I should have visited her for the Fourth, but she's underwater, and my aunt and uncle went away on vacation."

"Think of what we're doing, though. This is a great mystery adventure, something bigger than the both of us, like we're preserving the ocean."

"That may be your dream, Merri, but it's not mine." Jill dug her sunglasses out of her hair and hid her eyes behind them. "And it's Hailey's dream too. What if Marina needs another month to find her mom? Hailey will volunteer to stay down there again. What if something happens to her? We'd have no way of knowing."

Marina stirred, so Jill started the car. The cranking of the engine startled Marina, but when she realized what was happening, she sat up and reached for her seatbelt. Jill had driven forward and stopped at the intersection when Marina noticed something on the side of the apartment building. Not yet buckled in, she opened the door and ran outside.

"What's she doing?" asked Jill.

Meredith followed Marina, who stopped to peer through the dirty window of an abandoned shop. Inside were shelves and a few empty display cases.

"What are you looking for?" asked Meredith.

"I believe I have found the next clue." Marina pointed above her.

Stepping back and looking up at the windows, Meredith remembered the interior layout of the building well enough to know they were below Coral's former top-floor apartment, which had been looking out to the ocean. "We were already up there, and your mother doesn't live here—"

"Not there." Marina redirected Meredith's attention to the

sign hanging above the shop and squeaking as the wind blew. "There."

At that moment, a car horn honked. They turned to see Jill's minivan pulling up to the curb behind them. "Come on," called Jill through the open window.

"Look, Jill." Marina stepped to the car and pointed at the sign. "I know where we must go next."

Though most of the paint had chipped off the lettering, Jill recognized the faded logo. "The ferries will be crowded because of the holidays, so we're gonna have to wait till next weekend." She rolled her eyes. "That lady better have a good explanation."

The barely visible words on the sign were *The Mermaid's Lagoon.*

~ Chapter Eighteen ~

From the distance, Finn said, "There is nothing terribly unsafe about the waters ahead. Only a smack of jellies in the vicinity." Then he turned and swam back to Lorelei and Hailey.

"What's a smack?" Hailey asked Lorelei, who torpedoed forward to meet her father.

"I do not understand why Ray wishes to relocate the school." Lorelei slowed herself and gestured out to the open ocean. "These waters are to the northeast, farther away from the land."

"That may be the point," replied Finn. "Ray does not want us to be so close to land."

Catching up, Hailey breathlessly asked, "What's a—?"

"We would be more than a day's swim away when Hailey has to go back home." Lorelei turned to Hailey, who appeared confused. "I know what you are thinking, Hailey, but if we stay in the cave while the rest of the school migrates, Ray will grow suspicious."

Hailey flailed her hands in the water. "That's not what I'm thinking. What's a—?"

"And that is why we must find some fault with these waters." Finn put his arm around his daughter. "Even if we have to fabricate a reason."

"I am sure we can pull the scales over his eyes." Lorelei smirked deviously. "Meet you back here before sunset?"

They nodded at each other and then separated, swimming away in opposite directions. Hailey quickly headed after Finn, but then turned around to follow Lorelei, and then turned one more time before giving up and screaming, "O-M-G! Will someone please tell me what on earth a *smack* is?"

Turning around, Lorelei gestured for Hailey to join her. "A *smack* is the name for a group of jellyfish, just as a group of dolphins is a *pod*."

Hailey's mouth opened wide. "Oh! Makes sense. Silly word for it, though. But like a group of mers is a *school*?"

"Yes," said Lorelei, swimming northward. "Come help me find reasons not to move to these waters."

Hailey followed. "Like a group of sheep is called a *flock*. Or a group of geese is a *gaggle*?"

"Now *that* is a silly word."

Lorelei started scouting north of where they left Finn and then methodically made her way to the east. Unsure what they were even looking for, Hailey wasn't much help so she blithely swam about and enjoyed the freedom of open water. Always keeping Lorelei in view, Hailey tried swimming in different patterns such as figure-eights, corkscrews, and full loop-de-loops—anything that would give her practice and experience for when she became a professional mermaid performer at an aquarium or water park. She even mastered a variation of the backstroke with her hands resting behind her head while she flipped her orange fluke and watched the sun slowly cross the sky.

When the girls reunited with Finn before sunset, they shared their findings. No recent signs of humans other than scattered refuse at the ocean's floor either from boat wreckage or littering. No dangerous animals other than the smack of jellyfish at the outskirts of the area.

They headed back toward the cave but were met by Ray. "I expect that you found these waters to be satisfactory." Even though he barely moved his lips when he spoke, his voice was deep and his words as clear as the water.

Finn gestured his arm off to the side and slightly behind him. "There is a smack of jellies in that direction."

"Yes, I noticed that. The blue-tails should have little difficulty keeping them at bay."

"Though I did not see any human ships today, I suspect that they may travel by here."

Though through clenched teeth, Ray spoke louder. "We shall stay deeper than humans would notice."

Finn arched his back until he was floating directly in front of Ray. "You usually give me a few days to assess a new location. Why make such waves now?"

"Humans must not find the school." Ray's eyes glared at Hailey as he floated upward, his arms crossed in front of his muscular, bare chest. "Are you questioning my intentions?"

Startled by Ray's bellowing voice, Hailey ducked back and hid her face behind Lorelei's tail. She watched through the pale, translucent green of Lorelei's fluke as Ray trembled. His face turned red with anger.

Finn glanced over his shoulder. "Lorelei, Hailey, I think you maids should return to the cavern. Ray and I need to discuss our difference of opinion."

Lorelei grabbed Hailey's hand and started swimming away from her father and Ray. Whenever Hailey tried to say something, Lorelei shushed her and flipped her tail harder. When they were far enough away, Lorelei whispered, "Be careful what you say. Voices carry quickly in the water."

"That is correct," said a snide voice. "You would not want any other mers to hear what we have to say."

The dark-haired mer came into view, and Hailey gulped upon seeing the familiar purple tail.

"What do you want, Calliope?" asked Lorelei.

"When my father relocates the school, this orange-tail will not be welcome."

Before Hailey could protest, Lorelei said, "My father is telling your father these are not safe waters. Now let it float and leave us alone."

Lorelei abruptly changed course, pulling Hailey along with her.

Calliope followed. "When Marina returns, she will not know where we are, and our school will finally be rid of her kind!"

Letting go of Lorelei's hand and flipping her fin faster, Hailey passed ahead of her. "What's her deal? Why does she hate Marina and me so much?"

"Hatred is a learned behavior," replied Lorelei.

"So, like, what? Her dad taught her?"

Swishing noises came from one side, so Hailey and Lorelei turned toward the sound. One of Calliope's friends was quickly approaching. Lorelei cocked her head toward the opposite side, and Hailey got the hint to veer that way. Before long, the final member of the purple-tailed trio appeared ahead of them, and the three of them taunted Hailey with nasty names about the color of her tail.

"Is this an ambush?" asked Hailey, quickly switching direction again.

"You can swim fast, correct?" Lorelei glanced downward and then at Hailey, who nervously nodded her head. "We might be able to lose them if we—"

"We have not had a fun chase like this since that other odd orange-tail!" called Calliope to her friends, who snickered in agreement as they closed in on their prey.

"DIVE!" shouted Lorelei.

Hailey followed Lorelei's instruction, and they soared into the darker water below. Calliope and her friends swerved in different directions to avoid a collision and eventually, each of them stopped. Groaning in contempt, Calliope angled herself downward, but Lorelei and Hailey weren't visible in the darkness. "There is still enough time to catch her," she snapped before heading home with her two minions behind her.

Moments later, Hailey peeked out from behind an underwater boulder. "Sounds like they're gone," she whispered. "Good job hiding us, Lore. That really rocked."

"Yes, it is a rock." Lorelei swam over it and gestured for Hailey to follow her through the murky water.

On their way up, something sticky stroked Hailey's shoulder blade, burning her bare skin. "W-T-H was that?!" she squealed.

Lorelei winced as a similar sensation stung her outstretched arm. Pulling it back, she turned to her side to see the bell of a jellyfish staring back at her. Gasping, she said, "Jellies are descending. Sink slowly."

Hailey's heart started beating faster and louder. She curled her tail behind her and leaned forward until she was upside down and staring at more jellyfish. "They're below us too," she said while shuddering.

A tendril grazed her back, and she shrieked as she felt its shock all along her spine.

The water swooshed in a circle as Lorelei twisted her tail around Hailey and grabbed onto her, trying to compress her into the space within.

Hailey squirmed but couldn't shake Lorelei's grip. "What are you doing?"

"Keeping them from stinging you. Too many stings can be deadly to a mer." Lorelei's shoulder twitched from the touch of a descending jellyfish.

"But what about you? Who's keeping them from stinging you?"

"Marina must be able to return. I must preserve her tail." Lorelei grunted in pain, arching her back with her stomach pressed up against Hailey's side.

Hailey wrapped her arms around Lorelei, but one of her hands came in contact with the jellyfish that had dragged along Lorelei's back. She shook the pain out of her fingertips. "We've got to get out of this! How do we get out of this?"

Straining her weak muscles, Lorelei reached up and pushed Hailey under her. "Stay below me. I will shield you."

"No! I can't let you do that. You can't, like, sacrifice yourself for me! I won't let you!"

"My father says we must protect the orange—*augh!*" Lorelei wailed as her body writhed until it was limp, and her red hair floated upward in all directions.

Seeing that Lorelei's eyes were closed, Hailey started shaking her. "Come on, Lore, open your eyes. Please, open your eyes." In her periphery, Hailey saw a jellyfish descending toward Lorelei's exposed neck, and she splashed the water. "Shoo, jelly. Go away."

The slight movement of the water seemed to be enough to change the jellyfish's course, though Hailey's fingers had touched its tendrils. She ignored the discomfort and tried listening for Lorelei's breaths, but she didn't know enough about mermaid anatomy to know how they were breathing underwater. "Please, Lore, wake up!"

"Lorelei, are you safe?" asked Finn's voice from somewhere above them in the murk.

"It's me, Hailey!" She felt Lorelei spasm in her arms as another jellyfish floated by. "Lorelei—she passed out or something. Where are you?"

"I am above the smack. Where are you?"

"Right in the middle of the smack! Can you get us out of here?"

"There are far too many, but I believe *you* can do it. Concentrate."

"Me?" shrieked Hailey, wondering how she could concentrate on anything while Lorelei's unconscious body weighed her down. Curled as she was, she saw the dark form of her tail—her *orange* tail. From what she knew about the career destinies of mers, her tail wasn't the appropriate color for Finn's task. "But my tail isn't blue."

"Marina's father had a blue tail. You should be able to tell them to part around you."

"I…I…I'm not even sure I know what that means. How would I know how to make them do that?"

"Simply concentrate. Tell them to scatter."

A tentacle snagged one tip of her fluke, but she clenched her fists and mouth shut while she fought through the pain. As the sting subsided, she squeaked, "Scatter, you scary jellies. Please spread out and keep away from us."

The water grew darker from the enclosing jellyfish, and Lorelei convulsed again.

"It's not working!" called Hailey, unsuccessfully holding back tears before muttering to herself. "Please don't let us die here. Don't let us die."

"Hailey, listen to me." Finn's voice was firm but calming in a fatherly way. "Only you can part them. Once you do it, I will dive down and get you."

"I don't know how!" She held tightly to Lorelei's limp body, trying to keep it away from the jellyfish, but one grazed her wrist, and she winced.

"You must *persuade* them to leave."

Persuade them, thought Hailey, trying to find the courage. Suddenly, a thick set of tentacles descended toward Lorelei's collar bone. Could a shock at that point be fatal, she wondered. Her heart pounding in fear, Hailey shouted, "Stay away from my friend!"

The jellyfish stopped, the tip of its tentacle hovering mere inches above Lorelei's pale skin. Suddenly understanding that she got it to move away, Hailey shouted again. "Stay away from her! Stay away from us! Move away from here!"

Thin beams of light from the setting sun grew wider and pierced through the shadows. The water brightened temporarily and then darkened again as a thick green blur swished past her from above and scooped Lorelei from her arms. Startled by its sudden presence, Hailey floated back but quickly made sure there weren't any jellyfish behind her. They were no longer surrounding her, and many of them were descending into the darkness. *Did I do that?* she asked herself. *How could I have?*

She turned back around, but the creature that had snatched away her friend was gone. Once she realized it had been Finn, she shot upward until she saw his strong tail leaving a trail of bubbles in the distance.

When she finally caught up with him, Hailey asked, "Is…is Lorelei…?" Her voice stopped before she could bring herself to say the word *dead*.

Continuing forward, Finn didn't look back as he answered. "No, thank goodness. Only a few more stings and I would have lost her the way I lost Pearl."

Hailey flailed her arms in surprise, slowing the forward

motion of her torso. Her streamlined tail glided forward until she twisted at the waist. Inside, her brain was dizzy from the latest revelation. She knew Lorelei's mother had died, but she wondered if Lorelei and Marina even knew the truth. She didn't dare ask Finn for more information while his attention needed to be on his daughter. Hailey was grateful that Lorelei was still alive but terrified by the thought of what had almost happened, all because Calliope and her clique had chased them.

As she drifted far behind Finn, Hailey wondered if Calliope meant to lead them into the jellyfish smack. She knew Calliope had been behaving like a bully—not just to her, but to Marina for her whole life—but was she capable of almost getting them killed?

The pressure of so many questions throbbed in her head. How had she gotten the jellyfish to leave them alone? As far as she knew, they didn't have ears, so how could they have heard her? Could Marina—and she by extension—have some of the abilities of Marina's father? Or was the ability from the orange tail; something its solitary owner was supposed to do?

She was still lost in thought when she finally arrived inside the cavern's entrance. Finn had already laid Lorelei on one of the smoother rock surfaces and was floating beside her, caressing her cheek. Instead of rising upward, Lorelei's locks of red hair were draped almost lifelessly over the rock's edge. The scene was too somber, and Hailey turned no one would see her let her tears float away.

Moments later, she was startled by a large hand on her shoulder. She turned to see Finn hovering behind her, his face as empty of color as the jellyfish. "I believe she will recover before the time of no moon," he said, without the usual booming excitement in his voice. "Thank you, Hailey. You saved my daughter's life. I am grateful there was enough of Zale in that tail."

The floodgates holding back all Hailey's questions almost opened, and what sputtered out was, "But...but I-D-K how that works."

Finn's eyebrows pinched together. "How what works?"

"Like, if Marina's dad had a *blue* tail, how can Marina's be *orange?* I've known my color combinations since, like, kindergarten. Crayons and stuff. Blue and yellow make green, blue and red make purple, but I don't know what to mix blue with to get orange. It doesn't work that way, so how'd it happen?"

"You are correct; it does not work that way," replied Finn. "Mers inherit their tail color from one parent. Mine is green like my father's before me, and the tails of all maids match their mothers'."

Hailey gasped and said, "So Marina isn't—or wasn't—the only—?"

"That is correct." Finn released a long sigh as he bowed his head. "Coral's tail was also orange."

~ Chapter Nineteen ~

Meredith stood on the concrete deck at the edge of the large tank of water and scanned the incoming crowd filtering into the bleacher seats. Visitors wiped sweat from their brows or fanned themselves with aquarium guide pamphlets and baseball hats. It was hot and humid outside, so many of them chose the indoor arena to avoid the heat of the early afternoon sun.

She was trying to find Marina, who had spent the previous few days moping in the dormitory. Each morning, Meredith had tried to convince her to come along instead of being alone, and each morning she had failed. It took pleading with her before she agreed to come and see the interns' debut appearance in the sea lion show.

Wondering if Marina would gravitate toward someone familiar, Meredith glanced at the entrance. Jill was waddling around in her sea lion mascot costume, waving at passing patrons and letting them give her flippers high-fives. But there was no sign of Marina. Meredith took a few steps toward Jill but stopped and sighed upon remembering that she wasn't allowed to speak when she was in character.

"Who are you looking for?" asked Will from behind her.

"Just my friend Marina," she answered while continuing her search.

"Didn't you say she was your friend's cousin?" said Brittany, popping her gum in her mouth afterward.

"I can be friends with my friend's cousin, right?" Meredith kept her back to Brittany to prevent her flickering eyes from being noticed. "And you shouldn't be chewing gum near the tank."

"Whatever, dork." Brittany popped the gum again and stomped away.

"Wow. Good job getting rid of her," whispered Will. "I've been wondering how she even got into this program. I thought I had applied for one of only two positions, but I guess I could be wrong about that."

Meredith had barely registered Will's comment when he pointed across the tank and announced, "There she is!"

Sitting in the center of the front row, Marina had her arms crossed in front of her and a pale, unenthused look on her face. Uneasily waving at her, Meredith felt a little regret for making her come that morning.

"The show begins in a few minutes," Dr. Hatcher said from behind them. "Are you two ready?"

"We're ready, Sir." Will saluted him. "Are the *Zalophus californianus* ready?"

Dr. Hatcher patted him on the back. "I think they are."

The lights in the arena dimmed, and loud synthesizer music began the show. One performer acted as a game show hostess, interacting with the crowd and asking questions about the differences between seals and sea lions. With a correct answer, a child was awarded a gift certificate for a free ice cream at the snack bar. Meredith knew the obvious answers solicited from the crowd: sea lions had larger flippers, visible ear flaps, and could "walk" on land on their flippers instead of wriggling on their bellies. But she hoped Marina wasn't asked, for she probably knew other facts that humans didn't.

Then the primary trainer appeared on the deck and introduced the two stars of the show, the larger Donnatella and her son Stryker. Following hand and voice signals, the sea lions balanced on one of their front flippers and waved the other at the crowd until there was thunderous applause.

They demonstrated their visual recognition skills by pointing out a variety of simple shapes that the three interns were asked to hang on the wall. Donnatella displayed her impressive lung capacity with a loud, deep series of barks. The younger and smaller Stryker showed off his speed and agility by swimming in the tank, balancing a beach ball on his snout, jumping through hoops, and leaping high out of the water.

After each stunt, the crowd cheered, and the interns rewarded the sea lions by feeding them a small fish or two. Brittany shuddered whenever she removed a fish from the metal pail, and she wiped the slimy residue onto her lab coat as soon as the fish left her hand and went into Donnatella's mouth.

"Ewww, this is, like, so gross!" Brittany hopped up and down as if she stood on hot coals, and she loudly snapped her chewing gum.

From the far side of Stryker, Will leaned toward Meredith and whispered, "What did she think? That fish were dry?"

Standing between the two sea lions, Meredith glanced over Donnatella at Brittany, still squirming and popping her gum. Then she turned back to Will and muttered, "And why can't she follow rules? She could learn obedience from the sea lions."

Suddenly, Donnatella looked up at Meredith and barked. Thinking she wanted another reward, Meredith reached into her pail, but Donnatella shook her head. "What do you want?" whispered Meredith, nervously looking around to make sure the others weren't listening. "Can you understand me?"

And then Meredith received a kind of answer. Donnatella raised a flipper and whacked the back of Brittany's thighs, knocking her into the tank.

Following the splash, there was a mixture of gasps, howls, and laughs from the crowd. The trainers attempted to corral the sea lions, but Stryker dove into the tank and swam toward Brittany, eliciting more reactions. Donnatella followed after her son. Some people, mostly teenagers, were on their feet pointing and clapping and taking video with their phones. Parents were covering the eyes of their younger children or holding them close to them in case the situation got worse.

Brittany thrashed about, trying to swim back to the deck where Dr. Hatcher was extending his hand to reach her. Before she was close enough, Stryker swam in front of her, blocking her path. The waves left in the sea lion's wake pushed her in the opposite direction. She tried to swim against the artificial tide, but the larger Donnatella crossed her path, and again she was carried further away from the deck.

Security guards arrived to maintain order in the arena. They were keeping the walkway at the bottom of the bleachers clear in the event other emergency responders needed access to the tank. However, they couldn't keep the crowd's volume down, so Dr. Hatcher's instructions to Brittany went unheard.

While the sea lions circled her, Brittany treaded water as best she could. She swallowed and then spit back out the stale, salty water, which had been forced into her mouth from the waves and her own splashing.

She went under, and the crowd gasped. People stood on their toes to peer over the people in front of them, collectively releasing their held breath when Brittany popped back up for air.

Trying to tune out the cacophony around her, Meredith removed her lab coat and handed it to Will. He inquired why, but she ignored him and quickly studied the circling pattern of the sea lions. Other sea creatures were drawn to her, and if she jumped in, maybe her presence in the water would divert them away from Brittany to let her get out safely. When she had perfectly timed the space between the two sea lions, she jumped into the tank.

There was a mixture of cheers and shrieks from the bleachers. Marina took a step forward, but a security guard moved in front of her and emphatically gestured for her to sit back down.

Below the water's surface, Meredith saw Brittany's legs kicking wildly. Before swimming to save her, Meredith noticed a large, blurry, dark object pass in her periphery. She turned to the sea lion; it was Stryker, no longer swimming toward Brittany but approaching her. Donnatella had comprehended her, so hoping that Stryker would also, Meredith held out her palm and focused all her concentration on one word.

Stop.

The sea lion didn't change his course. Meredith opened her eyes widely, fighting the sting of the salt water, and glared at the oncoming animal. He slowed down and seemed to enter a staring contest with her. Neither turned away until Donnatella completed her circle and nudged her son's flipper as if to tell him he had taunted Brittany long enough.

Stryker squealed and turned around, joining his mother at the other end of the tank. Distorted voices from above the surface called out, and Meredith realized she had been under long enough to cause suspicion. She turned to Brittany, who had sunk under once again, the waterlogged lab coat weighing her down.

Meredith brought her ankles together as if they were fused into one tail, and in one swift motion, she kicked her feet and shot forward to Brittany's side. Grabbing her around the waist, Meredith hoisted her to the surface and then swam back to the deck where Dr. Hatcher and other aquarium employees, including an EMT, pulled her out of the water.

Will helped Meredith out and to her feet. "Wow," he said, stretching out the word in bewilderment. "Those sea lions, you got them to stop. I…I don't know what to say about that."

"Then don't say much about it." Meredith's response wasn't meant to be curt, but she feared Will would interpret it as such. She was busy juggling too many thoughts in her head. Was Brittany going to be all right? Had she done the right thing by jumping in, or had she jeopardized the status of her internship? Had she made a spectacle of herself and her otherworldly abilities? Would that expose herself—or worse, Marina?

She glanced at Brittany, who was sitting up and loudly

complaining to the security chief. "I'm fine, okay? I'm not the one who did anything wrong this time, so if you like your job, leave me alone."

Reassured that Brittany at least sounded the way she usually did, Meredith wrung water out of her clothes and hair. She surveyed the arena where the other security guards were waving the crowd out in an orderly fashion until she saw Marina. To catch up with her, Meredith dashed for the gate separating the far edge of the deck from the spectator walkway.

Marina's frowning face flushed, her eyes redder than her cheeks. Meredith took a deep breath and said with a nervous chuckle, "Quite a show, wasn't it?"

"I am leaving with Jill today and staying with her until we go to Hailey's island." Marina blinked quickly and wiped some tears away. "What you and your people in this place do to these beautiful creatures makes me uncomfortable."

"We're only doing it to learn everything we can. It's a pursuit of knowledge about life and the world."

"Your people only have false stories about my school. What if they learned the truth? Would we be confined in one of these—what do you call it?—one of these…" Marina thrust her arms toward the swimming sea lion as she remembered the word. "*Tanks*? Would we be expected—or commanded—to perform tricks for your people to watch? Would that make us nothing more than pets to you?"

"It's not like that, Marina. The scientists protect the sea lions and study—"

"Would your scientists keep *me* in a tank?"

Holding up a hand with an index finger pointed, Meredith wanted to tell Marina the answer was no, but she knew it probably wasn't the truth. As much as *she* would never keep Marina or any other mermaid in a tank, she knew that other marine biologists wouldn't feel the same way. They'd look at Marina's people as specimens instead of as humans with unique anatomical differences. A new discovery, perhaps a career-defining one.

She wasn't going to be that kind of scientist. After four years of college and graduating with a degree in marine biology, she was going to become a conservationist. Her internship at the aquarium was great practical experience, but it was merely a gateway to her real career goal. She was going to protect the ocean and all its inhabitants—mermaids included. But how could she explain that to Marina in understandable terms?

Before she could say anything, Will appeared with her lab coat. "You left this with me before you—wow—did something amazing."

"It certainly was amazing," said Dr. Hatcher from behind. "Are you sure you're not already a marine biologist? I've never seen anyone, student or colleague, so innately intuitive when it comes to our aquatic friends."

"Thank you." Meredith's face beamed while she put her glasses back on to look up at Dr. Hatcher, but her smile wilted back into a frown when she clearly saw Marina turn on her heel and walk away.

"We'll be returning the manatee to the ocean this weekend. I think you've earned some observational time with him before he leaves. Are you interested?"

Meredith enthusiastically nodded her head.

"How's early Sunday morning?"

"On Sunday, I have to..." Her voice trailed off as she looked for her friends. Jill was consoling Marina, gently stroking the side of her face with the mascot costume's plush flippers. They were planning to continue the search for Marina's mother that day. As much as she didn't want to let Marina down, she couldn't refuse Dr. Hatcher's generous offer. It wouldn't be polite or professional, and she would never get the opportunity again. "If Sunday's when you want me, I'll be there."

Dr. Hatcher grinned and patted her on the back of her shoulder before walking off in the other direction. Will congratulated her, but all she could do was let out a frustrated sigh. Too many decisions to make, potentially at the expense of Marina's feelings, and she was finding the pressure of balancing the two worlds too difficult.

Marina had already disappeared into the crowd and left the arena, so Meredith went to Jill and quietly asked, "Has Marina asked to stay with you through the weekend?"

Keeping her attention on waving goodbye to the departing guests, Jill nodded.

"I have a chance to see the manatee, so I can't come with you two."

Jill turned and dropped her flippers to her hips.

"You and Marina will be fine without me, right?"

Unable to speak while in character, Jill simply held out her flippers and shrugged, and then she waddled behind the final stragglers from the crowd. To Meredith's dismay, she didn't need any words to know she had disappointed not only Marina but also her best friend.

~ Chapter Twenty ~

"Do you really think Calliope knew the jellies were there?" asked Barney as he swam beside Hailey. "Do you think she led them to you? Or you to them? I know she is crabby, but why can she not let it float?"

"Who knows why she does what she does?" replied Hailey. "I could really make some waves, but I think I'll be the one who just lets it float. I'm just glad Lorelei's almost recovered."

"That makes you a wiser maid than she is."

The water flowing by tickled the dimples that formed in Hailey's cheeks. "Thanks, but I've got other things that I'm not gonna let float. I just can't. They're too big."

"What are they?" Barney swam ahead and quickly turned around until he was facing Hailey. "You can tell me. Are they whales? Whales are big."

"No, they're mysteries. Did you know that Marina's mother also had an orange tail?"

"That is no mystery. Her mother's tail had to be orange. How else would Marina have gotten hers? Every mer knows that." Barney turned and swam forward again.

"F-Y-I, I'm not a real mer. I didn't know how it worked until a few days ago."

"Sometimes I forget that." He slowed down to allow Hailey to catch up to him. "You are good at being a mer."

Again, Hailey couldn't keep herself from smiling at his sweet comments. She was halfway through her time as a mermaid, and she didn't want it to end. Putting on a costume tail and pretending at birthday pool parties was fun, and she imagined a job in an aquarium or water park as a performer would also be fun, but it would always be temporary. The unfortunate truth was that her legs would always be revealed once she wriggled herself out of the tail. If even mers recognized she was a good mermaid—maybe even better as a mermaid than as an ordinary human girl—then maybe there was a way she could remain a mermaid forever. *If only Marina was willing to stay on land once she found her mother…*

Hailey immediately shook the thought away. Though being a mermaid was more than a dream come true and much more than a career goal, she wasn't going to betray her friend. Marina deserved to be herself, even if Coral couldn't return to the sea. And Hailey knew her mother would totally freak out if she never returned to land. At least both she and Marina had mothers out there somewhere, and her thoughts drifted to the tragic fate of Lorelei's mother.

"Barney, did you know that Lore's mom was killed by jellyfish?"

"Where did you hear that?" asked Barney about as abruptly as he stopped swimming.

Nervously, Hailey answered, "From Finn. Why—?"

"Why did you tell me? Why did I ask? I did not want to know. I am not supposed to know. My parents and grandparents have taught me never to ask about Lore's mother. Some stories should remain in the deep. What if they find out?"

His arms flailed around like squid tentacles until Hailey took hold of them. "Hey, calm down. Your parents don't need to find out."

"I do not mean them." Barney looked around before whispering, "*They*. The purple tails. They can tell simply by looking at your eyes. Ray knows when mers do not tell the truth."

"I've been lying to Ray since I first met him. As far I can tell, he doesn't know. I hope, anyway."

"Maybe he cannot tell because you are not a real mer."

Hailey lowered her arms as she let go of Barney's. "I

thought you thought I was a good mer."

"That is not how I meant it. I did not mean to upset you." A boat passing by far above them interrupted their awkward silence until Barney finally spoke again. "Maybe Ray cannot tell because your tail is orange."

Not my tail, thought Hailey, *Marina's tail.* Barney wouldn't ever be able to see her wearing her fake tail, which was probably lying limply in the garment bag and not being used. Thinking of it only served to remind her that her mermaid status would never be permanent.

"I know you didn't mean it." Hailey stroked his smooth cheek but pulled her hand away. Whatever relationship she was developing with him—friendship or something more—could never be permanent either. "Let's just keep going. I want to enjoy as much as I can while I'm still down here."

They were swimming up toward some of the rock formations near where the coastal shelf dropped off into the open water. A few summers earlier, Hailey walked from her beach and into the water until she was submerged up to her neck. The waves were calm that day, and the water was clear enough to see the sandy slope continue into the underwater distance. Somewhere further out, it had to plunge deeper, but her mother called her back and grounded her for the rest of the week for endangering herself. That line of demarcation—between the human world and mer world—was finally accessible to her, and she wanted to explore it.

"Do you hear that?" whispered a voice from somewhere in the distance. The quieter response followed, "Something is swimming this way."

"Who do you think said—?" asked Hailey, who was rendered speechless when Barney suddenly took her hand. The jolt of his touch surged through her much more pleasantly than the jellyfish stings. They had healed, but she didn't think she'd recover from the secure feeling of his gesture of protection.

The whispers continued but were unitelligible by the whooshing sound of flowing water. Far to their right, two figures appeared from behind a large rock at the edge of the drop-off and started descending toward the direction where the school resided. Identified only by two faint glimmers of purple, Hailey wondered why they weren't swimming in a group of three until a familiar condescending voice screeched.

"You cannot just leave me here! My father will not be pleased!"

Barney tried to turn around, but Hailey flapped her tail vigorously and dragged him forward. Now that he had taken her hand, she wasn't going to let him go that easily.

"Do you understand who that is?" asked Barney. "Why would you want to swim toward her?"

As they curved up over the top of the drop-off, Calliope's silhouette came into view in front of the sunbeams piercing the water's surface behind her. Her fluke hung limply downward while her upper body writhed about as if she were unable to leave her current location.

"I think she needs help."

"You think?" Barney struggled to pull her back. "Is your head in a whirlpool? What if this is a trap?"

"I can't explain it. I-D-K how, but I can sense she's in some kinda trouble."

Hailey approached as quietly as she could, and Barney followed. Calliope was on the other side of a fishing net, trying to unravel her seashell top from the crisscrossed fibers. Upon seeing her, Barney released a chuckle and then immediately covered his mouth.

"Who is there?" snapped Calliope, furrowing her brow when she noticed them. "Go away. This does not concern you."

Calliope returned to fidgeting with the net and her seashells but only grew more frustrated. After a few minutes of watching and trying not to giggle, Hailey whispered to Barney to search for something that could cut through the netting. He swam back down, and then Hailey floated forward to get a closer look at the situation.

"I've gotten snarls in my hair lotsa times. I think I can

untangle you." Hailey reached for the net.

Calliope immediately turned to the side, so her shoulder was right in Hailey's view. "I did not ask for your help, orange-tail."

"It's not nice to call me just by my tail color. I have a name, you know."

"My father says you are not to be trusted. He knows that you are human. He can see it in your eyes."

"If I was a human, would I be trying to get you out of this? Wouldn't a human want you to get caught? Wouldn't I want to be the one to catch you?"

"That is why I am puzzled. You are behaving like a mer, so I do not trust your intentions."

"You're gonna have to trust 'em, or you'll stay stuck in there."

After releasing a not-so-subtle groan, Calliope turned and glanced at where she was caught, a signal that read more snooty than grateful.

Hailey traced her finger along one fiber, trying to find where it was stuck. Once she thought she had identified the location, she pulled gently, but either her hands weren't strong enough, or the mesh of Calliope's fishnet halter top had also gotten intertwined with the larger net. After several unsuccessful attempts, Hailey yanked on the net until she heard something snap. The tight mesh was still intact, but a piece of Calliope's seashell bikini top had chipped off.

While Calliope started complaining about the broken shell, Hailey said, "I don't get why you're even in this mess in the first place. How do I know that once I free you, you're not gonna wrap the net around me and bring me to your dad?"

Calliope's rants trailed off, leaving the two of them intently staring at each other for a few moments.

Shamefully waving her finger at Calliope, Hailey finally spoke first. "O-I-C. You and your friends were trying to steal the net so you could catch *me*. Gee, thanks."

"If you are human, then you do not belong here." Calliope's nostrils flared in disdain. "And it is not possible for you to be mer. My father says there is only one with an orange tail."

Hailey wove her arm through the spaces of the netting to try pulling it apart. Without thinking, she asked, "What if it wasn't always like that? What if there once was another?" She debated whether it was her place to tell Calliope—or any other mer—the truth. *Wouldn't some of them have to know?* The look on Calliope's face, a mixture of contempt and apathy, suggested that she had no idea about Marina's mother as if Ray was trying to hide it from his daughter. Or from the entire school. "Maybe your father's…" She didn't know how to call Ray a liar without offending Calliope, but she gulped and said the safest word that popped into her mind. "…wrong?"

"How dare you imply that my father—"

"I have returned with some shark teeth." Barney was swimming rapidly toward them. He grinned proudly at Hailey while speaking in his usual quick manner, almost like he was covering up the anxiety of being near Calliope. "Sharks are always losing their teeth. These look freshly lost. They might cut the net. I hope there are not any sharks nearby." He twirled around to inspect the area.

He gave one tooth to Hailey, who started to cut through the net's fibers. Barney followed her lead, beginning right below where Hailey started and working his way downward. Calliope cleared her throat and pushed her open hand through the mesh, waiting for Barney to give the third tooth to her. He raised his hand slightly above hers and let the tooth drop; it sank slowly into her grasp, and she chastised him for the childish way he gave it to her.

Fibers snapped apart, the sounds not in any discernible rhythm until a rumbling came from overhead. As a shadow was cast over them, they looked up at the underside of a large boat hovering at the surface. Without uttering a word, they each knew to saw more vigorously before the people on the boat could retrieve their fishing net and whatever was caught inside it.

The shadow moved forward, and the net shifted with it, dragging Calliope backward. Because Hailey and Barney's hands clutched the net as they were slicing through it, they were also pulled forward.

As the boat sped ahead, the net started closing around Calliope, who dropped the shark tooth and shrieked, "Get me out of here now!" She dipped her head and flipped her tail to propel herself through the hole, but the opening wasn't wide enough, and her seashells got tangled once again.

"Just stay calm, we're gonna get you out," said Hailey as she hacked through another fiber. "No mermaid gets discovered on my watch!"

Barney slashed with the tooth and separated Calliope from the web trapping her. She swam through but winced in pain when the scales at her hips got snagged on the netting.

"If you do not get me out, you put the whole school in danger!" Calliope squeezed through the opening, but it seemed to constrict around her as the boat kept moving in the opposite direction. She flailed her arms around frantically and knocked the shark's tooth out of Hailey's hand.

Hailey's arm swiped for it, but it had sunk out of her reach. The boat was dragging them too quickly, and if she and Barney let go of the net, they'd have difficulty catching up to it. Already, the nylon fibers were stretching.

"That's it!" She grabbed the edge of the opening with her free hand. "Barney, I think we can pull this apart enough for her to get out. On three, K?"

Hoping he understood what she meant, Hailey counted to three. As she heaved one way, she saw him go the other. The opening widened, and Calliope swam through it, rotating herself sideways so her fluke had less of a chance of getting stuck. As soon as Calliope had completely escaped, Barney and Hailey let go of the net. Hailey watched as he seemed to drift backward until she realized she was still going forward.

Her arm was still woven through the crisscrossed fibers of the net.

She tried to wriggle her arm free, but the boat was going

so fast that the netting was digging into her skin. Panicking, she called for Barney, but he and Calliope were getting further behind her, and she feared the roaring of the engine overhead was drowning out her shouts.

When the boat slowed down, Hailey's inertia carried her head and shoulders through the opening they had made, but she swerved to the side of her entwined arm. Her body continued into the net until her fluke got snagged on the frayed fibers around the opening. She frantically flipped her tail to free herself, but that only further tangled her.

In the distance, she saw only Barney approaching as quickly as his tail would take him. "I am coming, Hailey!" he called.

Before he could get to her, her arm was tugged upward. Realizing that the fishermen were raising the net, she screamed.

"I cannot believe Calliope left." Barney was closer but was swimming at an upward incline. "You saved her, and she left us."

Hailey's arm slipped free when that side of the net went slack, but as it bunched up, she lost sight of the opening they had made. Screaming herself hoarse, she thrashed around trying to find the way out until she started feeling lightheaded. Hundreds of smaller fish filled her vision as if the ocean was closing in on her, but when she squinted, she saw that it was the net surrounding her like a cocoon.

She sunk to the bottom of the sack, almost fully passed out, until Barney grasped her dangling fluke and shook her back awake.

"I…I don't know where to get out." Hailey wiped her eyes as if she was crying, but she couldn't tell if she was brushing away tears or ocean water. "I ruined everything. The humans on the boat are gonna see me, and it'll be all my fault. I didn't mean to—"

"I know you did not." Barney's speech was strained as he pulled himself along the net until he faced Hailey. "You are the truest mer I have ever known."

Though her eyelids grew heavy, she gazed into his gray eyes and pushed a hand through the net to stroke his cheek. "You're the flowiest boy I've ever met."

She leaned her face forward as best she could and reached around his neck to draw him closer to her. His face looked pained, a mixture of overexertion and not wanting to let her go. Right as her lips lightly touched his, the top of the net broke through the surface of the water so its lift speed increased, and Barney slipped right out of her embrace.

"You need to save yourself and get out of here," she pleaded while waving him away.

As he sank into the ocean, she closed her eyes. Whether due to overexertion, shock, or the sudden influx of outside air, Hailey had fallen unconscious by the time the net's contents were unceremoniously spilled onto the deck of the fishing boat.

~ Chapter Twenty-One ~

"I'm gonna go down there and talk with her," said Jeff as he stared out his bedroom window at the above-ground pool in the backyard.

Peering over his shoulder, Jill rolled her eyes upon seeing Marina swimming in Hailey's mermaid costume. "No, you're not." She turned her brother around and stood on her toes to give her already tall stature the additional height to look him in the eyes. "Remember how she disappeared last summer after meeting you? She's just gonna leave again in a coupla weeks, and I don't want to see you hurt again. You're kinda pathetic when you're sad, Jefferson." She said his full name with extra sass.

"I think I can take care of myself, Jillybean." He turned to the window and used it as a mirror to fix his tousled brown hair and straighten the collar of his white polo shirt.

"You just want to talk to her 'cause you're enchanted by her beauty and her bikini top."

"Do you think she and Hailey ordered matching mermaid tails?"

Jill suppressed a chortle. "Something like that."

Jeff kept his attention focused outside, mesmerized by the graceful movement of Marina's underwater silhouette. "You know, I've seen some of the videos Hailey sent us—the ones with her swimming in her tail. Don't get me wrong, Hailey's pretty good at it, but Marina's so much better. Like she's a natural or something."

"You have no idea," said Jill before she exploded into laughter.

Seizing the moment while his sister was distracted, Jeff turned to leave. Jill bolted ahead and stretched herself to block the doorway and appear taller than him.

Jeff groaned. "Move out of the way."

"Look, it's not really about you. It's more about protecting *her*." Jill could tell from his cocked eyebrow that he was curious. Rather than improvise, she decided to tell him a little bit of the truth. "I don't want you messing with her head."

"I'm just gonna say hi. That's not messing with her head."

"But with her, it might be. She's not like other girls. She's—"

"That's why I like her."

"She's innocent—naive, even—and she's got a lot on her mind right now."

"Then I'll let her know I'm here if she wants to talk. Or vent. Or whatever. You don't have to act like you're her mom."

Jill almost lashed out at him but didn't since he didn't know about Marina's mother. Sinking from her tiptoed stance, she slinked aside and said, "Just be nice to her, okay?"

~ ~ ~

Outside, Marina was swimming the length of the pool in one direction and then in the other, maneuvering the turns as agilely as possible given the limited width and depth of the pool. It wasn't particularly difficult, just awkward propelling herself by kicking with both her feet and a false fluke. The costume hugged her waist and legs, form-fitting like a second skin, but it certainly didn't feel like her own tail.

And it certainly didn't feel right occasionally poking her head above the surface to breathe. She went up for air as infrequently as she possibly could, completing two to three laps between breaths. With each inhalation, she caught a whiff of the same sharp scent as the pool on Hailey's island, and she wondered why on-land water smelled so different.

But the feel of the water was the same, enveloping and

comforting her like it did at home. If she closed her eyes, she could imagine herself in the ocean, but she couldn't keep them closed for long for fear of crashing into the side of the pool. The blue walls around her were as bright as the sky, even in the limited light of the moonless night, but they were still walls.

She was in a kind of tank, and she felt hypocritical for entering it willingly.

Maybe some of what Meredith says is true, she thought. Despite being confined, she felt calm and safe while resembling her natural form. Did the fish, sea lions, and others in the aquarium consider their lack of freedom an acceptable compromise for protection? She didn't know the answer, and she hoped that neither she nor any other mer would ever have to find out. Her school had evaded human capture for many moon cycles, so she chose not to dwell further and simply enjoy her relaxing swim.

Fortunately, Jill's backyard tank had one advantage over the tanks at the aquarium: she wasn't under constant observation. As she angled herself upward to take a breath, she was content in the knowledge that she wasn't being watched.

"Lovely night for a swim," said Jeff, crouching on the wooden deck at the pool's edge and smiling at her.

After a quick gasp, her natural instinct to flee kicked in. Arching her back, she twirled around and kicked her feet, flapping the fake fluke to thrust herself in the opposite direction.

But there wasn't any way to get away from him. Almost instantly after leaving the side by the deck, Marina found herself at the far wall of the pool. She reached for the rim and pulled herself up to peek over the edge at the ground below. Even if she could lift herself up and over, she'd fall and flop around on the grass with nowhere to go.

"You swim very gracefully," he said from behind.

Her heart skipped a beat. His compliment was nice, and it was said sweetly and sincerely like she remembered his voice to be. She almost turned around to swim back to him until images of him embracing the other maid flooded her mind. A combination of tears and water droplets from the pool trickled down her cheek. Softly, she said, "If you do not want me, then please leave me alone."

"You didn't call or write. I didn't know how to get in touch with you, like you wanted to disappear." Though his voice grew louder, Marina didn't detect any anger. His emotions seemed to match hers—a quiet longing of what wasn't meant to be. "I thought you didn't want me."

Lowering her head, she muttered, "I wish you wanted me instead of her."

"I never stopped thinking about you," he said.

His voice was unexpectedly close, and she could feel warm breath tingle the cool water on her shoulders. She looked up, and there he was. Right in front of her. Again, she quickly retreated to the other side, but she doubted she could hop onto the deck and shimmy out of the costume before he circled back again.

"I'm not just saying this because you're here." His sneakers clopped up the few steps to the deck. "I'm not that kinda guy, who's just gonna move on from one girl to the next. We only started dating a few weeks ago. If I had known you were coming back—"

"Jeff, please let it float." Marina submerged and returned to the far end. She couldn't have a real relationship with him. Though Hailey would probably keep her tail safe whenever she asked, her life was meant to be under the sea. Even if she came on land every full moon, it wouldn't be fair to make him wait like that, and he'd probably wonder why she couldn't stay. She considered telling him the truth, but without her own tail, she had no way to prove it. Fearing he was suspicious by how much time she had spent underwater, she popped her head through the surface only to see him right in front of her.

"Are we gonna keep going round and round like this?" He smirked as he hunched over and rested his arms on the pool's rim.

Marina caught a quick glimpse of his brown eyes before leaning backward into the water. She spun herself face down and kept her arms by her side as she crossed the pool once more. Anticipating that Jeff would circle around again, she abruptly reversed direction away from the deck.

"Do you know how stunning you look?" asked Jeff from the deck when she came back up for air. "You're making me believe that mermaids could be real."

"I am real, and I have feelings. It hurts that you are interested in someone else."

"Well, I don't think she's interested in me anymore." He sat in a white chair and took off his sneakers. "I tried to be all honest and tell her who you were—how our one date was the best first date I've ever had."

Marina glided to the center of the pool, where she curved the tail behind her to keep it from dragging on the pool floor. "It was a wonderful date," she said under her breath.

"Yeah, well, she didn't like hearing that. She was a little upset that I didn't say my first date with her was the best, and then she dumped me." Leaving his sneakers behind, Jeff walked to the edge of the deck and sat, dipping his feet in the pool. "She made me take her to a movie on our first date. Movies are an awful first date, you know? You can't talk to each other. I feel like you and I really connected last summer."

Slowly, she drifted toward him, as if she was caught in the water's current. "We did." This time, she knew he heard because he smiled and his eyes seemed to sparkle.

"I'm not trying to pressure you or anything. I wouldn't do that. If you still want me to leave you alone, I will. But I had to be honest and tell you how I felt and that I'm sorry if I hurt you and—"

With one flick of the tail, Marina rose up in front of him. She grabbed hold of his neck and kissed him, enjoying the light salty taste of his lips on hers. His arms reached around her bare shoulders, and she felt him leaning forward. As soon as she sensed him falling, Marina maneuvered herself out of the way and tried to cover her laughter while she watched him splash in the water.

When he finally stood, completely drenched, near the center of the pool, he smiled and said, "You think that's funny, don't you?"

Marina coyly turned away and heaved herself onto the deck, where she sat with the fluke dangling in the pool.

"I think it's your turn to walk off the plank!"

Jeff charged forward—as best as he could against the water's resistance—and she squealed in pretend fear. She lifted the tail out of the water and swiveled until it flopped on the deck. In the pool, she hadn't been able to evade him, but out of the water, she didn't want to escape.

He pulled himself out of the pool, water dripping off his soaked clothes. He reached down for Marina, ducking his head under her outstretched arm as he scooped her up off the deck and into his arms.

In a scratchy but playful tone, he said, "Arrr! I'm a pirate, and I've caught meself a mermaid."

She joined her hands around his neck, and they kissed again. Never had Marina imagined that getting caught would feel so good.

~ Chapter Twenty-Two ~

When he darted into Finn and Lorelei's cavern, Barney was panting so heavily that he couldn't speak. His overexerted body wanted to sink, but he kept his fluke flapping to maintain a constant depth. Though his sudden arrival startled them, his erratic behavior worried them more.

"What is wrong, Barney?" Lorelei sat on the smooth rock surface that she had been using as a bed, her green tail dangling limply over the edge. "Speak slowly."

"It is bad," he finally said. "Very bad."

"Where is Hailey?" Lorelei grimaced as she reeled forward, still recovering from the jellyfish attack.

Finn swam to his daughter and put his arm around her waist for support. "Did something happen to Marina's tail?"

"It is gone. Hailey too." Barney spoke between wheezes. "Fishing net. Big boat. Hailey. Caught."

Fighting through the pain, Lorelei shot forward and grabbed hold of Barney's shoulders, dragging him toward the cavern opening. "Show me where."

Before she could get him outside, Finn caught up and passed them, blocking the entrance with his broad shoulders. "You shall stay here and recover. I will find her."

"What if you cannot, Father? If she is already on a boat, she could be anywhere on land by now. I should look for her, and if I cannot find her, I must tell her mother." Lorelei hung her head. "I promised I would keep Hailey from danger. Her mother deserves an apology and explanation, even if I must crawl on land to give them."

"Then you must leave now. Tomorrow is the time of no

moon. If you are not in the water when the sun rises—"

"I understand, Father." Lorelei nodded solemnly and gave a slight shrug. "Sink or swim?"

Finn wrapped his arms around Lorelei. "I have dreaded the day that you would grow up and swim away. You have become an excellent scout, and I will always be proud of you." He slowly broke the embrace but caressed her cheek. "Now swim; do not sink."

The three of them emerged from the cavern, and Ray suddenly appeared in their peripheries. He had been swimming swiftly, so he extended his arms outward to brake, and then he curved upward into a vertical position where he stared directly into Finn's eyes. In a grim voice, he said, "My daughter has informed me that our unexpected visitor has been captured by humans. These waters are no longer safe. They may never be safe again. We must proceed with an emergency relocation."

Calliope appeared from around the side of the cavern and cowered behind her father.

Barney pointed at her. "Tell them the truth!"

Before he could say anything further, Lorelei yanked his hand and charged forward and away from the others. She wailed in pain with every forceful flip of her tail, as the largest and most sensitive sore was right at the start of her fluke. "Bring me to where you last saw her."

He led the way, and when they arrived, he reenacted what had happened and indicated the direction the boat had headed. Lorelei scurried ahead but changed her heading several times until she grew frustrated. Her father had taught her how to scout safe places for the school, but she had no intuition for tracking a human boat. With no way to find Hailey, she had to go to land and hope that Hailey's mother could enlist Marina and Meredith's help.

On the way toward the island, Calliope called out for them.

"What do you want?" Lorelei continued forward without even a glance at Calliope.

"The school is in trouble," replied Calliope in a trembling. "I want to help."

Barney, struggling to keep up with Lorelei, passed by Calliope and said, "You have done enough already."

Calliope propelled herself to Lorelei's side. "My friends and I were trying to cut that net to catch her when I got stuck in it. Then that orange-tail—human or whatever she was—she saved me. I did not expect her to be considerate."

"Maybe you should not judge a maid by her natural upbringing." Lorelei glared back at Calliope. "Or her tail color."

"What can I do? How can I help?"

Doubting Calliope's sincerity, Lorelei continued forward. Calliope stayed close behind and begged, almost desperately, to contribute to solving the crisis. Annoyed, Lorelei came to a quick stop, turned, and shouted, "If you want to help, then persuade your father *not* to relocate the school until after I or Marina return."

As abruptly as she reversed direction, Lorelei righted her course and signaled for Barney to keep up with her, leaving Calliope stunned and motionless in their wake.

They stopped near the island at a depth where they could poke their heads through the surface and graze the sandy ocean floor with their flukes. Lorelei stared straight ahead at the faint outline of Hailey's darkened house, barely illuminated by the back porch lamp of the house to the right and the light seeping through the drawn shades of the house to the left. She hoped she could crawl to Hailey's back door unnoticed, aided by the absent moon in the cloudless black sky.

"The sky does not look right," said Barney, looking up at the thousands of sparkling stars. "I should do this. You are injured. And I want to make up for not saving her earlier."

"I must do this," Lorelei spoke sternly. "I know the human world better, and I know Hailey's friends and mother."

She ducked her head just below the surface and let the

waves carry her forward until her stomach skidded along the packed wet sand. Her body dug a channel through the ground, bringing her to a complete stop, which she punctuated by smacking her fluke on the receding foamy water.

"Are you hurt?" called Barney.

Spitting out a clump of sand, she raised her head and looked over her shoulder. "Be quiet and hide."

While she watched Barney submerge, the next crest of the waves washed right over her, spilling her long, red hair over her face. She brushed it away, the dampness clinging her locks together haphazardly, and she saw the wooden footbridge about five or six body lengths away.

Lorelei had run on Hailey's beach before, even walked up to the house and back, so she had an idea how long it would take, on legs anyway. She hoped she had allowed enough additional time to drag herself across the sand, to the back door, and then return. At least the tide was at its highest so there'd be a shorter length of beach to traverse.

She clawed her hands into the sand and pulled herself forward, taken aback by how difficult it was. Underwater, she always glided so effortlessly and freely in whichever direction she desired, even if all she wanted was to float. But on land, she felt like an immovable sailing vessel trapped on the ocean floor. *I must not sink*, she told herself, *must swim*.

The uneven dry sand ahead was harder to navigate because the loose grains sifted through her fingers. The gritty surface irritated her wounds and made her itchy when grains lodged underneath her scales, but she hauled herself forward until her hand slapped the bottom step of the stairs to the footbridge.

The railings of the stairway and bridge provided Lorelei something sturdier to grab, but as she dragged her heavy tail along the wooden surface, she flinched. Splinters pierced the taut skin above her waist and pried off several scales below it. Willing herself to stifle the pain, she kept her eyes focused on Hailey's back door, which had slowly grown clearer to see.

When she finally reached the house, physically exhausted, she heaved herself into a seated position and knocked on the door. She waited a few moments, but no one appeared. Craning her neck to see the second-floor windows, she pounded louder, but there didn't seem to be any sign of life inside. All she heard were the waves rustling quieter and quieter.

She sensed some light from above, but it wasn't coming from the house. The sky had transitioned from black to violet, with reddish-blue streaks starting to appear.

From the distance, Barney yelled, "Lore, get back in the water!"

Lorelei threw herself across the deck, bracing for impact, but her tail slapped the wooden floor. She repeated the motion several more times, keeping careful watch on the brightening sky and the outgoing tide. When she got to the center of the footbridge, the tan sand of the beach loomed ahead of her, a larger expanse than she had previously crossed.

Then a curved sliver of bright, orange light broke through the horizon's seam, and Lorelei's entire body convulsed.

Having visited land many times before at sunrise on the day of a full moon, Lorelei knew what her tail concealing itself felt like. It was usually pleasurable, almost as if her scales were being lightly caressed by sea foam.

The sensation at sunrise on the day of the new moon was excruciating, and Lorelei clenched her mouth tightly in a futile struggle not to scream and thus reveal herself to the neighbors. Her fluke felt as if two sharks had clamped their teeth on both ends and were swimming in opposite directions. She was being torn apart, and sharp pain coursed through her like electric eels were nestling within the jagged space where her scales separated along her midline.

She tried to pull herself to the stairs, hoping she could get down them and to the water before the transformation was complete, but her lower body was paralyzed, and she fell forward. The agony was unbearable, like a piece of her soul was being ripped from her body, and all she could do was bury her face in her hands and cry.

"I am coming out to get you," called Barney.

"No, you will not. We can not lose both our tails." Sobbing, she looked out to the beach, where he lay in the shallow water. "Come back when the moon is full. For now, you must return to the school and tell my father that I have gone to find Hailey."

By the time Barney disappeared in the distance, the pain Lorelei felt had subsided, replaced by a tingling from mist spraying her legs. She knew the sensation meant her tail was dissolving into the air, but she didn't want to look. All she wanted to do was weep, but her eyes had run dry of salty tears.

When she finally turned over to see her bare legs, she saw that something was still around her waist. It wasn't translucent; it was a barely visible and tangible wisp of material across her thighs. Tucking her legs underneath her as she sat up, she noticed faint sparkling discs strewn about the footbridge—the only pieces that remained of her natural form. She gathered the scales to soak them in water, hoping they'd return to their vividly iridescent green. But she didn't possess the knowledge and tools necessary to do what Hailey had done to restore Marina's tail the previous summer.

Her cupped hands were overflowing with scales when a gruff voice said, "They're away on vacation. You might want one of these to cover yourself up."

Lorelei looked up at the old man, Hailey's neighbor. His face was turned away as he held a white beach towel down toward her. With a soft thank-you, she took it and started wrapping it around her waist.

"It's been a long time, but you're not the first young woman to appear lost on this beach." He extended a hand to help her to her feet. "And you look like you could use some help, lassie."

Having no other option than to go with him, Lorelei stood on legs shakier than she remembered them to be, as if it was her first time walking. If Hailey, wherever she was, had also reverted to human form, then at least any proof of her being a mer would have dissolved with the tail. For Hailey's and the school's sake, Lorelei hoped it was true.

But for Marina's sake, Lorelei hoped it wasn't true because it meant her closest friend would sadly never again be a mer.

~ Chapter Twenty-Three ~

Meredith stepped outside of the dormitory and instantly felt submerged in the humid air. The sky was overcast that Sunday morning, as rain was expected to fall later in the day. She set her backpack on a bench and tied her already frizzed long brown hair into a ponytail. Then she sat and took a textbook from the backpack to do some last minute manatee cramming.

Will sat beside her and asked, "Do you think Dr. Hatcher will mind if I tag along?"

"Probably not." Though Dr. Hatcher hadn't explicitly invited the other interns to come, he hadn't explicitly *not* invited them to come. Meredith didn't think Will would be allowed in the tank with the manatee, but she didn't mind him being there. She hoped he could take some photos. "It would be nice if you came along."

"Wow, okay." The dark blush on his cheeks was a sharp contrast to the pale skin of his forehead and his light hair. "I hope Brittany doesn't show up."

"I don't think it's her style to wake up this early on our day off."

Right after the sea lion incident, Brittany had called Meredith's dive into the tank an awesome act of rebellion. The odd comment sounded somewhat gracious, but Brittany's cold attitude toward her returned upon learning about the invitation to see the manatee. Since then, Brittany regularly muttered under her breath that Meredith was just another teacher's pet.

"I don't think it's her style to study marine biology," said

Will.

The shuttle arrived, and they switched their topic of conversation to the manatee. Meredith didn't want to waste any further time wondering how Brittany had been accepted, especially since she didn't seem to be an obstacle to advancing her own career goal.

At the aquarium, which was closed to the public, Dr. Hatcher didn't seem upset that Will had come with Meredith, but he didn't seem enthusiastic about it either. He took them to the marine life observation and rehabilitation complex, which consisted of two large cylindrical tanks connected by a gated and enclosed canal, and an interior examination area usually staffed by a few marine biologists. One of the tanks was open to the air with a taller wooden canopy over it, while the other tank had a domed roof.

After changing into her swimsuit, Meredith stepped onto the narrow observation deck along the inside perimeter of the open-topped tank. Between the clouds and the shadow from the roof, the space around her was dim. She drew her attention from above to below her, where she immediately focused on the large manatee. Her mouth slowly opened in wonder; the photographs in her textbook hadn't done its beauty any justice.

She estimated it at about eight to nine feet long, below average for an adult male so that it could have been an older calf. Its skin had a shade and texture similar to an elephant, except for the patches of algae growing on its back. Out in open water, more could conceivably be present, and maybe the aquarium staff had removed some. It swam in circles, leaving a path of oval-shaped ripples behind it, and it flapped its tail similarly to the way she had flipped Marina's. She giggled at the notion of old-time sailors mistaking manatees for mermaids.

Meredith heard footsteps, and she recognized the tentative gait as Will's. Trying to cover her one-piece strapless bathing suit, she squeezed her arms across her chest. He had seen her in the aquarium polo shirt and khaki shorts all summer, but she had yet to show him so much leg or exposed shoulders.

"Wow." Will stretched out the word in amazement.

On hearing his voice, her heart raced. Water beaded on her forehead, but she couldn't tell if it was her own perspiration or condensation from the humid air. She suspected he had a crush on her, and she enjoyed working with him, but why was she growing anxious? Did she like him in that way too, or was she suddenly self-conscious that he was checking her out?

"That manatee's cool," he said. "Wow."

Meredith dropped her arms by her side, releasing the tension in her shoulders. She felt deflated and couldn't shake a twinge of jealousy toward the aquatic mammal in the tank.

"Are you ready to meet Manny up close?" Dr. Hatcher handed her a snorkel, diving mask, and a pair of flippers. All of them were a shade of blue that closely matched her swimsuit.

While she sat and slipped her feet into the flippers, Will asked, "So he's Manny the manatee? That's not very original."

"You can take that one up with Brittany. She named him." Dr. Hatcher released a contemptuous groan.

Meredith and Will turned to each other. As if by telepathy, their shocked facial expressions asked each other the same questions about how, why, and when Brittany would be given naming honors. Lowering the mask over her eyes, Meredith shrugged. The answers were moot because no matter what arbitrary name the manatee had been assigned, it probably received an actual name from its parents—in a language they'd never understand.

Dr. Hatcher said, "Manny's quite docile and has been mostly friendly since he's healed. He's been a little lethargic the past few days, so I'll be right here ready to jump in if I sense any trouble."

Nodding in understanding, Meredith lowered herself into the water. As soon as she broke the surface, the manatee across the tank stopped, but she didn't notice because she was having difficulty using the flippers. From being on her school swim team, she had gotten used to swimming with her legs, and two flippers were far less effective than the single orange fluke she had borrowed the previous summer.

Once she got the hang of it and stopped flailing her feet, she bit down on the curved end of the snorkel. Floating right below the surface, she turned to face the manatee and found it hovering in place at the other end facing her.

Manny chirped and shook one of his flippers, almost as if he was beckoning her to approach. She cautiously kicked her feet but propelled herself forward a little faster than she intended. To let the water resistance slow her down, she extended her arms and opened her palms. As she drifted to a stop, Manny's sounds got louder and more frequent, like the tuning of a radio dial searching for a station, until they were coherent.

You are not like the others. Where is your tail?

Meredith gasped into the snorkel, thinking about her so-called superpowers. Rays, crabs, and sea stars flocked to her. Fish inside their tanks pointed at her through the glass. Even the sea lions understood her, though she couldn't understand them. Something made her communication with Manny possible. She wondered if it was because she was fully submerged in the water or if the connection between manatees and mermaids was stronger than with other sea creatures. Unable to speak under the water, especially with the snorkel in her mouth, she concentrated all her thoughts on an answer: *I don't have a tail.*

The manatee grunted. *You have had one. I can sense you are mer.*

She wasn't sure how to convince Manny that she wasn't a mermaid without revealing how she and Marina accidentally switched places. Later that day, the aquarium was returning him to the ocean, and she feared others in the ocean learning the truth.

Your secret is safe with me. I need your help.

Why do you need my help? She pointed at her chest while she treaded water in the center of the tank. Only the top of her head and the open end of the snorkel were above the surface.

Manny rose to take a breath and then submerged again. *To return to the ocean. I have been kept here against my will.*

They were nursing you back to health, thought Meredith.

My mother was teaching me travel routes. We are far from home, and I fear I will not find her.

Meredith felt her heart sink. She and Jill were already taking care of one motherless sea dweller, and now she had encountered another, almost like they were seeking her out for assistance. *They're bringing you back to the ocean later. Trust me. You'll be home soon.*

I do trust you. Manny veered to the side to swim along the tank's circumference, and he stopped when he was facing Dr. Hatcher directly. *It is them I do not trust. They have done things to me.*

They've been trying to help you. Meredith swam alongside Manny and gently stroked his back, hoping it would console him. *And they were also studying you, to learn more about your kind.*

Is that why they have attached something to my tail?

Manny sped up while Meredith floated in place. As he passed, she noticed a thin gray nylon belt, almost matching the color of his skin, wrapped around the narrowest part of his tail. It wasn't tightly secured to him, but it was constricted enough that it wouldn't slide off in ocean currents.

A thunderclap cracked loudly across the sky, followed by heavy rain pelting the wooden roof above the tank. Dr. Hatcher called for Meredith to get out of the water, so she quickly thought *Goodbye* to Manny and swam to the deck.

"Wow!" Will handed her a beach towel, which she quickly wrapped around herself and then dragged the mask up onto her head. "That looked amazing, almost like the two of you were having a conversation."

"Don't be ridiculous." Meredith patted his arm in a somewhat patronizing manner. Trying to reach Dr. Hatcher before he went inside, she stumbled in her flippers and almost knocked Will over. "What's that around Manny's tail?" She pointed at the gray belt.

"We're going to attach a radio transmitter to it so we can track his movements—migration patterns and what not." A gust of warm wind howled as it blew over the tank, interrupting Dr. Hatcher's answer. "The board of directors wanted to keep Manny in captivity, but we may learn more by letting him go. All in the name of science."

Dr. Hatcher disappeared inside. Will followed, still commenting how wonderful it was simply watching her experience. Meredith stepped out of her flippers and stood there on the deck, the strong wind flapping the towel against her legs. As Manny circled the tank, she kept her eyes locked on the gray belt. Tracking a manatee didn't matter much since humans knew about their existence.

Meredith looked at the sliver of sky visible between the top of the tank and the bottom of the canopy roof. The storm clouds were the same shade of gray as Manny's tracking belt. When a lightning bolt flashed, she was struck by how correct Marina was.

But if a single mer was ever caught and eventually tagged like Manny, that unfortunate mer could unknowingly lead the scientists directly to the school. More mers would be caught and studied…or worse.

Then thunder rumbled in the distance.

~ Chapter Twenty-Four ~

Jill pushed open the door, clanging the bell above it so hard that its screws were almost pulled out of the door frame. Finally out of the drizzle, she wrung her hair dry and marched straight across the square retail space and past the smattering of customers to the counter where the old shopkeeper stood. "You'd better have a good explanation."

"Welcome back to *The Mermaid's Lagoon.*" Isabel locked eyes with Jill. "Are you sure you know what you're looking for?"

Her stare intensified, almost like she was looking right through Jill, who uncomfortably turned away and revealed Marina behind her.

The woman's intense expression brightened into a wide grin that revealed an incomplete set of dentures. "Why hello again, dearie. I had a feeling I'd be seeing you sooner or later, but this is certainly a little on the sooner side."

Marina smiled, but before she could speak, Jill asked, "So you know about the wild goose chase we're on?"

Isabel glared at Jill, but the bell above the door rang and broke the tension. "Have a pleasant day! Enjoy your stay!" She waved at the pair of tourists, a young woman enjoying her time stopping in every island souvenir shop and her husband who probably would have been golfing if it hadn't started raining.

"Please, we need your help." Marina laid the print of her mother's painting on the counter.

"How very interesting." Isabel leaned forward to look closely at Marina's face. "Your ocean blue eyes are calmer than before. Something unexpected and uplifting has happened, though you're still adrift."

Marina thought about Jeff, the source of some recent happiness, and then about the difficulty she'd been having finding her mother. A quick glance at Jill rolling her eyes was a reminder that she doubted Isabel's ability. Smirking, Marina gestured toward Jill and asked, "Can you read my friend's thoughts?"

"Oh, no no no!" Jill swung her arms in front of her. "None of that mumbo-jumbo on me."

Isabel gave Jill a sideways glance but spoke to Marina. "I saw enough already. Her eyes are brown like the land. She wants to stay grounded, but she's feeling buried under frustration that's soon going to get deeper."

Jill rolled her eyes. "You're quick with the puns, aren't you? I can do improv too, *dearie*. Tell us about your other store."

Isabel stepped back and looked away. "I don't have another store."

"I don't need special powers to know you're lying. We've been there. It's empty now, but it's got the same sign."

"That store was already closed down when my husband bought it for me from some woman who lived above it." Her voice grew more airy than usual at the mention of him. "He passed away after we packed up the inventory, and then last summer, I opened up here instead." She spread her arms like a game show hostess showing off a contestant's grand prize. "More tourists. I can charge more."

Marina tapped her finger on the image of Coral. "My mother once lived in that building, and I am trying to find her. That is my mother, and I am the baby—"

Pressing her index finger to Marina's lips, Isabel cocked her head to the side indicating the one pair of customers remaining in the store. A pre-teen girl and her mother were looking over the collection of mermaid figurines on display. As Isabel floated over to them, the hem of her black dress hovered just above the floor without showing her feet or legs, as if they didn't exist underneath.

"I think this one suits you best." She carefully picked up one exactly like the one on Meredith's desk. "This color's the rarest in the shop and in the sea. That makes it quite special."

The girl's face beamed as she nodded at her mother, and then Isabel guided them to the cash register. During the interaction, Marina pulled Jill aside and said, "I appreciate how you are watching out for me, but I can speak for myself."

"Then speak up," said Jill. "You didn't give up your voice to get those legs."

After the transaction, Isabel followed her customers to the door and waved as they left. After shutting and locking the door, she turned the *Come in, we're open* sign around to *Sorry, we're closed*, and then she drew the blinds. "Now we can get down to real business."

Jill pointed at the door. "Locking us in against our will is probably illegal. And it's at least creepy."

"The door's only locked on the outside. You can leave whenever you want." Isabel glided to Marina and put an arm around her. "But you need to be careful, dearie. You shouldn't tell just anyone who you really are."

Jill blinked and thrust her open palms forward. "Wait! You mean you know that she's a—?"

"Mermaid? Of course." Isabel chuckled as she turned Marina to face her. "I've known since I first saw your eyes. Never met a mer with an orange tail before." She took a hold of the sides of her dress and curtseyed. "It's an honor to officially make your acquaintance."

While Marina stood there dumbfounded, Jill shook her head in such confusion that her hair went everywhere, even over her face. "Why didn't you tell us any of this before? We're trying to find her mother! It could've helped."

Isabel looked up and waved her finger at Jill. "Stop being so overdramatic, dearie. I didn't know for sure that you knew who she was when you first walked in. And I certainly didn't know if you were trustworthy until Hailey kept coming around." She gently squeezed Marina's hand. "You've got a true friend in that sweetheart, and I'm sure she's keeping your tail safe."

Jill's hands and arms made quick, jerky motions. Her head rocked back and forth while sounds sputtered from her mouth. She only uttered one coherent thought: "O-M-G."

"That's Hailey for you." Isabel drifted to the counter, Marina in tow. "I envy her. Just imagining all the sights she can behold and the freedom of the water, I wish I could go back down there."

"I think I've gotta sit down for this." Jill's knees buckled, but she collapsed safely into a chair that Isabel wheeled out from behind the counter in the nick of time. Jill massaged her temple, which ached from trying to process the revelation. "Does that mean you're one too?"

"Did you think Hailey was the first person to switch places with a mer?" Isabel turned from Jill toward Marina. "Or the girl who accidentally left you ashore last summer? I beat them both by several years."

There was a roll of distant thunder, and then Marina asked, "Did you know my mother? She left our school before the picture was made."

"I'm afraid I didn't, dearie. That was painted before my time under the sea. I met my dear Marlin about fifteen years ago." She sighed wistfully then fanned her hands in front of her face until she smirked. "Oh, the fiery red tail that beautiful, hot creature had."

Jill blocked her ears, "As Hailey would say, T-M-I!"

"He and his sister came ashore one morning while I was walking the beach. I saw what they were. They panicked at first, but I calmed them down, and then we were able to come to an agreement." She snickered. "Marlin's sister wanted to leave the ocean and explore land, and I wanted to escape my life for a while. Marlin was intrigued by my spunk, and I was intrigued by his—"

"Rock hard abs? Or hot red tail?" Jill rolled her eyes and spun her wrists around to get her to tell the story quicker.

"Go on. We get it."

"One moon cycle turned into two, which turned into three, and then into eleven years. His sister never wanted to go back."

Marina asked, "If you were part of our school for so long, then why did we never meet?"

"Because we weren't part of your school, dearie." Isabel patted Marina's hands. "We were our own little pod, about a dozen or so of us. Eventually, Marlin felt bad that I had sacrificed my life on land, so we let our tails disappear and planned to spend the rest of our time up here."

"His sister must have been a wonderful scout. There is much more land to explore that I have imagined." She looked into Isabel's green irises. "Her tail would have nicely matched your eyes."

"Well, not exactly."

"Question." Jill stood and held up her hand, stopping the natural flow of the conversation so she wouldn't lose the idea that had popped into her head. "Is that why you can do what you can do? You got your psychic-ness from being a mermaid so long, right?"

Isabel grinned and tapped her temple. "You're a clever one. Definitely a residual effect of being mer. Marlin told me I'd make a great counselor or advisor, like the best of the purple-tails."

Marina felt the color drain from her face as she staggered backward. "You had a *purple* tail? You are far too kind to have been a purple-tail."

Jill wheeled the chair over to Marina and stood behind her. "Maybe *you* need to sit down for this."

Isabel stepped out from behind the counter but stopped when she saw Marina flinch. "Most of our little pod had purple tails, dearie, and they were the most generous—"

"No, they are *not*," said Marina firmly. "They have treated me like an urchin my entire life."

"Calm down, killer shark." Jill put her hands on Marina's shoulders to ease her down onto the chair. "Isabel can be right too. Maybe they're not all bad."

Marina quivered as she recalled all the name-calling, taunting, and teasing she had endured, especially from Calliope and her friends. "I have been treated differently all my life because of my tail. Had my mother never left the school, I would not have been the only orange-tail. I would not have been alone." Her face sank into her hands, and her tears fell as fast as the pouring rain outside.

Gently rubbing Marina's back, Jill knelt beside her and spoke in a soft, soothing voice. "You're not alone. Meredith and I are here for you. Jeff too. We're your friends, and we're not gonna give up on you. And I'm sure Hailey will stay down there living her dream as long as you need to find your mother."

Isabel bent over and stroked Marina's cheek down to her chin, gently tilting her head back to make eye contact. Squinting, the old woman said, "You know why your mother left the school, don't you, dearie?"

Marina nodded solemnly. "She went looking for my father."

Isabel held her gaze to infer what she could from Marina's eyes. "Because he was the one who was truly lost?" She squeezed Marina's hand, eliciting an exhalation and a nod from her. "That must mean she loved him deeply."

"Before I returned here, I learned the story from an old mer, who insisted I keep it secret. That is why I want to find my mother—to learn if it is true." Marina sniffled between her sentences. "My father was banished from the school, yet my mother maintained his innocence. They say he was responsible for another mer's death. Maybe that is why I am treated poorly."

There was a knock on the window pane. Isabel drifted to the front of the store and peeked behind the shade before eagerly unlocking and opening the door. The bell rang in sync with a loud thunderclap. "If it isn't the girl with the cloudy green eyes." Isabel stepped aside. "Come in out of the rain, dearie."

"I did not know where else to go." Shivers impeded Lorelei's speech as she entered the store. She wore a faded floral house dress, a few sizes too large but clinging to her because it was soaked. Her arms were faintly bruised, and her long red hair was matted down and dripping.

Recognizing her best friend's voice, Marina turned to the door but quickly looked away and wiped the tears from her eyes. Jill looked also, and the three girls exchanged curious glances until Lorelei started an explanation.

"I waited with Hailey's neighbor for a few days, but her parents have not returned since I...since I lost my…" Her voice gave way to sobs as she removed a capped plastic bottle from a pocket of the dress. Pale green scales floated in the water inside.

Marina embraced her friend and asked, "How and why did this happen?"

"If you're out here, then where's my cousin?" Jill trembled as she raked one hand through her long hair. "Where's Hailey?"

"She is why I am here and why I sacrificed my tail. She is in a tidal wave of trouble, and we need to find her."

~ Chapter Twenty-Five ~

The booming thunder jolted Hailey awake. Before she popped into a seated position, her head crashed into something, and the clanking of metal reverberated around her.

She lay back down in the cloudy water and rubbed her forehead, hoping she could prevent a bump from appearing. Strands of her damp, dark hair got into her eyes, and she brushed them away to get a closer look at her cramped surroundings.

Four stained white walls rose not too far above the filmy surface of the water. The rectangular compartment looked like an oversized bathtub, but it was deeper, without curved edges, and the two walls to her sides were much longer than the other two narrow walls.

Her head throbbed, and she glanced upward at the cause of her injury. A section of chain-link fence covered the top of the basin. Beyond the rusty crisscrossed metal, a wide open lid ran along the longer rim to her right. She was inside a freezer typically used to keep fish fresh, but instead, it was defrosted and keeping her confined.

Hailey remembered getting caught in the fish net but had no recollection of how she got inside the freezer. She had drifted in and out of consciousness a few times, catching vague glimpses and sounds of her surroundings, but this was the most alert she had been. For all she knew, days could have passed. The new moon had most likely come and gone.

She looked down the length of her body and kicked, weakly splashing water which rippled back to her face. The span of her tail was wider than the freezer, so the ends of her fluke curled against the walls and sagged inward.

At least I still have Marina's tail, she thought, desperately remaining optimistic.

The thunder roared again, and Hailey's head and shoulders tilted backward while her tail rose upward. The water level rose over her face while her tail broke through the surface on the higher, shallow end. Her motion reversed until her head was higher than her submerging tail, though not as steeply. She felt dizzy, a queasiness forming in the pit of her stomach that she could only equate to human seasickness. *Mermaids shouldn't get seasick, right?*

The back and forth rocking eventually made sense to her. She was on a boat.

Maybe she could convince the people who had caught her that she was a human wearing a realistic-looking costume. She could show off her social media sites where she had posted a few videos and dozens of pictures of her with her custom-made tail. They showed her immediately after removing the tail from its box, hugging it and squealing happily, putting it on for the first time, swimming in it, even lounging around on the sofa wearing it. It was close enough in color to Marina's tail, so maybe they'd believe.

Until they asked her to remove the costume. She wiggled her fluke. It was a part of her that wasn't coming off and proof that she wasn't a human. If they had caught her—an *actual* mermaid—then what was stopping them from starting a search for more?

She reached her fingers through the fence and took hold of the links. If she could lift it up and push it aside, then she could pull herself out of the freezer. She'd have to be careful that her tail didn't flop too loudly on the floor, and then she'd have to drag her legless body up to the main deck of the boat. But once there, she could dive back into the ocean and swim deep enough to avoid being recaptured. Then she could look for the school, and if she couldn't find them, she'd revert to her true form at sunrise on the morning of the full moon.

The fence wouldn't budge. Hailey was able to push up on the metal lattice and create a bulge in the center, but the frame stayed put. She submerged her head and slid her back down toward her tail, which forced her fluke upward. Then she flipped her fluke as powerfully as she could, hoping the force would knock over the fence.

All it did was clang the metal loudly.

Tilting her head back, she scanned the perimeter of the freezer's rim. A padlock secured the fence at the narrow end closest to her head. She lowered her tail and noticed another at the far end. Whoever had caught her intended to keep her.

I'm in a cage, she thought. *Like an animal.*

In her frustration, she grabbed the bars of her makeshift jail cell and shook them violently until her knuckles turned white. She cried aloud, but the water distorted her voice, so she sounded like a dolphin wailing in pain.

Footsteps clopped on the deck above, and Hailey froze. Sawdust drizzled down from the cracks between the wooden planks. "I think it's awake again," said a muffled voice.

"Don't worry," said a deeper, gruffer voice. "There's no way it'll get out of there."

It?

Hailey's fingers slid from the bars, and her arms sank limply to her sides. She flicked her fin. From the waist down, she was definitely more fishlike than human, but from the waist up, she appeared just as human as the men upstairs probably did. She didn't have any noticeable gills—confirmed by a quick rub along the tense muscles on the sides of her neck. She studied her hands, which had regained their normal color; they weren't webbed. She wasn't an *it*, and as she glanced at her clamshell bikini top, she grunted at how obvious it should be to the men that she was a *she*.

"Mermaids aren't natural," said the first voice, in which Hailey detected a tone of worry. "They're dangerous. The stories say they'll bring bad luck. We need to throw it back."

Hailey nodded, lightly splashing the stagnant water.

"Throw it back?" The gruff voice laughed. "What are you,

crazy? It could be worth a fortune!"

"If we accidentally snagged a dolphin or a seal…or…or a…a sea turtle, we'd get in big trouble. Imagine the kind of trouble we'll be in for catching this."

"Trouble? It's the only one that's ever been caught."

Hailey turned her head to the side and sobbed. No mer had ever been caught before. She was the first.

"What if it's not the only one? What if the government already knows about it and the whole species is endangered?"

All mers are in danger now, Hailey thought. *And it's all my fault.*

By performing a selfless gesture—saving another mer—she managed to put the entire school in jeopardy. The grimy surface before her didn't cast a reflection, but she didn't want to face herself—any part of her body, human or mer—because she had let so many others down.

Gruff-Voice spoke again. "Shut your trap and make sure below deck stays locked."

"What if it makes more noise?" asked the whinier voice. "What if while we're docked, someone comes on board and hears—?"

"We tell 'em we got nothin', and they'll go." Gruff raised his voice in anger. "We could make more from one of *it* than from millions of fish."

There was a rumble of thunder, and the boat rocked sideways. The dirty water splashed to the unhinged side of the freezer and some spilled over onto the floor. Meanwhile, the upstairs footsteps scrambled to another end of the ship, and any continued conversation was too far away to hear.

Squirming in the restricted space, Hailey flipped herself onto her stomach. To them, she wasn't a person. She was a creature, a possession, a commodity. To the school, she probably wasn't welcome anymore as a mer. And to her family, she'd be forever lost at sea. *What's going to happen to me?* Thinking about the real possibility of never seeing them again only made her submerge herself in a mixture of tears and dirty water.

The attitudes of the fishermen made her ashamed to be human, and her unfortunate capture made her embarrassed to be mer. She cried herself to sleep, unsure which she wanted or deserved to be.

~ Chapter Twenty-Six ~

The storm got worse before it moved east out to sea, delaying ferries to and from the island for most of the afternoon. When Jill and Marina returned to the mainland with Lorelei, the setting sun was streaking the sky red beyond the buildings and trees to the west.

Waiting for them to disembark, Meredith paced the terminal and tried to formulate a plan for finding Hailey. She could tell from the volume and tone of Jill's voice—alternating between loud, angry shouts and quivering mutterings—that Jill wouldn't be in the right state of mind to think calmly or even to drive home. Without a car of her own, Meredith asked Jeff to drive her to the terminal. Since it was the weekend, he was fortunately able to borrow his father's car.

He sat relaxed, one leg up on his other knee and an arm stretched across the back of the bench like he was missing a girl to put it around. Meredith envied how he could sit there so calmly while her stomach was tightly knotted, but he had no reason to be worried. She hadn't explained why she needed to pick them up. How could she tell him that his cousin had been masquerading as a mermaid but was missing after being caught in a commercial fishing net?

Jill barreled through the door, her hair a tangled mess from the rain and her nervous twirling it around. "Nice of you to make time for us in your busy schedule, *Meredith*." Her tone had bite to it, causing Jeff to stand up and approach. Noticing him for the first time, Jill pulled Meredith aside. "What's *he* doing here? Shouldn't you have called the coast guard or something?"

"He was the only way I could get here," whispered Meredith.

"Why so riled up, Sis?" Jeff patted her back. "And why would you need the coast guard?"

His attention was stolen when he noticed Marina standing in the doorway. Upon seeing him, she ran and threw her arms around him. Though there were some streaks on her face from crying, she allowed herself a thin smile as she nestled against the warmth of his chest.

"When did *that* happen?" asked Meredith.

Jill held up her hand and rolled her eyes. "Don't get me started."

Meredith approached Lorelei, who stood alone by the door, and gave her a comforting hug. "It's good to see you again. I'm sorry it's under these circumstances."

"I am wearing my tail under this dress, but I can barely feel it." Lorelei revealed the water bottle and pointed at the scales inside. "These are all that are left."

"We'll figure it out."

Her arms crossed while she tapped her foot, Jill scoffed, "Just add it to the list of otherworldly emergencies to solve. Can we get going?"

She reached into her purse for her keys, but Meredith grabbed them from her and said, "I'm driving."

"Whatever." Jill stomped toward the door.

Meredith gestured the others to come along. Lorelei followed disconsolately while Marina and Jeff lagged behind, hand in hand. "If you don't mind, Merri," said Jeff, "Marina can ride with me."

Taking Marina's other hand and pulling her away, Meredith said, "Not tonight. We need all the girls together right now."

"You're not all here. You're missing Hailey."

Marina gasped. "You know what happened to her?"

"Of course, we're missing Hailey." Meredith extracted Marina from Jeff and nudged her toward the door. She stammered while she tried to channel some of Jill's improvisational skills. "We're um…we're doing something… special…for her birthday." She shook her head in dismay, knowing she didn't sound convincing.

"A surprise party?" Jeff's forehead crinkled. "Her birthday isn't for another few months, but I get it. I'll follow you girls home, okay?"

Meredith sighed in relief and then dashed away with Marina to the parking lot. Jill leaned against the passenger door of her car, her hands on her hips while her thumbs fidgeted with the belt loops by the pockets of her cut-off denim shorts.

Inside the car, Meredith adjusted the driver's seat forward a few clicks before starting the engine. Jill slouched in the passenger seat, resting her forehead against the window and staring blankly outside.

Behind Meredith, Lorelei tried deciphering the map she had been given to pinpoint the location where the fishing boat had caught Hailey. The folded paper had an arrow indicating north, but Lorelei didn't recognize anything else. The bright blue region representing the ocean was the wrong color, and she didn't know how to determine distances.

Motion in the corner of her eye distracted her. Sitting beside her, Marina waved out the back window at Jeff driving in the car behind them.

"You have strong feelings for him," said Lorelei softly. "It is easy to read your face."

"It is?" As Marina turned to Lorelei, her eyelids fluttered. "I do."

"Does he know who you really are?" Lorelei paused while Marina shook her head. "To know how he truly feels, you will have to tell him. Some secrets should not stay in the deep."

Marina thought about the night before at the pool. It would have been easy to tell him while she had the appearance of a mer. He seemed to like her that way, and she liked being held in his arms, so why wouldn't he like her in that form most of the time? If he liked her enough, they could find a way to see each other every moon cycle. It would be challenging, but it would give them both something to look forward to. Except that until they found Hailey, she didn't have a tail.

The thought of spending all her time with Jeff made her happy at first, but when she caught a glimpse of Lorelei's legs, her shoulders slumped. The longer she stared, the more shame she felt. If she hadn't chosen to search for her mother alone and leave Hailey her tail, then Lorelei would have stayed safely in the ocean. Whether deliberate or not, Marina—and her father—had caused far too much loss in Lorelei's life.

She squirmed in her seat and looked away at the shadows passing by on the side of the road. Until a better time to tell her came, that secret was going to stay submerged.

Lorelei watched the scenery go by. "I have always dreamt of spending more than a day on land. There is so much to see out here."

Over her shoulder, Meredith asked, "How's it coming with the map, Lore?"

"I have never viewed the ocean like this." Lorelei rotated the map for the others to read it correctly. "I cannot tell for sure, but I believe the boat headed in this general direction."

Jill twisted her body and watched Lorelei sweep a finger across the coastline on the map. Rolling her eyes, she moaned, "That's gotta be over a hundred miles. It'll take weeks to go from one marina to another—"

"Am I not the only Marina you know?"

Meredith chuckled, hoping Marina's misunderstanding would relieve some of the tension in the car, but Jill scowled at her. The light turned green, so Meredith drove ahead.

Marina leaned forward and asked, "What is so funny about my question?"

Meredith explained, "Your name is *Marina*, but up here, a *marina* is also a place where boats dock."

"Your language is confusing," said Lorelei.

"A *marina*?" Meredith muttered the word a few times until

a startling recollection made her eyes bulge, and then she turned the steering wheel to pull the car over.

Lurching to the side as the car swerved, Jill yelled, "Hey, what gives?"

Meredith brought the car to a stop at the side of the road and turned to face Jill. "Remember the people in the apartment building who knew Marina's mother? Do you remember *exactly* where they said Coral went?"

Jill was rubbing her forehead. "I've got other things on my mind right now, Merri. Like Hailey."

"They said my mother went to look for me," replied Marina.

"But maybe that's not what they meant." Meredith turned to Marina and waved her arms around as she explained, "Some of them said that your mother was moving on and something about *a marina*. They used the indefinite article *a* in front of your name. We must have assumed they meant you—a girl named Marina. What if she was going to an actual *marina*—the place, not the person?"

Jill released a loud and obviously fake cough. "No offense to any of the mers in the car, but right now, searching for a lost-long mother *isn't* the top priority."

"I'm not suggesting we focus on Marina's mother right now. I just had a brainstorm."

"That's right, you and your precious brain. How can you even think about something like that right now? Why would you stop the car to tell us? Have you spent so much time with your face buried in books that you can't recognize how frightened I am for Hailey?"

"Maybe if you'd actually stop and use your head for a change instead of thinking with your temper, a gut feeling, improv, or whatever you want to call it, then maybe you'd have come off that ferry with some semblance of a plan instead of shoving people around!"

"Fighting like this will not help!" shouted Marina. "Neither of your abilities is any less important than the other's. We need to work together before all is lost. Already too much has been sacrificed."

Marina turned to Lorelei and gently wiped a tear from her cheek. In the front seat, Meredith and Jill looked down and away from each other. Then a knock at the window startled all four of the car's occupants. Outside, Jeff asked if everything was all right. Jill turned away to hide her reddened face while Meredith gave him a thumbs-up and waved him back. Before he got back to his car, Meredith drove ahead and onto the highway onramp.

"You don't have a clue, do you, Merri? Let me sum it up for you." Jill itemized on her fingers. "We've got two stranded mermaids, and Hailey the not-a-real-mermaid who's been caught and mistaken for one—maybe even turned into sushi by now—on our hands. But we can't ask anyone else for help because either they'll think we're crazy, or we'll run the risk of exposing all the mermaids in the ocean. We should call my aunt, but we shouldn't because she'd freak out more than I am right now! As I see it, we're really up the creek, and my improv's not gonna solve this problem." Wheezing to catch her breath, Jill sank into her seat, her long legs oozing onto the car floor. In a strained voice, she continued, "Since you're such a *big expert* on marine biology, how do we find a missing mermaid?"

Except for the whirring of the engine, the car fell silent for a few moments. Meredith's knuckles had turned white from nervously clutching the steering wheel.

Lorelei held the water bottle close to the window and noticed her scales glimmer faintly in the twilight. "I am a scout by birth. Maybe when we go to one of these marinas instead of looking at this map, I will gain a better sense of direction."

"She has my tail," said Marina. "Maybe when we are close, I will be able to sense it."

Shaking her head, Jill raked her hair to the side. "Your combined superpowers might not be enough out of the water. You have to think like us self-centered humans. What would be the first thing a fisherman would do if he caught a mermaid?" She glanced at Meredith, who was opening her mouth as if to answer, and immediately continued, "He'd probably take a picture and post it online."

"Where is this *online*?" asked Lorelei.

Jill quickly lectured about the internet and social media, explaining how if the person posting tagged a location, their search could be narrowed. It could conceivably lead them to a specific marina or even a specific boat. She showed the results of a search with the terms *mermaid* and *caught*, but when it produced thousands of results, the optimism in her voice washed away.

"Though it may seem like a small step, it is something." Marina reached forward and massaged Jill's shoulder. "We will find her, and we will not give up until we do. If my mother is out there, she can wait."

"You really mean that?" asked Jill.

"Yes. You are my friend, and so is Hailey. If something were to happen to her, I would never forgive myself. It is my duty to find her and protect my school."

Lorelei took Marina's hand and squeezed it. "You have grown much since I last saw you. Your mother, wherever she may be, would be proud of how well you took the lead."

Marina didn't feel like much of a leader, keeping secrets from her best friend. Instead, she felt adrift and afraid, but that was another secret she refused to reveal.

~ Chapter Twenty-Seven ~

Though she didn't see any direct sunlight, Hailey could tell the difference between the next few days and nights. The below deck area of the boat alternated between dimly lit to near pitch black, but her mermaid eyesight compensated as if she were underwater.

She chose to remain under the surface of the tepid water with her eyes closed most of the time. She even contemplated playing dead with the hope that maybe they'd believe and throw her back into the ocean. She never looked at the fishermen when she heard them enter, and while they were in the room, she never reacted to the daily meal of sardines they dropped in the water. Rumbles of hunger thwarted her opossum-like charade, and she ultimately couldn't resist devouring the salty, crunchy little fish. She had tried them once before on land but hadn't liked the taste or texture. Desperation for food must have changed her appetite, she concluded, or becoming part fish had.

With such limited space to move, Hailey waded in her thoughts while becoming acutely aware of her surroundings. She knew all the rust spots on the chain-link fence imprisoning her. She knew from the gentle rocking and lack of the engine humming that the boat had been moored for a couple of days. She knew how the floor creaked when people walked above. She could distinguish the voices and footsteps of the two fishermen, though she occasionally noticed a third person walking with much lighter steps. She saw the ring of grime around the walls as the water level gradually lowered, but she didn't know for sure if the freezer had a leak, if the water evaporated, or if she was digesting or absorbing it somehow.

She glanced down the length of her tail. The scales were dull, not their usual shimmery vivid orange, and her tail looked sickly with a film around it. Hailey hoped the discoloration was caused by soaking in filthy water instead of some illness. *Mermaids belong in salt water*, she thought, *not in this yuck*.

Either the water was going to contaminate her, or the fishermen were going to do something with her—she didn't know quite what; she hadn't been able to hear their plans—but she couldn't wallow there any longer. She grasped the chain links but kept herself perfectly still while she listened.

The boat swayed gently. The room was dim but not dark, so she guessed it wasn't night. Seagulls squawked faintly in the distance, almost sounding like they did every morning on the beach at home. A few minutes passed without any sign of the fishermen; either they were asleep or weren't there. Hoping for the latter, she thrashed back and forth, trying to rip the fence loose from its padlocks.

She shook until her muscles were numbed so much that her arms felt gelatinous like they belonged to an octopus. No one came to check on her, so she tried to wedge her fluke in the narrow space between the fence and the freezer's rim. It could propel her through the water, so she reasoned it was strong enough to bend the fence post.

One of the chain's sharp points nicked her fluke. A sudden searing sting, like from a paper cut at the flimsy skin between fingers, shot all the way up her spine as her tail recoiled from the fence. She pounded her clenched fists on the water's surface, splashing some into her face, which scrunched up as she tried to withstand the pain. Hyperventilating, she lay on her back on the freezer's bottom with her tail twisted upward to keep the injured point out of the water.

When her breathing returned to normal, she heard shuffling coming from the floor above. Slowly, she lifted her head into the air and searched for the source of the sound. Light footsteps were walking back and forth, stopping periodically as if their owner was searching for something. Wiggling the free end of her tail, Hailey knew that the most interesting thing hidden on the boat was the mermaid down below. Without knowing what the stranger's objective was, Hailey closed her eyes and focused on the sounds being made.

The footsteps got fainter as the person crossed above her, then got louder and closer, echoing off the wooden walls. There was a knock on the door, followed by a muted voice. "Is everything all right in there?"

Hailey gulped as she considered answering the question. Speaking or making any noise would reveal that she was there and being kept against her will. Maybe the stranger would be sympathetic and find a way to help her. But she'd also reveal her identity, and she didn't know what kind of reaction the person would have upon ultimately seeing her. Maybe the stranger would be opportunistic and steal her from the fishermen. *Friend or foe?* she thought. *Sink or swim?*

"I can sense you are in there." The voice was louder but soothing, almost melodic, and undeniably female. "If you are in trouble, please tell me so I can help."

Something about the voice sounded familiar and trustworthy, so without a second thought, Hailey said, "I'm here, and I wanna get out."

The doorknob jiggled, but the door didn't open. "It is locked. I will be back in a moment to help you. I know where they keep a spare key."

The stranger's footsteps got softer as she walked away, and then almost immediately afterward, they got louder and were accompanied by jingling—a keyring, she hoped.

"Hey, lady out there, before you come in, I just wanna warn you, okay? Don't be shocked and faint or scream or anything like that when you see me." Hailey curled her tail underneath her back to hide it as best she could in the confined space. Her face pressed against the lattice pattern of the fence. "You might not believe it, but I'm a…well, I'm a…" She couldn't bring herself to say it; she felt like it would be betraying the school. Again.

The door opened, and the woman firmly but calmly said, "Do not be afraid. I know what you are."

The voice floated through the air, overcoming Hailey with a sense of tranquility. She watched the ripples in the woman's salmon skirt swish and flare outward as she walked. In sharp contrast to the flowing fabric below, the dress was fitted tightly at the waist and above. The woman was shapely, and when Hailey glanced upward to see if her face was similarly beautiful, she gasped.

Staring back at her was Marina's face, only slightly older. The woman's cheeks were smooth like porcelain, and her eyes as blue as the ocean. The few signs of age were in the fullness of her lips and the slight creases in her forehead. Her hair, without the platinum sheen Marina's had when in mermaid form, was wavy and layered, giving it a windblown look and making her appear almost exactly like she did in Daniel's painting.

Coral.

"O. M. G." Her mouth agape, Hailey reached through the fence for Coral's hand, but the opening was too narrow, so her fingers squeezed together. "I…I can't believe—"

"No need to speak." Coral held a finger to her lips. "Conserve your energy."

Hailey's head filled with questions and comments, but she simply nodded. Coral's presence was comforting, and Hailey didn't want to show any disrespect by disobeying.

"However a maid like you got in a riptide like this does not matter." Coral knelt beside the freezer, taking hold of Hailey's fingers and caressing them. "You should *not* be here."

As much as Hailey wanted to explain what had happened, Coral's gentle touch coaxed her into remaining silent.

"I knew they were hiding something. They are usually forthcoming and boisterous with their daily catch, but they have been far too secretive lately. I had to force my way on deck to get their numbers. That is when I sensed you, my dear maid. You needed protection, but I could not get on board until they left this morning. I do not know when they will be back, so we must hurry."

She guided Hailey's fingers back down and then reached for the padlock closest to Hailey's head. None of the keys unlocked it. Standing, Coral studied the fence from above and for the first time caught a glimpse of Hailey's scales dimly sparkling in the murky water. Her chin quivered as she said, "Please show me your tail."

Hailey squirmed out of her contorted position and flapped her fluke upward until it struck the fence, the clang reverberating around the room. Coral brought a hand to her mouth, and what little color there was in her face drained.

"I do not know why you have that tail or where its true maid is, but you *cannot* be here. You *must* return to your school."

Coral clutched the fence from above and pulled, while Hailey pushed up from below. Creaks came from the end by Hailey's tail, but neither the fence, padlock, nor U-hook secured to the freezer snapped.

"I will go get something to cut through the lock." Coral ran to the door but stopped and turned back. "If they return before I do, please remain calm and do not talk to them. I will be back to set you free as soon as I can. Too much is at stake." She waved before closing and locking the door.

Hailey watched the ceiling, and her eyes followed Coral's harder, more urgent footsteps across the deck. As soon as the sound faded into the distance, Hailey blinked her eyes and shook her head. She felt groggy as if waking up from a nap, with only a muddled recollection of what had happened.

Then waves of memory crashed in her brain. She had met Marina's mother! More accurately, Marina's mother had found her. *Why didn't I tell her I knew where Marina was? Why didn't I tell her Marina was looking for her? Why didn't I ask where we were?* Hailey shook her head as she covered her face with her hands. *Why did I only do whatever she told me to? Was she even really here?*

She sighed and smoothed out her wet hair until her hands were at the back of her neck. There wasn't a need to chastise herself for withholding the information from Coral since she'd be back. She could tell Coral all about Marina later and play a part in their mother-daughter reunion, just as she had hoped for an entire year.

But Coral wasn't the first to return. The fishermen boarded with another few people, and their steps and voices were loud just outside the door.

"We were thinkin' of sellin' it to a sideshow or maybe runnin' our own and chargin' people money to see it," said Gruff-Voice as keys jingled. "I showed some pictures to some friends, but they said it looked like a lame costume or doctored image or somethin' like that."

The door squeaked open, and Hailey closed her eyes and stiffened all her muscles. Coral had told her to stay calm, but her heart was racing too turbulently. It took all her concentration just to stay still.

Whiny said, "And its scales were looking—I don't know—kind of unhealthy, so I convinced him that calling you would be a better idea."

"Part of me's regrettin' it already. Like not buyin' a lottery ticket for the big jackpot."

Hailey flinched when the padlock near her head clicked open. She hoped they didn't notice, and she was better prepared when they unlocked the other. She heard them grunt as they lifted the fence, and she contemplated whacking one of them with her tail, but she knew the attack would be futile.

She sensed a shadow looming over her—someone staring at her, looking for signs of life. The silence was uncomfortable, and Hailey felt the hairs on the back of her neck standing on edge.

After the prolonged pause, a professional sounding voice said, "She's exquisite."

At least this one knows I'm not an it.

"You did the right thing, gentlemen, and we'll discuss terms later." The voice got closer as if the man was kneeling beside the freezer. "I apologize if this hurts."

Hailey's scaly skin was pierced right where her thigh would be. By reflex, her eyes popped opened, and her fluke kicked, splashing water up and over the rim. Likening the pain to a jellyfish sting, she wailed and noticed the tranquilizer dart sticking into her tail

She looked up at the three men, but everything started getting blurry. The man standing in the center wasn't dressed in rubber overalls like the other two, so she kept him in her sights, trying to get a good enough glimpse of him before her eyelids grew too heavy.

He was tall with broad shoulders, and his hair was gray around his temples. His other features weren't particularly distinct, but she recognized the green and white insignia on his navy polo shirt and white coat.

Hailey's lifelong career dream of being a mermaid at an aquarium was beginning right as she drifted to sleep.

~ Chapter Twenty-Eight ~

After three full days of searching, there wasn't a sign of Hailey. Not even a clue.

On Monday morning, Lorelei had chosen a starting point based on the direction she believed the boat had headed. The four girls spent the day driving east along the coast, stopping at every seaport to look around. Marina and Lorelei would sit on the docks with their feet in the water trying to scout the area and sense if Hailey had been close by, but either she wasn't there, or they couldn't tell if she was.

The tension between Meredith and Jill was thick, so Meredith stayed at the aquarium on Tuesday while Jill took the day off to search with the mers. They headed west from the starting point. As the day progressed without success, Jill grew more nervous, noticeably trembling while steering the car.

Meredith pretended to be sick on Wednesday to take over driving duties, and they picked up where they had left off the day before. She joined Marina and Lorelei when they dangled their feet in the water, hoping that her "superpowers" would magnify their senses. After another unsuccessful day, they returned home long after sunset.

Hiding her tired eyes under sunglasses, Meredith waited for the other interns and Dr. Hatcher by the whale tank on Thursday morning. The aquarium hadn't yet opened, so she used the free time to scroll through more *caught mermaid* images on her phone, hoping to find one of Hailey.

"Want some breakfast?" said Will, holding a cup and a bag. "Some orange juice in case you're still feeling under the weather, and a cranberry muffin because…well…because I've seen you eat one for breakfast before."

Meredith smirked and thanked him, and then she reached into the bag and picked off a piece of the muffin.

"It wasn't the same without you yesterday." Will anxiously tapped his fingers on the railing. "I was stuck alone with Brittany at the Investigation Station. And wow, that girl doesn't care for this place. She didn't want to touch anything, let alone even be there, and eventually, she disappeared to who knows where."

"What did Dr. Hatcher have to say about that?" Meredith swallowed a sip of her juice. "What did he have to say about me not being there?"

"I don't think he knows. He wasn't there. Apparently, something urgent came up, and he had to leave before our day even started. So you didn't miss that much yesterday. And he's not going to be here again today, so we're with the rays this morning instead."

Sipping her juice through the straw, Meredith watched the larger of the two white beluga whales surface to take a breath. "Oh, I'm sorry, Will. You were looking forward to working with the whales more than anything else here."

He held the top of the safety rail and leaned forward. "I guess *Delphinapterus leucas* will have to wait till later. We still have a few weeks left, right?"

When they arrived at the touch-tank, Brittany was leaning against the back wall with her arms folded across her chest. Once the attraction was open to the public, Will circulated through the visitors and showed them the proper way to interact with the rays. Meredith followed and participated, but she wasn't as enthusiastic as she had been all summer.

Her thoughts were preoccupied with Hailey. They weren't any closer to finding her, and with each additional day, she could be further and further away. Meredith stared at the rays circling the tank, ultimately going nowhere, and she began to wonder if Jill was right about her. Maybe she was more concerned with her internship and career goals than her friends.

"Why so down, Nerd-Girl?" asked Brittany, after snapping her chewing gum. "Bummed that you can't be teacher's pet when the teacher's away?"

Meredith wasn't in the mood to listen to her, so she squeezed through the crowd over to a mother whose young daughter clung to her, too afraid to reach into the tank or even look at it.

"I doubt he'll be here tomorrow too," called Brittany. "He's a busy man now."

Will approached and looked down at Brittany. "Wow, you don't know when to leave things alone, do you?"

"Standing up for your girlfriend? Very sweet. Didn't know you had it in you." Brittany chuckled as she watched Will's face flush. "Since Hatcher's not coming, there's no point in me staying here." She took a step away but turned back and cocked her head toward Meredith. "She'd probably be interested to know that Hatcher's made a big discovery. He's got himself a new pet to study, and I saw it before anyone else. The little girl in her would *definitely* want to see it."

She turned on her heel and walked away.

The crowd of people dispersed enough for Meredith to make her way back to Will and thank him.

"You didn't hear what she said, right?" asked Will, still somewhat red.

Calling me your girlfriend? she thought, letting a smile make its way onto her face. "No, not really."

"Oh, wow," he stammered. "Well, she thinks you'd want to know that Dr. Hatcher discovered some new sea creature that no one's ever seen. Oh, and she saw it before you."

At first, Meredith shook off Brittany's obvious attempt to one-up her, but when she thought further about the comment—*some new sea creature?*—her eyes bulged. She pushed Will away from the crowd until his back was against one of the posts holding up the tent. Poking his chest, she asked, "Did she say what he found?"

His pink cheeks blushed deeper as he slouched and tried

to hide his head like a turtle. "No, just that you'd definitely want to see."

Hailey? Meredith's heart raced as she considered the possibility. Instead of taking pictures of a mermaid to post online, the next sensible—the most humane—course of action would be to call an aquarium. If only she and Jill hadn't been so caught up in their unnecessary fight, she might have thought to investigate right in her own backyard. But none of it mattered until she could confirm it was true.

"Thanks so much, Will." Standing on her toes, she leaned forward and kissed him on the cheek.

She dashed out of the tent and toward the main concourse. She looked around to find Brittany, who had vanished somewhere like she usually did. Groaning and letting her arms fall to her side, Meredith couldn't understand how Brittany seemed to know how to get around the aquarium without being seen.

But she didn't need Brittany's help. If Dr. Hatcher had somehow obtained Hailey for study, the only logical place to keep her was the observation and rehabilitation complex. She sprung forward and into the main gallery, weaving her way through a maze of slow-moving families with easily distracted children. She had to brake and change direction abruptly whenever people in front of her stopped suddenly, but she kept moving until she was outside at the back of the building.

Fewer visitors milled about, so she sprinted through the aquarium grounds, her open lab coat billowing behind her. She stopped at the path to the complex and hunched over with her hands on her thighs as she caught her breath.

The sign on the gate warned that only authorized personnel were allowed to enter. She scanned the area; only a few scattered groups of people passed, heading to or from the outdoor seal and sea lion exhibits. The unlocked gate was nothing more than a narrow right triangle of yellow pipe that swung open and closed, but it served as enough of a deterrent to visitors. Standing up straight, she pulled on the lapels of her lab coat—her self-approved authorization—and pushed through the squeaky gate.

Jogging forward, she passed the first tank, which had the open top, and stopped at the tank behind it. If they had Hailey—or any mer, for that matter—they'd want to study her in the most secure facility on site. She just needed to get inside to make sure before informing the others.

She went to the examination building between the tanks and tried the door. It was locked, and she didn't have a key card to get inside. She held up her fist to knock but took some deep breaths to calm herself first. A few short taps would sound less desperate than a longer series of rapid beats.

A marine biologist opened the door wide enough to stick out her head. Meredith recognized the woman by her tightly wound bun of auburn hair.

"Sorry, but Dr. Hatcher has a hectic schedule today," said the woman. "He should have left you an assignment."

"He did," said Meredith, trying not to appear too petulant. "But I wasn't feeling well yesterday, and I wanted to know what I missed."

"Please send him an email. When he has a free moment, I'm sure he'll get back to you." She shut the door before she finished speaking.

The way the woman kept the door mostly closed. The distinct tone of annoyance in her voice. The quick brush-off. They were more than enough pieces of evidence to suggest that they had something unique inside. All she needed to do was find out if it was Hailey.

Meredith walked around the second tank until she was out of view of the main walkways and examination building. There was no longer a path, only gravel surrounding the structure. She stepped close enough to the tank to touch it. Cold, but that was normal heat conduction from her hand to the metal. She was hoping for a feeling, something extrasensory, that Marina's tail was inside. Stretching her arms out as wide as possible, Meredith leaned forward and pressed her cheek against the curved surface. She closed her eyes and concentrated.

There wasn't any wind. Even the birds momentarily stopped chirping, as if something magical had lowered their volume. Meredith felt relaxed, but as much as she willed herself to perceive beyond the thick wall, she sensed nothing. *Maybe it only works in water*, she rationalized without trying to get too discouraged.

"Hugging the building? What's wrong, Blushy-Boy not good enough for you now?"

Brittany. Meredith's eyes popped open, and she wondered how long she had been watched.

"It's okay, don't let me interrupt you." Brittany stepped forward slowly, her footsteps crunching the gravel in time with her mouth munching on her gum. "Unless you have x-ray vision or something, you're not gonna find out what's inside that way."

Gulping, Meredith lowered her arms, turned around, and took a step toward her. "How did you find out what's inside? I doubt you even know what's in there."

"I have my ways, and I can't wait to see the look on your face when you find out what it is." Brittany unfolded a piece of paper and handed it to Meredith.

The image was gray and grainy—a bad printout of a poor photograph—but the silhouette swimming in the water was unmistakably that of a dark-haired mermaid. Holding the paper so tightly that it started to crinkle, Meredith staggered back until she hit the wall of the tank, which clanged loudly. She couldn't be sure from the overhead view of the mer's back if it was Hailey, but Dr. Hatcher and other marine biologists at the aquarium had proof that mermaids existed. Before long, the whole world would know. The entire school was in grave danger, and she had to do something to help them.

"Its tail is bright orange." Brittany snickered. "Just like the little one on your desk."

There's only one orange-tailed mermaid, thought Meredith as she broke into a sprint. She had to contact the others and tell them where Hailey was, but she couldn't in front of Brittany. Given the friction between them, Meredith would have preferred to avoid speaking to Jill and send a text message instead, but she couldn't while running.

The phone call went straight to voicemail. Groaning, Meredith stopped at the gate and whispered her message, "Hailey's here at the aquarium. Call me back."

Brittany tapped her on the shoulder and snatched back the paper when Meredith turned. "You steal my picture, run away, and make a phone call. Suspicious. Almost like you're planning something."

"This doesn't concern you, Brittany."

As Meredith took hold of the gate to swing it open, Brittany pushed it the other way and said, "It concerns me now. I never thought you were one of those save-the-whales kind of girls. I figured you'd be begging Dr. Hatcher to help him study it."

Meredith's bottom lip quivered, and she squeezed her eyes closed. "You mean *her*," she whimpered.

Brittany grinned then laughed, and Meredith keeled forward, supporting herself with both arms on the gate's crossbar. A few visitors passed by, and Brittany gave them a feeble wave until they were out of view.

"It's pretty obvious that you don't like seeing *her* in captivity." Brittany put extra patronizing emphasis on her pronouns. "I think a part of you wants to break *it* out."

Tears fell from Meredith's eyes. "You don't understand how much bigger than the two of us this is."

"I don't think you fully understand that you'd much rather have me on your side than against you. My father's on the board of directors of this stupid place. Do you want me ratting you out for trying to rescue his precious new fish-girl?" Brittany walked around the gate and leaned forward, mirroring Meredith's pose. "I doubt it. I know how to get around here unnoticed, even after closing time. So if you really are planning on setting her free, I want in."

~ Chapter Twenty-Nine ~

"Are you sure she can be trusted?" asked Marina. "I have seen the way she behaves toward others. I would not trust her."

Meredith shrugged and said, "She knows her way around the aquarium, including the underground tunnels between the buildings."

Leaning against the desk in Meredith's dorm room, Jill scoffed, "And you believe her?"

"Her father's on the aquarium's board of directors. She's been coming here since she was little, and she's sick of it. She didn't want to do the internship in the first place, but he made her, presumably to keep an eye on her."

"So this is her way of sticking it to her father?" Jill folded her arms and shook her head. "All the more reason *not* to trust her. The minute things go wrong, she turns us in."

"She may turn us in if we do anything *without* her. We don't have many other options. At least we know where Hailey is."

"Face it. We got lucky that she ended up at the aquarium."

Sitting beside Marina on the bed, Lorelei asked, "Is Hailey safe…there?"

Marina replied, "The fish I have watched in this aquarium appear well protected, though they are confined. I do not like it. They and Hailey deserve to be free."

"Yeah, but those are fish they know about." Jill flung her arms around as she spoke. "As far as we know, this is the first mermaid scientists have ever seen. What if they decide to *dissect* her?"

"Stop being so dramatic." Meredith reached up to put her hand on Jill's shoulder. "Dr. Hatcher's not going to do that. At least I don't think he'd do that to the *only* mer they have." She felt chills from Jill's icy stare down at her, so she withdrew her hand and turned away to see Marina and Lorelei leaning forward with their mouths dropped open in fear.

"We cannot let that happen." Marina stood. "How do we get her out?"

"First, I've got to get in." Meredith held a hand out toward Jill, hoping to stop her from rolling her eyes disapprovingly. "I'm going to persuade Dr. Hatcher to let me see her."

The next day, Meredith sent Dr. Hatcher three emails and came looking for him twice at the observation and rehabilitation complex. At the end of her scheduled day, she skipped the shuttle bus to stay in the aquarium and wait outside the tanks. As time dragged, she fidgeted, tying and retying her ponytail tightly to keep it from frizzing near her face. Even in the evening shade, the air was hot and humid.

When he finally came out, his body looked exhausted, but his eyes were bright and full of life. "I'm sorry that I've been absent the past few days, but we've made a remarkable, potentially world-changing discovery." He gave her a sheepish grin. "I wish I could tell you more, Meredith, but it's top secret until we have complete confirmation that—"

"I know what you've got in there." Meredith breathed quickly and nervously while she watched Dr. Hatcher's expression change from wide-eyed wonder to cocked-eyebrow concern. "Brittany showed me a picture."

He tightened his gaze on her, and her throat went dry. She feared that mentioning Brittany would complicate matters on all fronts, but she had to say something. Implicating Brittany was both a truthful and plausible excuse.

Sighing in contempt, Dr. Hatcher shook his head and said, "I told her father she wasn't qualified for the program and that I didn't want to babysit. I'm sorry she dragged you into this, but please tell me you haven't told anyone else."

Beads of perspiration clung to Meredith's hairline. She

wiped them away, hoping he'd conclude they were from the heat and not the lie she was about to tell. "No one else," she said in a monotone, and though she knew the answer to her next question, she posed it as inquisitively as possible. "Is she real?"

His face beamed, glowing in the sun rays that pierced through the trees. "She's real, and she's absolutely amazing. If I weren't seeing her with my own eyes, I would never have believed she could even exist."

Under different circumstances, Meredith would have enjoyed Dr. Hatcher's childlike enthusiasm, but all she could think about was persuading him to let her see Hailey. She clasped her hands behind her back and stood on her toes. "Is there any chance I could—?"

"See her? Meredith, I have no doubt you're going to be an exceptional marine biologist, but this is beyond what the aquarium allows student interns to experience."

"I understand that, Dr. Hatcher, but imagine the long-term opportunities it will open up when I apply for grad school or a job." She hated what she was saying, for it sounded like she was selling out a friend to advance her career.

Meredith watched his chin move from left to right as he contemplated the request. "Unfortunately, I have to keep the aquarium's interests in mind as well. She may be the greatest single aquatic discovery of this century, and we don't want information to leak out before confirming—"

"You don't have to worry about that with me. I'm not the one who's leaking information." Meredith gulped, worried that calling out Brittany would jeopardize a potential and necessary alliance with her.

He sighed and shook his head. Then with a grin, he whispered, "Be at the front gates tomorrow morning an hour earlier than usual. No one but you. Understood?"

Barely getting any sleep that night, Meredith awoke the next morning at the crack of dawn. Dr. Hatcher met her at the front gates, and they walked briskly but silently through the main gallery. The aquarium staff wasn't there yet, and Meredith couldn't shake the eerie feeling that all the fish were watching her.

When they got to the complex, Dr. Hatcher rushed her inside and said, "The rest of the team would disagree with what I'm about to ask you, but they haven't seen your progress. We could use your assistance."

Meredith stared dumbfounded at him. She didn't want to think like a marine biologist; she was on a reconnaissance mission, using his good nature to gain access to Hailey.

"We're trying to communicate with her, but she's not responsive. Our X-rays, CT scans, and ultrasounds show that her voice box—her whole body above the pelvis—is anatomically identical to humans, except for what look like gill slits in her trachea. It's amazing how it appears she can breathe underwater!"

Scientific questions that Meredith had wondered the previous year resurfaced, but she didn't want the answers. Mers were people too, even if their lower anatomy wasn't human, so they didn't belong in the aquarium with other animals. "What do you need me to do?" she asked, trying to mask her impatience with a tone of curiosity.

"I apologize. The more we learn about her, the more it redefines our understanding of human and marine evolution." Dr. Hatcher took a breath to control his scientific giddiness. "We have no way of knowing the lifespan of her species, but from all outward appearances, we estimate that she's about your age. Maybe she'll trust or understand you more than the adults."

Meredith sighed in relief, grateful that he was willingly giving her what she wanted.

Before long, she was wearing her swimsuit and holding the snorkeling gear. Once Dr. Hatcher unlocked and opened the squeaky door to the tank, there was a loud splash. Both startled and excited, Meredith ran out onto the deck.

The mermaid vigorously flapped her fluke, creating waves that distorted their view of her. She reached the far end of the tank quickly and lifted her head above the surface. She slicked back her hair while treading water with her back to them.

Meredith instantly identified the dark hair as Hailey's and the orange tail as Marina's. As she recalled fond memories of her temporary mermaid experience, she grinned at how natural Hailey appeared and behaved. She resisted calling out to her—to say hello and to calm her down—and instead let Dr. Hatcher speak first.

"Don't be afraid." His tone was gentle. "We're not here to harm you. I've brought someone I'd like you to meet. Her name is Meredith."

Hailey flicked her tail to turn around slowly, and upon seeing Meredith, her face brightened. Dr. Hatcher crouched down, reaching forward and beckoning her to come closer. Meredith held her finger to her lips, hoping Hailey wouldn't respond like her usual excitable self. Without asking permission, Meredith sat to put her feet in the water and then leaned forward to dive in.

She stopped in the middle of the tank, and Hailey swam toward her. Once they were face to face, Hailey whispered, "What are you doing here?"

"Did she just say something?" Dr. Hatcher jumped up. "What did she say?"

Looking back over her shoulder, Meredith answered, "She wants to know…wants to know what *she's* doing here."

"That's the first time she's spoken since we brought her here!"

Though Meredith had some difficulty imagining Hailey being quiet for so long, she was relieved Dr. Hatcher believed her improv. "You wanted me to communicate with her, right? Just doing what you asked me to."

Dr. Hatcher fumbled with the pockets of his lab coat and took out his phone. "I should be getting video of this!"

Meredith groaned and turned back to Hailey. With Dr. Hatcher recording, she had to speak carefully. "I'm sure you're confused. There's nothing wrong with that."

Hailey nodded. "I do not want to be here. The

examinations they have done are scary. I want to go home."

No contractions. Hailey was becoming more mer-like, just like Meredith had the previous summer. Maybe spending so much time without talking to anyone had triggered the shift in her speech.

Meredith shook her head. She couldn't think like a scientist. She had to save Hailey by giving her some cryptic information about an escape plan they hadn't fully developed. She looked up at the high domed ceiling, where a security camera at the top pointed straight down—probably the one that recorded the image Brittany had given her. There were several fluorescent lights around the blue walls so an escape attempt would be caught on camera. Hopefully, Brittany knew how to darken the place.

Dark? Night. She associated ideas and words in her mind. *Moon!*

"It must be very different than home in here. You can't see the night sky."

Hailey looked up then cocked her head to the side and squinted. "What?"

"The stars and the moon. In a few more days, the moon will be full."

"A full moon?" Hailey's eyes opened, and her smile widened. "When is the full moon?"

"Four nights from tonight. I hope you get to see it."

Dr. Hatcher shouted, "This is incredible! She can understand us! I don't know how you're doing this, Meredith, but this aquarium—heck, the whole field of marine biology—should recognize your contribution."

Meredith drifted toward Dr. Hatcher as he praised her, but Hailey lunged forward and pulled her back.

"I must tell you something," said Hailey. "Coral is near where they caught me."

"Did she say a coral reef is in the area?" asked Dr. Hatcher. "It's not impossible, but it's unlikely for one to develop so far north."

Hailey shook her head and grabbed hold of Meredith's

hand. "Oh. My. Gosh. Coral is near the boat that caught me. *Coral*."

Meredith repeated the word and then realized it was a name. One of their problems was solved, and she wished she could react accordingly without looking suspicious.

"But I do not know where that is." Hailey frowned.

"It's okay. I understand you miss your home, but *we're* going to take care of you." Talking in code again, Meredith hoped Hailey understood that *we're* meant she, Jill, Marina, and Lorelei.

Without letting go of Meredith, Hailey leaned to the side and started swimming, taking Meredith with her. "If I did not end up here, I would have wanted to be like this forever."

Meredith doubted Dr. Hatcher could hear them over the splashing water, but she didn't respond to Hailey's dream desire. A part of her agreed. Becoming a scientist was ethically complex, and she wished sometimes she could just let things float.

After a few laps, Hailey brought Meredith back to the deck. Dr. Hatcher crouched down and thanked Hailey, but she dove under the surface and swam swiftly across the tank. He extended an arm to help Meredith out of the tank and was still shaking her hand and congratulating her when she stood. Waving his phone, he said, "I'm going to show this to the rest of the team. You communicated with her, and she trusted you enough to swim beside her. You made breakthroughs we couldn't—breakthroughs we only dreamed of. I'm going to recommend we allow you to shadow our research."

Meredith reached for her towel. "That would be such an honor. Thank you." She knew she was saying it mostly to be polite, but if it meant keeping an eye on what they were doing to Hailey, she'd agree to it. "But I need to know where she was found."

"Wondering if there are more, aren't you?" Dr. Hatcher walked through the doorway and waited until Meredith had followed before speaking further. "So have we. If we had a few more, think of what we could learn…"

While he kept talking and walking to a nearby examination table, Meredith froze. She shivered, but clutching the towel tighter around her body didn't stop her fearful trembling. Meredith couldn't let them find the other mers, and she had to get Hailey out, but the best chance of escape was the full moon almost a week away.

Unless there was a way to get her out sooner.

Meredith rushed to the examination table where Dr. Hatcher was looking over his research on Hailey. Staring across the table at him, she said, "Could you put a tracking device on her tail, like you did to the manatee?" She hated the idea of using Hailey as bait, but if she could tell Hailey to avoid the school and wait it out alone until the full moon, no breakout would be necessary. Hailey could shed the tail and tracker that morning, and she and the school would be safe.

Dr. Hatcher smiled. "I like how you're planning ahead. We discussed that possibility, but we don't want to lose the only one we have. And the directors would love to have her on display before the end of the summer." He shook his head in disapproval. "For them, it's all about attracting more visitors and making more money. They've probably already planned marketing and merchandising strategies."

"No!" Meredith composed herself after the outburst. "She wants to go home. If there are more, she'll lead you right to them."

"She's obviously intelligent and far more flexible than the manatee. With opposable thumbs and arms instead of flippers, she could easily take it off." He looked down at the papers laid out on the table. "We haven't done it yet, but any tracking device on her would have to be something she couldn't remove, something surgically implanted."

Meredith stumbled back. An implanted tracker would either stay in Hailey after the full moon, or it would permanently stay in Marina's tail and lead the scientists to the school.

~ Chapter Thirty ~

Right before the aquarium's closing time on the night before the full moon, Jill and Meredith sneaked Marina and Lorelei into a small electrical control room Brittany had left unlocked for them. The sparsely populated area outside the room wasn't covered by security cameras, and it was unlikely that the maintenance staff would enter.

Jill had already changed from her mascot costume into a black hoodie and leggings, and Meredith gave similar clothes to the others. Watching them stretch the fabric and squirm as it hugged their legs, Jill couldn't contain her laughter. Meredith glared at her, so she went out into the corridor, lugging her heavy duffle bag back with her.

"This feels like a second skin," said Marina.

Lorelei shrugged. "I suppose I will have to get accustomed to coverings made for separate legs."

"Once we get Marina's tail back, we'll work on restoring yours." Meredith unzipped her backpack and placed it on the floor. "Put your old clothes in here, underneath the towels. I'm going outside to talk to her."

Leaning by an emergency exit, Jill was convulsing with giggles, covering her mouth with one hand and clutching her stomach with her other arm. "Sometimes, they're way too funny. Like fish out of water!" She slapped her thigh.

"Shouldn't you be more worried about Hailey instead of making jokes?"

Jill's demeanor suddenly changed, and she straightened her tall form and looked down at Meredith. "I'm trying to keep positive and loose. Do you know how much is riding on this?"

"Of course, I do. Why else would I risk my position here—?"

Jill rolled her eyes. "Always back to you, isn't it? We can't blow this tonight."

"We're not going to. We've got all the bases covered. Our phone alarms are synchronized and set. Brittany knows what areas don't have cameras and how to kill the lights in the areas that do."

"I still don't trust her."

"We need her help to get around undetected, so if you don't trust her, then do you really trust me?" Meredith watched Jill cross her arms and scowl at her. "I guess I know the answer to that. So where does that leave us? What do we do now?"

"I'm sorry, but there's only one way to solve this problem." Jill pushed open the door and shoved Meredith outside.

Meredith stumbled forward, regaining her balance without crash-landing on the pavement. Before she could turn herself around, she heard the gray door click shut. Even if the door had a handle, it led to an area of the aquarium where patrons weren't admitted, so it would be locked.

"Jill, let me in!" She pounded on the door until her fists were red. "This isn't funny!"

When there was no answer, she pulled her phone from her pocket to call Jill, but it went directly to voice mail. In the middle of leaving a message, there was an incoming text.

For your own good. Can't jeopardize your internship.

Under normal circumstances, Meredith knew not to impose emotional states on text messages, but she was irritated and assumed Jill was being angry and snarky. She huffed and stomped toward the main entrance, which was already closed to the public.

Turning a corner, she ran into someone. Before she was knocked backward, a pair of arms reached around her to stop her from falling. She looked up and found Will's ocean blue eyes staring back at her.

They held their poses for a moment, and his face flushed. He made sure she was standing steadily before letting her go, and then he immediately hid his hands behind his back. "Wow, Meredith, didn't see you there." He nervously rocked back and forth. "I hope you're alright."

"I've got to get back inside," she said, scrambling toward the main entrance.

Will followed. "Your friend told me to meet you here. She said you were interested in maybe going out for pizza. There's this place about a mile up the road they say is world famous."

"My friend?" Meredith reached for her phone to call Jill and shook her head upon reading another text from her.

We'll be fine. I'll keep you posted. Relax and enjoy a "date" for once.

"Pizza?" she asked, trying not to let her combined frustration and relief at Jill's performance taint her tone. When Will nodded eagerly but shyly, she sighed and smirked. "You won't think I'm weird if I want mine with anchovies, right?"

"*Engraulis encrasicolus*?" He scrunched up his face. "Wow. On your half of the pie, I guess."

The restaurant was crowded, so they sat at a counter by the front window. Meredith nibbled on her slice while anxiously clutching her phone and avoiding Will's gaze.

"I've eaten three pieces while you've taken three bites." Will wiped tomato sauce off his mouth. "What's wrong?"

Meredith didn't answer. She tapped the screen of her phone, trying to will it to show her a text message.

"This isn't because of the other day, is it? Because you haven't said much to me since you…since you…kissed me." He turned away as she turned to him. "I know it was only on the cheek, and that doesn't mean as much as, wow, on the lips, but did I do something wrong?"

She dropped her phone onto the counter. "No, Will, don't think that way. I've been busy with a lot on my mind. You're sweet, and I kissed you because you helped me figure something out and because I wanted to." She took hold of his hand. "Because I like you."

"Wow!" His head bobbed up and down as his eyes and mouth opened widely in surprise. "Okay. That's…that's great. So you've just been preoccupied. It was weird because you're usually so focused on the internship."

Meredith lowered her head to glance at her phone. "Have you wondered if we're doing the right thing? I've spent the past year dreaming of this career. All I wanted to do was protect life in the ocean. Is that what we're doing at the aquarium?" She extended one arm in one direction, and then she swung the other in the opposite and raised and lowered them like she was balancing two weights. "Or are we removing life from the ocean and using science to justify it?"

"We're doing both, I guess." He waited while she let out an exasperated sigh. "This is only a first step. Your career, your dreams, they're still ahead of you. You can work wherever you want. You can approach the career however you want. You don't have to work in an aquarium."

"Do you want to work in a place that…that does what it does?" She wanted to ask him if the aquarium had the right to keep a mermaid in its possession without consent, but she knew she couldn't. "Are the marine biologists right?"

"Wow, that's a tricky question, and I don't really have an answer. All I know is that I came here wanting to study whales. Haven't had that chance yet, but I met you. I see what you can do, and wow, I want to be at least that good."

Meredith grinned, but when she thought about her superpowers, the grin sank. "But what I do isn't natural."

"You're right, it isn't," he said. "It's extraordinary."

He leaned forward and kissed her. As restless as she was about her career choice and Hailey's breakout plan, she let herself savor Will's soft, gentle lips against hers. As she felt herself relaxing, she uttered a breathless, "Wow."

~ ~ ~

"Why did you throw her back?" asked Marina when Jill had returned to the electrical control room. "She helped create our plan. Will we not need her? Is she no longer your best friend?"

"Even though we've kinda been at each other's throats lately, she'll always be my best friend." Jill sat on the floor, bending her knees up to her chest. "That's why I can't let her do this. It could ruin her chances to follow her dream."

Lorelei said, "You are a loyal friend, Jill. It is nice to know Meredith has someone like you protecting her."

Marina immediately crossed to the far corner of the room, keeping her back to the others. Like Jill had always watched out for Meredith, Lorelei had always watched out for her. How could she deserve such unconditional support when her family had hurt Lorelei so badly?

She felt warmth on her shoulder. "Is something bothering you?" asked Lorelei.

Sniffling, Marina turned around to see Lorelei's comforting grin, which only made her look away again.

Lorelei said, "Jill, may Marina and I speak alone for a moment?"

Jill shrugged and flicked her wrists in circles. "Nowhere else I can go right now. I'll tune you two out best I can, but that's about it." She took her headphones out of her pocket and plugged them into her phone to listen to some music.

Slowly turning Marina around, Lorelei said, "I have known you long enough to know something has sunk you down."

"I should have told you sooner. Please know that I withheld it only to protect you." Marina's voice wavered. "I recently learned that my father may have been responsible for your mother's death."

Lorelei stepped back and stared at her for a moment. Other than the faint music emanating from Jill's headphones, there wasn't any sound. Then tears streamed from Lorelei's eyes.

"I am truly sorry, Lore. And I feel guilty being out here looking for my mother while you…" She reached for her friend's hands, but Lorelei kept them clasped together in front of her stomach. "If I must stay on land longer to find her, you may wear my tail. I know it cannot make up for your loss, but—"

"You know I cannot wear your tail. It is forbidden. If I were to return to the school with an orange tail instead of my scouting green, I would instantly be banished."

"I hope you can forgive me."

"Forgiveness is not necessary because you have no need to apologize. Even if what you say is true, *you* did not do anything to my mother. You are and always will be my dearest friend."

They embraced, and when Jill noticed, she rolled her eyes and turned her volume up.

The door opened, startling all three of them. Lorelei and Marina separated while Jill sprung into a ninja-like pose. Brittany, also dressed completely in black, slinked in and closed the door behind her. "All right, time to move." She reached for Jill's duffle bag to sling it over her back, but it had more weight than she expected, throwing her off balance. "What the heck do you have in there, Mascot-Girl? A baby sea lion?"

Jill wrenched the bag out of her grip. "Back-up plan. Now let's move."

Throughout the night, they relocated several times, gradually getting closer to the observation complex. After casing the place for a few days, Brittany was exceptionally adept at avoiding cameras and the night security guard. She kept them in the dark shadows with their hoods drawn while creeping through the underground tunnel system. She knew the locations of storage closets, staff bathrooms, and other empty spaces—all of which were left unlocked because they were only utilized by the maintenance staff and weren't high-security areas. Lorelei and Marina occasionally dozed off, but Jill had packed a thermos of coffee—and found more in a break room—and Brittany didn't seem to want sleep.

Meredith promptly texted every hour for status reports. Jill kept her responses short, only because she wanted to apologize later in person for her act. A part of her felt terrible for deceiving her best friend, but Jill didn't want Meredith to be implicated in what they were doing.

Shortly before sunrise, Brittany entered the low-ceilinged passage connecting the two observation tanks. On the narrow walkway alongside the canal, she slid flatly against the wall, staying out of the camera's view until she was directly beneath it. She took a few final chews of her gum before spitting the pink wad into her palm, and then she stretched it over the plastic shield in front of the lens.

"I don't know how long we've got before they notice," whispered Brittany as she returned to the others. "We should've done this at night, but you guys insisted on sunrise."

The three of them made their way into the passage to join Brittany, who jumped into the shallow water to unlatch the gate.

Upon hearing the splash in the canal, Hailey swam toward the gate. Her face exploded into a smile when she saw them. "Oh. My. Gosh. I am so happy to see you all! Lorelei, what are you doing out here? Did you come to help save me? That is so sweet of you!" She reached through the gate and beckoned with both hands for someone to come to her.

Jill shooed her away. "We'll hug it out it later. Just get out of the water and dry yourself off."

"Wait, a minute!" said Brittany. "You *know* her? What the heck is going on here?"

Jill removed a beach towel from the backpack and tossed it over the gate and onto the deck. "And cover up while you're…well, you know."

"But *she* will see what happens." Hailey cocked her head at Brittany. "She should not learn the secret."

"She already knows mermaids exist, Hailey. She can see you." Jill checked the incoming text on her phone. "That's Merri telling us it's two minutes till sunrise. Now get on the deck and stop speaking like a mer!"

Hailey swam to the side of the tank and heaved her dripping tail out of the water. As she sat on the deck, her fluke flopped loudly on the concrete surface. She bent forward, repeatedly pushing the towel down her tail from her waist, but not the other way or she'd painfully snag the fabric on her scales.

Brittany pushed the gate shut to keep it latched and held up her soaked phone. "If someone doesn't tell me what's going on right now, I'm calling my father and turning you all in."

Marina jumped into the water beside her. "You have helped us, so you have proven yourself worthy of knowing the truth. Our friend Hailey is wearing my tail. I am the true mer."

"Mer?" asked Brittany. "Is that shorthand for mermaid? Oh, that's lame. And so is your whole tail-switching story."

Jill and Brittany's phone alarms rang in sync. "Sunrise," announced Jill.

Lorelei joined Marina at the gate and gestured toward Hailey. "If you watch, you will see that it is true."

Hailey closed her eyes, waiting for the pleasant tingles she felt when her legs first transformed into a tail, but she felt no such sensation. Opening her eyes, she stared at the glistening orange scales and waited for them to disappear, but they remained.

Figuring she wasn't dry enough, she wiped herself off more quickly. More vigorously. More frantically. But still, nothing happened.

"Uh, guys? Nine-one-one here." Her body trembled as her voice filled with panic. "Why am I not changing back?"

~ Chapter Thirty-One ~

"Come on. Please come off." Hailey furiously scrubbed her tail. Her fluke smacked loudly on the deck whenever she felt the occasional pain of the towel bending a scale the wrong way. "I want to be an aquarium mermaid but not like this."

"Calm down, Hailey," called Jill from the passageway. She turned to Marina and Lorelei. "One of you two better tell her how to change back!"

Brittany shouted, "One of you *four* better tell me what's going on here, or I call my father!"

Marina held her hand up to Brittany. "If you please let us figure out what is wrong, then you will witness something you have never seen before."

"Five minutes," grumbled Brittany. "That's all I'm giving you."

"I do not understand what is wrong," said Lorelei. "The sun has risen, and she is out of the water. She does not need to be fully dry. That must be a myth your people have created. I have transformed many times, and it always happens as soon as I am out of the water."

"Then what's missing? Let's think logically." Jill rolled her eyes at the notion of applying logic to a mermaid's tail turning back into a skirt. She tapped her temple, trying to activate her overtired brain, but the thought to which she kept returning was that Meredith would know what to do.

Her phone buzzed with a text message: *Status report?*

Jill didn't hesitate to call. "She's not changing back, Merri. What do we do?"

"She's out of the water, right?" asked Meredith.

"Yes."

"Is she dry?"

"Apparently not necessary."

"Interesting." Meredith paused to ponder. "It's after sunrise, so we've got the timing right. Unless she actually needs to be in the sunlight."

Both tanks were brighter than the dimly lit passageway, but the quality of the light was different. Hailey's tank was flooded with an artificial white glow, while the empty tank on the other side was paler, more natural.

Jill put her phone on speaker and turned to Lorelei and Marina. "You need the sun, don't you?"

"I have only shed my tail on a beach," said Lorelei. "And the sun was always visible."

"Get her to the other tank!" Meredith's voice sounded metallic as it crackled through the phone's speaker.

Jill said, "Hate to break it to you, Merri, but we won't see the sunrise there either. The walls are too high, and—"

"Your plan stinks," barked Brittany, holding the gate closed to prevent Marina and Lorelei from opening it. "I knew we should've done this at night."

"Someone tell me what to do!" called Hailey. "I am freaking out here!"

"Quiet!" The shrill screech came from the phone, and everyone turned to it. Then Meredith explained, "As long as she can see the *sky* from the other tank, she'll be seeing light from the sun that the atmosphere scattered. Blue light scatters the most, and hence, the sky is blue."

Brittany said, "I thought the sky was blue because it reflected the ocean."

"No, it's the other way around," said Jill. "The ocean's blue because it reflects the sky."

Meredith groaned. "It's neither. You seriously should take a physics class sometime."

"Then why is it red at sunrise?" asked Lorelei, genuinely curious.

"Same principle, different geometry. The blue is scattered

away, so the red—"

"Enough with the science lesson!" Brittany pointed at the wad of gum covering the camera and then at Hailey. "They're probably not watching us in here, but they're watching her out there. If I let her into the other tank, security will figure things out."

Marina said, "Please trust us. If you allow her to transform, she can walk out on her own."

Brittany stood in the shoulder-deep water but held onto the gate to keep herself steady. She spent a moment fixated on Marina's blue eyes and her soothing voice asking once again to be trusted. As if in a trance, she unlatched the gate. Then, shaking her head, she said, "If we end up getting caught, this better be worth it."

When the gate squeaked open, Hailey dove into the water and propelled herself toward the others. The water inside the narrow passageway was shallow, no more than five feet deep, but more than enough for her to swim beneath the surface. She kept her hands by her side as she passed between Brittany and Marina on her right, and Lorelei on her left, while Jill stood on the walkway.

Marina smiled. "I knew she would make an exceptional mer."

"Hailey flows," said Lorelei, looking up from Hailey to Marina. "But no mer inhabits that tail better than you do."

Jill rolled her eyes. "Are all mers this corny?"

"So what if they are?" asked Meredith through the phone. "What's going on there?"

Before Jill could answer, her phone signaled an incoming call. She put Meredith on hold to say good morning to her Aunt Susan.

"You'd better have an explanation, Jillybean," said Susan. "This is the morning you and that fish-girl—whatever her name was—promised me Hailey would be back."

"We've got her here. Everything's good," said Jill, imagining a skeptical look on her aunt's face.

Hailey reached the gate and pulled her head above the

water's surface. "I am fine, Mom!"

"I was woken up at the crack of dawn by someone knocking at the back door and looking for you. I hope you have a good explanation why…" Susan's voice got quieter. "Why he wasn't wearing any clothes."

"Mom!" Hailey's face turned red as her tail flipped. "Too. Much. Information!"

Jill took the phone off speaker and handed it to Hailey, who said hello and then heard the most unexpected but most welcoming voice she could imagine.

"Is that you, Hailey?" he asked. "Are you inside this glowing little box? How did you get in there? It is very thin."

"Barney! You are out of the water! I am so proud of you."

"It is scary. But it also flows. Your mother gave me some clothes. Is that what they are called? They feel strange. Lorelei told me I had to come here. In case you were in danger. Are you safe? Is Lore safe?"

"Everything is fine, and she is here. Tell my mother to take care of you."

"I must return tonight. Ray wants to relocate the school, but Finn convinced him to stay at least through moonrise."

"Please do not leave until I see you later today."

"There won't be a later if we don't get on with it!" Brittany made her way across the canal and unlatched the other gate.

Hailey tossed the phone to Jill and then swam through the open gate. The little bit of sky visible above the tank walls and below the canopy was turning from orange to blue. Hoping it would be enough light, she pulled herself onto the deck. As soon as the tips of her fluke left the water, her tail started feeling tingly, and she rolled into a seated position.

"Something is happening," she squealed, clapping her hands. She had tried to flap her tail on the deck, but it had gone numb and wouldn't cooperate.

Jill grabbed another towel and the bottom half of a bathing suit from the backpack. Before she could toss them toward Hailey, Brittany took them and swam through the open gate.

Hailey had expected the transformation to be painful like Meredith's the previous summer, but it was a smooth and pleasant caress like someone was slathering sunscreen up her legs. She figured since Meredith had changed at the wrong time of a cycle—the new moon—while she was changing at the right time, the experience would be different. Whatever the reason, she was happy that she'd be able to escape from captivity, but she was equally sad that her month as a mermaid was over.

Brittany's jaw dropped when she made it to Hailey. The orange fluke had separated into two pinkish halves that were rearranging into two feet, each with five toes inflating like little balloons. She climbed out of the water and stood at Hailey's feet, using the towel to shield the transformation from being caught on the security camera.

"Thank you for keeping this private," said Hailey, as more scales disappeared to reveal her knees.

"Can you walk yet?" called Jill from the passageway.

"The change takes some time," said Lorelei, peering through the open gateway. "She appears halfway done."

Hailey pushed down on the deck and was able to raise her backside, but her not-fully-formed legs were paralyzed. Then her thighs reappeared, and Hailey felt the frayed end of the beach towel suddenly tickle her toes. "Laughing Out Loud! I feel feet!"

She tried to lift herself again and was able to pivot her ankles enough to plant her feet firmly on the deck. Unable to bend her knees, she leaned too far forward, but Brittany broke her fall and stood her up straightly.

"Almost there." Hailey glanced down to see the final scales lose their pattern as they became the iridescent skirt.

It detached from her waist and slid like a swath of silk down her legs where it pooled around her feet.

"Fully me again!" Hailey grabbed the bathing suit from Brittany and almost tipped over.

"Then we've gotta go!" Jill waved her over. "The sooner we leave, the less chance we get caught."

Hailey couldn't keep her balance while she tried putting on her bathing suit. "A-S-A-P, Jill. You gotta wait till I'm decent. And I think I forgot how to use these legs."

Without warning, the gate slammed shut. Marina and Lorelei slogged through the water and tried to undo the latch, but they couldn't get it to budge.

"What is wrong?" asked Marina. "Why will this not open?"

Brittany wrapped the towel around Hailey and jumped into the water. "They can close and lock them from the examination area." She swam to the gate. "You guys have got to get out of here. My father might let me slide, but who knows what he'll have them do with you."

Marina asked, "How will we get back without you?"

"I am a scout," said Lorelei. "I watched carefully and remember the way we came."

Jill cleared her throat. "I'm not leaving without my cousin!"

"And you can't leave without Marina's tail." Hailey picked up the sparkling tail-skirt and went to the end of the deck. The gate was too far out of her reach, so she sat on the edge and eased herself into the water. Despite being an excellent swimmer, she found the task foreign without a single tail, especially while she struggled to keep the skirt above the surface. She had no idea what would happen to it if it got too wet while nobody was wearing it, and she didn't want to find out. Before her head sank, Hailey grabbed onto the gate's metal cross bars, and Marina took the skirt from her.

"Thanks so much for trusting me with it," said Hailey, reaching through the bars and embracing Marina. "I'm sorry that I ended up here and whatever mess it causes for your school, but until then, it was the best time of my life. Now go find your mom. She's wherever the aquarium found me!"

"I'm not leaving you here," said Jill.

"You've got to. It's not like they can turn me back into a mermaid now."

Suddenly remembering the duffle bag, Jill passed it to

Marina and Lorelei so they could squeeze it through the bars.

"What's this?" asked Hailey, taking the densely packed bag.

"Back-up plan." Jill held open the door leading out of the passageway until Marina and Lorelei were out of the water and out of sight. "We'll find a way to meet up later, right?"

"Sink or swim." Hailey gave a thumbs-up signal and watched Jill disappear through the exit.

Brittany peered over Hailey's shoulder and asked, "So what's inside?"

Hailey unzipped the bag and squealed upon seeing its contents.

~ Chapter Thirty-Two ~

Two security guards emerged through the door and onto the deck of the roofless tank. They stopped short at the edge upon seeing something unexpected swimming in the water. Though they had heard that the aquarium had recently obtained an extremely rare sea creature, nothing prepared them for what they were witnessing.

A young man with matted hair stumbled out behind them, almost bumping into them. "I don't know what happened. I must have dozed off." He tried to straighten his rumpled lab coat. "It's supposed to be in the other tank. I have no idea how it got in here, but when I saw that it did, I auto-locked the gates."

The dark-haired mermaid reversed direction and sputtered toward the deck from the center of the tank. She propelled herself by bending at the knees and then straightening her orange tail, all the while sweeping her arms in wide sideways movements. When she reached the deck, she pulled her head out of the water and smoothed back her slick, wet hair.

"That's not an *it!*" said Hailey, sitting off to the side and kicking her feet in the water. "That's a *she!*"

The older security guard looked down at the figure in the water and groaned when he recognized her. "Why am I not surprised to see you here?" He turned to his partner. "Contact her father."

Walking away, the other guard sarcastically said, "I'm sure he'll be thrilled."

"Tell him I say hi!" Brittany waved and then kicked off the wall of the tank with the rubbery tail. "I think I'm getting the hang of this."

Hailey applauded. "You totally are. You'd be a great mermaid!"

The man in the lab coat put on his thick-rimmed glasses. Seeing Hailey's face clearly for the first time, he pointed and stammered, "But *you're* the mermaid!"

Hailey giggled. "Nope. I'm just a girl."

"With one kick-butt costume!" Doing a kind of backstroke, Brittany smacked the fluke on the water's surface. "I've gotta get me one of these things. Do you think they make 'em in jet black?"

The marine biologist's face crinkled while he mouthed the word *costume*. Then he shook his head and staggered to the door. "I need to call Hatcher."

Brittany's father arrived first, impeccably dressed in a gray three-piece suit and a maroon bow tie. "Why do you continually disappoint your mother and me?"

"Because I don't want to be the fish-loving girl you want me to be. That's your dream, not mine." Brittany floated on her back. "I just want to do my own thing."

"And what exactly is your own thing?" he said contemptuously.

"Haven't figured it out yet, but I'll keep you posted. Maybe I'll be a professional mermaid." She turned herself over and dove under the surface.

"That's not a real career!" As he shouted, his face gradually matched the color of his tie.

Hailey raised her hand. "Excuse me, Sir, but F-Y-I, it kinda can be." Her voice turned into a squeak when he glared at her.

One of the security guards approached and said, "We found wet footprints in the underground corridors. They lead away from here but eventually fade."

"Do your job and don't bother me!" commanded Brittany's father. "Can't you see I'm trying to deal with my unruly daughter?"

Brittany hoisted herself out of the water, and the tail

flopped on the deck. Sitting up, she grabbed hold of the costume's waistline to start peeling it off.

"I tolerate your behavior, your attitude, your dark makeup. I send you to the best schools, private tutors, this internship, but all you do is let me down. I don't know what else to do with you." He crouched by her costumed ankles. "This might have to be the last straw."

"Or this might be." Brittany lifted her feet and swung her legs, whacking her father with the fluke and knocking him into the tank.

He flailed in the water, shouting a litany of her past transgressions. Brittany ignored him, shimmying out of Hailey's costume and leaving it flat on the deck. "This was fun," she said to Hailey. "But being a fish-girl's not for me." She smirked at her father being helped him out of the tank by the security guards, and then she turned her head and strutted toward the door.

Slinging the heavy orange tail over her shoulder, Hailey sighed and smiled, relieved to be her full human self once again and no longer under observation. Though the costume allowed her to transform into a pretend mermaid whenever she wanted, it could never replace her experience as a real one. A unique one. A good one.

The door closed, and Hailey skipped ahead to catch up with Brittany until the two of them were away from the tanks where they had been kept.

~ ~ ~

Meredith rode the shuttle to the aquarium like she usually did. Exhausted and anxious from staying awake all night, she leaned against Will and enjoyed the comfort provided by his arm around her. Their future after the internship was uncertain, but she refused to dwell on it. She only wanted to enjoy his company while it lasted.

More pressing on her mind was the fate of her friends. Jill had stopped replying to texts and answering calls. Hailey had started changing back, but whether everyone was safe or in big trouble was unknown to her.

When they arrived in the parking lot, the aquarium seemed normal. There were some cars, families who had arrived a little too early for their day trip, but no indication that an attempted mermaid breakout had happened. Meredith sighed in relief, though she wasn't sure if the lack of police presence was a good or bad sign.

The shuttle stopped, and Meredith kissed Will quickly before excusing herself and darting outside. Once she got inside the gates, she slowed down to catch her breath. Running around would draw unwanted attention. She had to convince people she had nothing to do with the events of the previous night, or Jill's selfless act of protection would be undone.

Sandy the Sea Lion dawdled to her starting position. Meredith ran to meet her and asked, "That's you in there, right?"

When Sandy nodded, Meredith threw her arms around her friend. Jill maneuvered her plush flippers to return the hug, but they wouldn't bend around Meredith's back.

"Where is everyone?" whispered Meredith.

"I called Jeff to get the mers," replied Jill. "He came as quickly as he could, like a knight saving a princess."

"And Hailey?"

"Haven't heard yet, but I'm sure she's giving Brittany's dad quite a show."

"Like the show you gave me last night?" Taking a step back, Meredith cocked her head to the side.

Jill shrugged her flippers. "A fish has gotta do what a fish gotta do."

"Mammal."

"Whatever. You were great figuring out how to turn Hailey back. We're a good team."

"Yeah, we are. Thanks for keeping my internship safe." Meredith covered her mouth while she yawned, then she rubbed the back of her neck. "Although I have no idea what kind of internship it'll be now."

The aquarium was about to open, so Meredith left Jill to welcome the guests. She wanted to go to the observation and rehabilitation complex to see if Hailey was inside, but she feared an appearance there would be an admission to being a co-conspirator. Instead, she went to Dr. Hatcher's office like she had done several mornings that summer.

Grunts and slams came from inside, so she peered through the halfway open door. Dr. Hatcher had a stack of books in his arms, and there were boxes on his desk. Meredith could tell he was packing up, and her heartbeat raced with guilt as she assumed losing the mermaid had lost him his job.

When he noticed her standing in the doorway, he put down the books and welcomed her inside. "I don't know what you've heard already, but I'd rather you hear it from me." He released a long breath. "The mermaid's not a mermaid. It's all a hoax. She's just a girl—a girl with an intricate, probably expensive, costume—and she's friends with Brittany. Somehow, they fooled her father. Were you fooled?"

Not fooled at all, she thought. *I helped do the fooling.* Perspiration appeared on her brow as she stammered a noncommittal reply. Dr. Hatcher was respected in his field—he was her first mentor—but he certainly wasn't the enemy. He was merely doing the job he loved, but by saving Hailey, they might have ruined his career.

"I advised against Brittany's inclusion in the program, but my hands were tied. I don't know what her father's going to do with her now, but I won't have anything to do with it. I'm sorry I'm not going to see it through with you, though. You're going to be—you already are—an extraordinary marine biologist, Meredith. Hopefully, Will can learn a thing or two from watching you."

Meredith gulped. "They…*fired* you…because of all this?"

"Fired me?" He laughed. "I resigned."

"What? Why?"

"Brittany's father wants to brush this whole incident aside as just another rebellious thing she did. She admitted to having the other girl pose as a mermaid. I don't know how she did it—I doubt she even did it—but he let the other girl go. Probably gave her a lifetime visitor pass to keep her quiet. Holding a teenage girl here for a week would be a scandal, and he doesn't want any bad publicity for the aquarium." Dr. Hatcher examined the spines of his books, choosing to pack some of them in a box on the desk. "They want me to forfeit all my research and pretend she wasn't here, but there's no way this *didn't* happen. You can't erase scientific facts like that."

"Scientific facts?" Meredith could feel herself trembling, and she started to stutter. "Wh…what facts?"

"I watched her spend more time underwater than any human could without breathing. She had gill slits inside her throat. The X-rays show her skeletal structure below the waist was similar to a dolphin, not a human with two legs. A costume can't fake that." He itemized the facts on his fingers, and Meredith flinched with each one. "It wasn't a costume. Her skin merged into scales; I have some that shed off. I collected blood samples. What more proof could there be that mermaids exist?"

Meredith stepped back, frightened by his transformation. For a month, Dr. Hatcher had been mild-mannered and friendly, but he was behaving as someone obsessed, even crazed.

He walked to the window, which overlooked the whale tank. "Mermaids have been part of folklore for hundreds, even thousands of years. Sailors claimed to have seen them, but the sightings were often written off as figments of their tired, weary, heat-stricken imaginations. When I was younger, I thought I—" He stopped his sentence and sighed. "I thought they were real but hiding out deeper than we could look."

Trying to avoid his eyes, Meredith scanned the room until she noticed a map unfolded on his desk. In thick red ink, an area in the ocean was circled, and a spot on the coast was marked with an X. She didn't need an explanation to know that the locations were where Hailey had been caught and kept.

She had to get a closer look to find out where Marina's mother was.

Quietly, she sidled to the desk and glanced down, grateful that her enhanced vision could read the seaport's name. She jumped back when Dr. Hatcher braced himself on the edge of the desk.

"I don't know what happened this morning, but last night, we had a real mermaid in that tank—a real mermaid who displayed humanlike intelligence. She can't be the only one. Every organism has at least one parent, and most complex ones have two, so I refuse to believe she was alone. There must be more, most likely a community of them." He frantically tapped his finger inside the circle on the map. "And that's where I'm going to start looking."

~ Chapter Thirty-Three ~

Jeff got a text from Meredith with instructions to take the girls to a specific seaport, though he never received an explanation why. After parking the car, he got out and walked to the passenger side to hold open the doors for Marina and Lorelei. A gust of wind blew by, rippling their sundresses. Lorelei dropped her hands to her side, while Jeff put his arm around Marina and held her close to him.

"Where do you think she is?" asked Lorelei.

Without answering, Marina stepped forward, letting Jeff's arm slide across her back and down her arm until their hands clasped and their fingers interlocked. Drawn by a deep longing in her heart, she led the others to a gangway heading down to the docks. The metal rattled as she stepped upon it.

"I'm not sure if we're allowed down there." Jeff stopped and tried to pull Marina back, but she let go of his hand and kept walking. "Marina, are you okay?"

Lorelei stepped in front of Jeff and looked up at him. "If you care for her, you will trust what she is doing."

"I do care. I do trust her."

"Good. Then wait here." Lorelei slowly descended the gangway.

Standing on the weathered wood of the dock, Marina focused her gaze ahead on a woman in a billowing peach dress conversing with two burly fishermen while holding a clipboard tightly at her side. The woman's back was to her, but as the breeze blew her blonde hair to the side, Marina was overwhelmed with an air of familiarity.

She felt a soft and gentle touch on her shoulder. "Lore, I

know that is her. What shall I do? What shall I say?"

Lorelei asked, "What would you like to say to her?"

A tear trickled down Marina's cheek. "Hello, Mother."

At that moment, the woman raised her shoulders and turned her head to the side, as if she heard something within the whistling wind.

The woman's face came into view, and Marina's eyes widened. Like a reflection in a faraway mirror, her mother's expression matched her own. They stood there, transfixed for a moment while the waves rustled. Then Coral stepped forward, dropping the clipboard as she broke into a run. Marina followed suit until the distance between them closed, and they met in an embrace.

"My dear Marina!" said Coral. "I never imagined I would see you again."

Nuzzling her face against her mother's collar bone, Marina wept tears of joy. "I never imagined I would meet you. Hello, Mother."

"How can you be here? You should be in the ocean. You should be with the school. You should *not* be here on land. What are you doing on land?"

"I came to find you."

Moments later, they were standing near the end of an empty pier away from Lorelei, Jeff, and any other people. Coral squeezed Marina's hand. "I am grateful you came, my dear daughter, but you cannot stay. Your place is in the ocean, and mine, unfortunately, is forever here on land. You need to return."

"Can I please stay with you, as a mother and daughter should?"

"I would like that more than anything else. You have grown into a beautiful maid." Coral stroked Marina's hair and then held Marina's cheeks in her hands. "But today is the full moon. You can only stay until sunset."

"I can stay longer. My friend Hailey can borrow my tail for another cycle. I suppose Meredith might again. Possibly Jill if I asked nicely enough. Lorelei has lost hers, but she refuses to take mine."

Coral stepped back and raised her finger in a reprimanding but motherly way. "You must not let others—mers, and especially humans—wear your tail. It comes with certain abilities."

After wearing the tail, Meredith had become a better swimmer and was able to communicate with the aquarium animals, but those were skills Marina had always possessed. Perhaps Hailey would gain those abilities as well. Isabel was able to read people's moods and secret thoughts from having worn a purple tail, so Marina wondered what powers her orange tail granted her.

"The first time was an accident." Marina shuffled her feet and swayed her arms. "This second time was so I could find you. I promise that I will not do it again."

"If other mers learned that a human-maid wore your tail, the punishment would be severe. If the leader of the school ever found out…" Coral stepped toward the pier's edge and stared out at the ocean. The waves seemed more turbulent that morning than originally forecasted. "It has been many years since I was last there. Who is leading the school, and what color tail does the mer have?"

"Purple," replied Marina with a disheartened sigh. "His name is Ray."

Coral turned sharply toward Marina. "Ray?"

"Have you heard of him?"

Looking back out to sea, Coral watched the white-capped waves crash against the boats. The mention of Ray's name brought memories back up to the surface—memories of a life she had chosen to give up. And a daughter she had given up—a daughter who came ashore without fully understanding why she shouldn't have left the school. Coral wiped her eyes, but she couldn't control the flow of her tears. She couldn't let Marina see her cry. She had to be strong, for there would be stormy waters ahead.

"Is there something wrong, Mother?" Marina stepped forward. "Do you know Ray?"

"Yes, but do *you* know who he is?" Coral turned and clasped her daughter's hands tightly until together, their arms trembled. She had her answer; Marina didn't know, and it was time someone told her. "This Ray who leads the school is…*my brother.*"

Sneak peek at *Tripping the Scales* ~ Chapter One ~

"Mother!" gasped Marina. "You should *not* have done that!"

Before Coral could respond, Hailey squealed from a few benches over. They were on the top deck of the ferry. Marina had asked Jeff to give her some time with her mother, and after kissing her forehead, he went to the snack bar one deck below. Meredith and Jill had tried to convince Hailey to join them with Jeff, but Hailey insisted she stay with the mers in case they needed her.

Waving at Hailey, Marina said, "I am sure she would like to hear why you chose to sit out on those rocks. She can be trusted."

"As you trusted her with your tail?" asked Coral, one of her thin eyebrows slightly raised. "Should you have done that?"

"I would not have found you without trusting Hailey."

"I know that, my darling sea star." Coral smirked while she stroked her daughter's long blonde hair.

Lorelei stretched out her arms. "You should have seen her in the water. If I had not first met Hailey with legs, I would have believed her to be mer."

"Mer or human does not matter," said Marina. "Hailey is one of my dearest friends."

Coral said, "I have lived among the humans long enough to learn that a majority of them are trustworthy. It seems like you have found several in so short a time, including a special young human-man."

Marina could almost feel her cheeks flushing from embarrassment, and she stammered a defense of her relationship with Jeff, but Lorelei interrupted by asking, "Could you continue with your story?"

"Yes, tell us more, please." Marina let out a deep breath, relieved that Lorelei's well-timed question had rescued her.

Gathering her windblown hair, Coral scanned the deck of the ferry. Other than Hailey bouncing anxiously in her seat and peering over at them, there were only a few scattered people. It was late afternoon on a weekday. According to Hailey and the others, it wasn't a popular time for people to head to the island. For the same reason, there was plenty of space down below for Jill's minivan. Marina and Lorelei were amazed by the concept of transporting cars over the water, and they had whispered to each other about humans thinking of so many different ways to get around.

"Please do not be secretive," said Marina. "I have finally found you, and I want to learn all I can about you. Why would you have done something like that?"

"Because when I was your age, it was something adventurous." Coral snickered. "That is what happens when your closest friend is a scout."

"You mean Pearl?" Marina grasped Lorelei's hand and turned to face her friend, who leaned forward, equally eager to hear about a mother she never knew.

"Every new experience flowed to her, and I followed along." Holding back tears, Coral sighed. "How odd it sounds to say that I merely wanted to follow. Perhaps I was not yet ready for anything more."

Like mother-maid, like daughter-maid, thought Marina, fondly recalling all the times she had followed Pearl's green-tailed daughter. Without Lorelei's persistence, Marina would have never taken her first steps on land.

It wasn't until the previous moon cycle began when Marina had finally taken the lead and decided to search for her mother. And she had found Coral, who welcomed her after so many moon cycles with open arms. Never had Marina instantly felt so much love and warmth but also confusion and fear about her place in the school. It may have been her birthright, assigned to her by the unique color of her tail, but she wasn't ready for it.

And she wasn't sure if she wanted it.

"I would have followed Pearl anywhere. It was Shelly who always complained to my parents and brother—your uncle Ray—about the deep water we often found ourselves in."

Upon hearing the name of the school's leader, shivers coursed down Marina's spine and all the way to her toes. If Ray was her mother's brother, then it meant that she and Calliope—who had teased, taunted, and tormented her—were cousins. Marina shuddered at the thought. All her life, she had believed she was an orphan, but the mers she never knew were her relatives had refused to acknowledge her existence.

"I have many questions, mother."

"I will answer what I can." Coral looked to the sun in the western sky, well past its highest point but far from the horizon. "There is still time before you must put back on your tail. And you *must* put on your tail and return to the school. Because your friend over there was caught, and now the human scientists know of our existence, you need to make Ray understand the danger the school may be in."

"Why would he listen to me?" Marina's list of questions was long, and she wasn't sure where to start. Closing her eyes, she took a deep breath before continuing, "Why did Ray and Shelly never tell me I was their niece? Why did no one in the school tell me? Why—?"

"You deserve a better mother than I." Coral took Marina's hand and squeezed it tightly but gently. "I am ashamed I cannot answer those questions. I had already left the school by then." She hung her head.

"Then why did you leave? And where is my father?"

"I do not know where he is, but I can tell why he—and then later I—no longer have our tails. Sadly, there is far too much in my past that I should not have done."

~ ~ ~

"Coral, Pearl, you should *not* be doing that!" Shelly's head bobbed with the waves, and she kept her purple tail submerged, unlike the two mers openly displaying themselves while sitting on adjacent rocks.

"Will you let it float?" Coral smacked her fluke on the water's surface. "Stop living your life inside a clam shell."

Pearl elbowed Coral in the side and said, "I came out of my oyster shell long ago!"

Coral and Pearl laughed and flicked their tails to splash Shelly in the face.

"That is not funny," said Shelly, flipping her tail to back herself away from the spray of water. "What if the two of you are seen?"

Pearl said, "I have already scouted these waters. There are no boats near us."

"Boats are fast. One could appear without us realizing it."

Coral extended her arms. "Look around you, Shelly. The nearest land is far behind us, and there is nothing but clear water in every direction. This is the perfect place to get away and relax." She leaned back on the smooth rock and swung her tail back and forth.

"Get away? Does your family know you feel that way?"

"No, they do not." Pearl slid off her rock into the water and then drifted toward Shelly. "And you are *not* going to blubber to Ray about this."

Shelly avoided Pearl's intense glare and swam around the rock until she was closer to Coral's head. "We are no longer little maids. It is time for us to grow up and accept our destinies."

Stretching her arms behind her, Coral groaned. "That is easy for you to say. Yours is easier to accept. Do you understand the pressure that comes with mine?"

"Do *you* understand? Ray seems to think you do not."

Shelly was suddenly dragged under the water. She struggled to escape until she realized Pearl's hands were clamping her at the waist. Pearl released Shelly to turn her around, and Shelly seized the opportunity to swim upward. Before Shelly could surface, Pearl yanked her fluke back down.

Sinking to Pearl's depth, Shelly asked, "Why are you behaving like a shark?"

"Do you understand that you need to let it float?" Pearl flicked her tail and rose enough that they were no longer looking eye to eye. "Just because you and Coral's brother have chosen each other, it is not your place to advise her."

"She should have a purple-tail advising her." Shelly curled her tail behind her and flapped it sideways. "One who would have prevented her from lounging on a rock."

"Are you jealous?"

"I am one of her closest friends, and Ray is her brother. We should be the ones to advise her, but she spends so much time with Zale. What could a blue-tail possibly offer her?"

"Protection. By virtue of his tail color, he will keep the school safe." Pearl grinned. "And because he and Coral love each other, he will protect her to the ends of the ocean."

"But she will need to place the school above her own needs. Ray says—"

"Are all your thoughts dictated by Ray?" Pearl folded her arms across her shell-top. "I trust that when the time comes, Coral will rise to the challenge."

There was a splash at the surface, and then a faint shadow passed over them.

"You do realize that I could hear you," said Coral, hovering above them. "My tail was touching the water, so I heard everything."

Shelly dropped her arms against her side and slowly approached Coral. "I am sorry for not saying these things directly to you, but I am not sorry for saying them."

Shooting forward, Pearl said, "Is your head in a whirlpool, Shelly? That is no apology."

Coral groaned until she had caught their attention. "All I wanted today was to spend time with my friends and do something we have never done. Can you please give me that?"

Pearl and Shelly fell silent, floating in place while Coral returned to the surface. Once there, she grabbed hold of the rock and with a forceful kick of her tail, she jumped out of the water and spun herself around, ultimately landing in a seated position. Then she heaved herself backward and reclined, keeping the tips of her fluke underneath the soothing ripples of the waves.

The sun shined high in the sky, and the golden light reflected off Coral's tail and made it sparkle. She could feel droplets of water from underneath her scales evaporating into the moist air. Sighing, she imagined her tail dissolving and leaving her with a pair of humanlike legs. "If only I could…"

Her voice trailed off with the realization that she would never have that experience. While Pearl had occasionally ventured onto land at the full moon, Coral knew it was forbidden. She could recite the rule from memory. *An orange-tail should not drift too far from her school and must never walk on land.*

No longer dazed, Pearl and Shelly poked their heads through the surface. "We are sorry," said Pearl.

Shelly added, "There are still several cycles until you—"

"Not thinking about it." Coral swayed her wading fluke back and forth.

Pearl sprang up to her waist and bobbed with the larger incoming waves. She jerked her head to one side, then another. "We are not safe here."

As Coral sat up and looked around, Shelly vanished into the ocean.

With one abrupt quarter turn, Pearl looked toward the same direction Coral was facing and saw a sailboat. "Coral, we must go!" she said, reaching for Coral's hand before ducking her head below the bubbling sea foam.

Coral remained transfixed on the passing boat. Humans

weren't supposed to see her, but she had never seen one of them. Her eyesight was exceptional in the water, but not above it, so she squinted, trying to catch a glimpse of someone. Anyone. Anything to show her there was more than her impending role in the school.

Pearl flung some water up at Coral. The sudden splash knocked Coral out of her daydream, and she dove into the water. Grabbing Coral's hand, Pearl kicked vigorously and steered them deeper and deeper until the water was a dark blue.

"Maybe Shelly is right," said Pearl. "We should *not* have sat on the rocks. You might have been seen."

"I do not think I was," said Coral.

Meanwhile, a young man standing on the sailboat lowered a pair of binoculars from his eyes. Speechless, he continued staring at the distant spot where he saw what he thought he saw.

One of his friends on the boat patted him on the back and asked, "See anything yet?"

"I thought I saw a…" The man with binoculars couldn't bring himself to admit it out loud. His friend wouldn't believe him. There were many plausible explanations why he *thought* he saw a mermaid—a beached manatee, a trick of the light, an overactive imagination, the beverage in the red plastic cup his friend handed him.

"A whale watch was a great idea to celebrate your Ph.D.," said another friend, raising his own cup to make a toast. "Congrats again, Hatch."

ACKNOWLEDGMENTS

I'm writing this series first and foremost for my daughters. When I started *Flipping*, I had no idea what its ending was, never mind that it would become a trilogy. Thank you for all your love and encouragement, especially how you said you liked the twists, danger, and mysteries (some resolved, some remaining) in this part better than in the first. It's all for you. I love you lots. Fist bump, whoosh back.

Thanks to Tatiana Vila for another beautiful cover design. It's always a pleasure working with you. I hope we can figure out which side of the page the tail comes from for the third part.

Special thanks to the best support team I could have possibly assembled: Amy Astorga, I showed you my mermaid sequel, and I can't wait to see yours! Andrew Bradley, a comment of yours inspired me to add scientific names, but you're probably happier to know more about the shopkeeper. Chris Jones, thanks for the final spell-check; you're an ace at predicting things. Sabrina Rucker, your feedback equals what the adults give me, and of course, you can beta the next book. Susan Soares, I wouldn't have started this series without you, and I'm impressed that I impressed you. Kyla Stan, thanks for your unbridled enthusiasm, fin friend. Sioux Trett, thanks for the advice at the eleventh hour. And finally, the inimitable and prolific John Barker, where do you find the time to write that much about my work? Thanks so much for everything and the updated website too!

And finally, thanks to everyone who read and enjoyed the first part…and waited patiently for the second part. It took longer to write than expected, it came out later than I wanted, but it's better than I imagined. Thank you for supporting an indie author with a dream to tell these fanciful tales of tails.

ABOUT THE AUTHOR

Pete Tarsi writes stories he hopes his daughters will enjoy. Two down, and so far, so good.

He graduated from MIT with a degree in Creative Writing and Physics, and he considers himself fortunate that he still gets to do both. When he's not writing, he can be found teaching high school science, directing theatre, or spending time with his three lovely daughters. He grew up in a small town north of Boston and still lives in Massachusetts.

OTHER WORKS BY PETE TARSI
Flipping the Scales

Visit Pete online at **petetarsi.com**

Made in the USA
Charleston, SC
13 July 2016